Dawn, —
There is a journey
here and I hope you
Enjoy it!.
Brenda Sorrels

ALSO BY BRENDA SORRELS

The Bachelor Farmers

The Way Back 'Round

Brenda Sorrels

ISBN: 978-1-4834-0505-6 (sc)
ISBN: 978-1-4834-0504-9 (e)

Because of the dynamic nature of the Internet, any web addresses or links contained in
this book may have changed since publication and may no longer be valid. The views
expressed in this work are solely those of the author and do not necessarily reflect the
views of the publisher, and the publisher hereby disclaims any responsibility for them.

Lulu Publishing Services rev. date: 11/25/2013

FOR MARGARET DOUD

ACKNOWLEDGMENTS

ONCE AGAIN, I MUST THANK my editor, Margaret Doud, for guiding me through the ins and outs of growing a small story into something much bigger. We work so well together because of her intelligence, patience and extraordinary ability to push me to become a better writer.

My friend, Cathy Vanden Eykel, also had a huge hand in my decision to write this novel. She not only read the short story several times, but sat me down and pointed out key areas where she thought I could expand. Her enthusiasm and great instincts gave me the confidence to move forward.

My husband, Barry, and my stepdaughters, Quincy and Avery, were there full force. Quincy did not hesitate with her opinion, and Avery edited and went out of her way to give me notes and ideas for character development. They graciously read all that I thrust at them and always got back to me with their feedback.

I am lucky to have brilliant friends and again, Bari Ross and Angela Brady, stepped up and read critically for me. Their contribution was generous and greatly appreciated. Libby Miller read an early draft of the book and gave me feedback as did Carol and John Carr. Evelyn and Jimmie Joynt, Sandy Lief, Beth Scott, Gary Udashen and my sister, Carla Friedman, have read and encouraged me from day one. Ina Chadwick will always be a mentor and a friend. I can't thank everyone enough!

The Midwest continues to be an inspiration for me. I thank my parents for the life they provided and my friends and family for their love and support, wherever they may be.

PROLOGUE

THE YOUNG BOY EASED THE tarnished metal knob to the left, cracked open his bedroom door, and leaned into the hallway to eavesdrop on the conversation he was determined to hear. The topic of his Aunt Liddy had come up at dinner when his traveling salesman uncle made a rare stopover at the farm and inquired about her. The boy's father had glanced at his son and then suggested to the adults that they wait until later that evening to re-visit the topic. No sooner had the dishes been cleared and the boy sent off to bed, than the uncle pulled a bottle of Beefeater and a shaker out of his suitcase and masterfully mixed up a round of gin sours.

"Try this," he offered. "It's all the rage in Omaha." He shook the icy concoction into the glasses that the boy's mother drew from her china hutch only on the rarest of occasions.

After the three of them exchanged pleasantries, his father's voice rose to an animated timbre, and the boy popped his head into the hallway even further, intent on not missing a word.

The story hailed from his father's side of the family and had taken place somewhere in Kansas, a place that, except for the tornados, was not unlike the long, grainy fields of Minnesota where the boy and his family now lived.

The boy's father cleared his throat and paused for a sip of his drink. "Well, there was Liddy, twenty-eight-years-old and still living at home with no prospect of a husband in sight. The word "spinster" had been whispered on occasion and our Pa, as a nod to the tongue-wagging, took it upon himself to introduce her to a farming man, Delmont something-or-other ... ten years her senior, who was rumored to be looking for a wife."

"Sounds promising," said the uncle.

"Well, it might have been, but the farmer turned out to be a real dandy. He was cocky and good-looking, but what set him apart most was that he owned his own car, a Ford Runabout. There wasn't much around in those days that could compete, and Liddy fell hard."

"He sounds like a bona fide dandy alright," replied the uncle, who had guzzled his first drink and was busy mixing up another. The boy didn't know what a dandy was, but, judging from the disgust in his father's voice, he decided that whatever it was, it wasn't good.

"The real question, or the real trouble, depending on which way you look at it, was why the man had never married before. He'd long held the deed to his acreage and had been plowing his own fields for years. Claimed he just never met the right woman, and of course we all wanted to believe him, Liddy most of all."

"Marry me, Liddy," he begged not too long after they'd met. "I've been looking for a woman like you since I was old enough to provide for a wife. I can promise you all the finest things life has to offer, everything a beautiful woman like you deserves."

"Sounds like a perfect match," the uncle interjected. "Him lookin' for a wife and Liddy so ready to become one."

"Well, that's what we all thought. Nobody paid any mind to the fact that Liddy hadn't taken more than three rides in the Runabout with him before she accepted his proposal. None of us had met his family, either. I believe he said they were somewhere out West in Montana or some such place. Liddy and mother spent weeks sewing her wedding dress. They even made a special trip to Kansas City and spent every nickel of their egg money to buy lace. I'd never seen a girl sort through her hope chest so many times. Heck, Pa joked she could have opened a store she had so many linens and what-not."

The boy's father took a hard swallow of his drink. "About a week before the nuptials were to commence, Liddy and Delmont met with the priest and handed him a copy of the marriage license before driving into town for a couple of sandwiches at Ida's Café, a popular local haunt.

After making themselves comfortable at a center table, they placed their order and relaxed in the high spirit of the day. Ida brought the plates out herself, insisting that lunch was on the house. Less than two bites later, however, a woman who had been eying them from a back corner booth rushed up with a baby in her arms. 'Was told I might find you here,' she snarled at Delmont, before turning to Liddy. 'Here,' she said, plunking the baby into Liddy's lap. 'This is his, too. Might as well take all of him.' You can imagine the shock!"

Like a crazy twist on 'Hot Potato' Liddy forced the baby into the arms of their startled waitress and ran 'outta there, knocking over a couple of chairs on her way out. Nobody knew what hit, the whole mess caused such a scene. It wasn't 'til much later when Liddy could talk about it without breaking into sobs that she told us the rest of the story."

"Well, don't leave us hangin' on the edge of a cliff now," the uncle insisted. "What happened?"

The boy was hanging on every word too and was grateful his uncle was there to tease more details out of his father.

"Well, Mr. Big Shot jumped into his car and took off after Liddy. Liddy ducked into the cemetery when she heard the car barreling down the road. She knew no vehicle could get in there with all those gravestones set so close together, but Delmont pulled the Runabout to a quick halt and chased after her on foot, dodging in and around the sacred markers just as the sky cracked open and a drenching rain let loose. Liddy snatched up a stone and heaved it at him, but she lost her balance and landed in the mud. Her fiancé fell onto his knees beside her, scooped her up and begged her to forgive him. He'd made a mistake, he admitted that much. But all he really wanted was a proper wife, and he insisted that Liddy was the woman of his dreams."

The uncle's wooden chair squeaked as he shifted his weight and tipped his head up, draining the sweaty ice in his glass. "What'd she do?" he asked, smoothing out the edges of his damp moustache. "She didn't forgive the two-timer, did she?"

"Well," the boy's father continued, "Liddy was all hard tears with her head bleeding and soaked to the skin, but he somehow coaxed her back into the Runabout. They motored out to the farm. She never did say what happened on the ride over there, but bottom line is he could have been makin' a delivery of milk the way he dumped her on the porch. Sped away before Liddy could even get the door unlatched."

The uncle shook his head. "That's quite a story. A storm of a whole 'nother sort, it sounds like."

"Sure was," the boy heard his mother chime in. "You know, Liddy has a heart of gold. She didn't deserve to be treated that way."

"No one does. Especially not Liddy," the boy's father agreed whole-heartedly. "Pa wanted to go after the man himself, but Liddy begged him not to. She'd suffered all the humiliation she could handle and didn't want to make things any worse than they already were."

"Damn," the boy's uncle said in a mix of disgust and compassion. "I had no idea Liddy'd been through somethin' like that."

"Yup. A bona fide tragedy it was. Never did marry, you know. Didn't have the mind for it after that. Spent the rest of her life on the farm nursing Ma and Pa 'till they passed on."

"Mmm," the uncle murmered. "Last I heard she was still living in Kansas."

"Kansas City." The boy's mother broke in again. "She's the nanny for a large dry-goods family by the name of Keller. About the only thing that stayed intact through the whole mess was her sweet nature."

At the conclusion of the story, the boy silently closed his door and tiptoed to bed.

Laying there in the darkness, he pulled the blanket up over his head, rubbed his eyes and wondered about this Aunt Liddy. He was too young to know how she would figure in his own life, a bigger, even more painful story that would be retold for decades to come to distant relatives and long-removed friends when he wasn't around.

PART I

*"You can't keep trouble from visitin', but
you don't have to offer it a chair."*

---anonymous

CHAPTER ONE

Rural Minnesota, 1932

"**P**LEASE CAN WE GO, MOM? It's a perfect day outside and there's nothing to do around here."

Truth is, any activity to break the routine of the farm was a relief. I was itching to drive the wagon with my father even more than I cared about a picnic, but my mother was not into having fun these days.

"Stop begging me, child," she snapped, spot-cleaning her Sunday gloves with a damp cloth. She propped open a loose kitchen window with a small block of wood and laid them on the sill to dry. "I already told you, no, and I've got plenty around the house to keep us busy if you're so bored."

"Aw, Mom!"

Things had been strange in our house lately, and it was hard for me to get my mother's attention, let alone convince her to do anything out of the ordinary. Her latest miscarriage had taken a heavy toll. All she had done for the last few weeks was cook, clean, and lie in her room with the door closed, in spite of my constant pleading and my father's hopeful encouragement. In all of my eight years, I'd been through enough of these scenes to know when to give up. I sat at the table letting my scrambled eggs run cold, so angry I couldn't even look at her.

My father, as he often did, stepped in to pick up my begging in his own more reasoned way. "It's been three weeks, Sarah. We can't risk wasting a day like this. You know how fickle spring weather can be around here. Come on, I'll even help you pack up the lunch." He pushed away from the table and lifted a carver to the leftover brisket.

This got my mother's attention, for the kitchen was her domain and she would never have anyone messing with her food. Sure enough, as if my dad had choreographed the whole thing, she rushed to the counter and elbowed him out of the way. "I'll do it," she said, pulling the knife from his hand. "You'll just make a mess of things."

"Now that's more like it." My father gave her a quick peck on the cheek and threw me a nod. "Come on, Jake. Wash up and let's go hitch up those horses."

"All right!" I scooped my plate off the table, clattering it on the counter as I hurried to rinse my hands under the faucet.

By the time we had mucked out the last stall and brought the wagon around, my mother stood waiting, the dark outline of her shadow visible behind the screen door. She took a hesitant step out into the sunlight as we pulled up, the picnic basket in one hand, our jackets and a Crazy quilt tucked under her other arm. The wagon seat gave its usual rusty bounce as my father jumped down to help lighten her load before hoisting me onto his lap. I took up the well-worn reins, anxious and proud to show my mother what a good driver I was as my father circled his rough hands over mine and whispered to me to give the go-ahead to the horses. As I snapped the reins to urge them forward, I shifted my eyes toward my mother and was rewarded with the first smile I'd gotten in weeks. "Good job, Jake," she said. I swelled inside with a pride I knew I'd be admonished for if I were to admit it. We moved along at an easy pace. The simple enjoyment of such a fine day was conducive to keeping our thoughts to ourselves. I was riding high, hoping we'd take a longer than usual route, but about three miles down County Road Two we came upon our favorite spot, and my father tugged my arms to pull back on the horses, slowing them to a stop.

The wide prairie field was dotted with buds of purple and yellow wildflowers poking up through the spiky grass. To the north, the land was so flat it looked as if I could walk straight off the face of the earth, and I still secretly believed this was possible, in spite of what I'd learned to the contrary in school. After unloading the wagon and choosing the perfect spot, my mother paused to let the wind settle down, taking her time to open the food basket and lay out a generous luncheon feast. There was no reason to rush here, just miles and miles of prairie land and crop fields, a quiet disturbed only by an occasional fly or mosquito looking to crash in on our picnic. In time, she passed us plates and forks and we lunched, squinting our eyes in the bright daylight, our pale winter faces as hungry for the sun as our stomachs were for food. I ate fast, since I hadn't eaten my breakfast, and was restless to strike out. I stood up with the last bite of pie still in my mouth. "Where's my jar, Mom?" I asked, referring to a large Mason jar that, if I was lucky, would be filled to the lid with every color, shape, and size of insect that the prairie had to offer by the end of the day.

My mother dug inside the picnic basket and handed it to me. "Wipe that cherry off your chin first." She wet a napkin and I reached for it, averting my face as she made a move to wipe it herself.

"Come show us when you've got something good," said my father. He was already leaning back on his elbows, a sure sign that a nap might be in the plans.

"I will!" I shouted over my shoulder, venturing out through the coarse native scrub toward a rocky creek that flowed not too far off in the West. How wonderful it was to be running outdoors at full speed after the long winter, the warm rays of sun on my back, the land around me springing to life. Catching my breath at the edge of the creek, I spotted two large beetles and hurried to scoop them up. Within an hour my jar was brimming and I lay on my belly at the edge of the narrow bank letting the shallow water trickle through my fingers. Much later still, when the frog I'd spied got away, along with several small fish that had slithered from my hand, I wandered back.

"Where have you been, Jake?" My mother said as I walked toward them. "I was about to send Dad out to fetch you."

"Look, I got some good ones," I grinned, handing my father the jar of insects. "Got two huge water beetles too."

"Well, you sure as heck did." My father admired the bugs by holding the jar up to the sky for better light. "You've about outdone yourself, Jake."

My mother laid back on the quilt and moved to make room for me. "Come and settle down with us, son. We're about to take a nap."

"Aw, Mama, I'm too old to take a nap. I'll just sit here real quiet for awhile. I promise I won't go anywhere far and I won't bother you."

"Well, okay then, but see that you keep your promise and stay within sight. I don't want to open my eyes and not know where you are."

Sprawling on the quilt, I admired my bug collection and daydreamed of an even bigger jar that I would bring along next time. When my father rolled on his back and broke into a light snore and my mother covered her eyes with the quilt corner, I stood up wondering what other treasures I might find nearby. Roaming through the grasses, there was plenty to keep me occupied: lots of grasshoppers and small colorful rocks that I dropped into my pockets. I was careful to stay within sight. When I finally played myself out, I plunked back down on the blanket between my sleeping parents and dozed off.

It was some time later when I felt the bulk of my father's body rustle beside me. "Sarah, wake up," he said, "We overslept." My father reached over and nudged my mother, who stirred at his urging. "I got cows in the pasture needing to be milked."

My mother raised up on her elbows and brushed the dark strands of hair from her face. "Oh, no, Albert," she said as she pulled herself to her knees. "I can't believe we slept so long."

"Hurry now, if you can. Cows know no patience," my father said as he ran off to ready the wagon.

My mother gave me a look. "Jake, why didn't you wake us? Surely you noticed how late it was getting."

It was just like her these days to strike out at me.

"I'm sorry, Mama. I was just playing with my bugs. Look here. This one is green on the bottom and brown on the top. Why do you think that is? The rest of them have the color on the top if they have any at all." I was about to tell her that I had collected four large grasshoppers while she and dad were napping, but my mother interrupted me.

"Jake, we have no time for such foolishness," she snapped. "Didn't you hear your father?"

My mother threw me another one of her unsettling looks like she did when I let the screen door slam behind me or took too long collecting eggs. Her lips tightened and she lifted her chin. "Come on, help me gather up our things. Be quick now."

Anxious to feel the reins in my hands once again, I hustled to tighten the lids on jars of peaches and plums and hand her wrappings of uneaten pie to stuff into the wicker basket. Folding the quilt just as my father brought up the wagon, my mother pulled a light shawl over her shoulders and tossed a jacket my way. "Put this on, Jake," she said without looking up. "Air's getting cooler already!"

Tugging my arms into corduroy sleeves as fast as I could, I climbed into the driver's seat settling myself in my father's lap and reaching for the reins. "Not this time, son. We're in a hurry." He lifted me from between his legs and nudged me toward my mother.

"Please, Dad," I begged, my eyes tearing up against my will. "I'll be real still. Won't say a word. Please!"

"Sorry, son. Can't do it. It's coming on nightfall. I've got to push the horses at a faster clip than usual, and I have to be in total control. Scoot over now."

My mother grabbed my arm and anchored me to the seat just before my dad snapped the leather straps across the backs of the horses, lurching the wagon forward. I slumped down, angry and hurt. Who knew when I'd get my next chance with our outings as rare as they were these days. It was so unfair.

The horses kicked up the familiar scent of earth and manure as they trotted up to speed. My mother fiddled with her kerchief in the rough prairie wind and readjusted the basket at her feet. The road was dark and bumpy, and shadows filled the spaces between the trees, surrounding us like strange, ghost-like figurines. In the dim light, I spotted shallow patches of snow that had refused to melt, and I shivered as I sank deeper into the seat. By the time we approached a tree grove at the edge of our land, there was nothing to be heard but the sound of the rusty wagon and the horses' clomping on the half-frozen ground. My stomach grumbled. It had been hours since we'd eaten our lunch. I thought about the cooked ham my mother had promised for dinner and the fire she would light. As angry and hungry as I was, the rhythm of the horse's hooves and the rocking of the wagon lulled me into a trance and I daydreamed that I was a grown man in charge of driving these horses whenever and wherever I wanted.

CHAPTER TWO

"**M**Y GOD!" MY FATHER SHOUTED. "Whoa!"

I bolted upright, wide awake now, jolted by the tremor in his voice that ran a quiver of fear down my back. My mother screamed, "Jake! Jake!" as the horses reeled their thick necks upward and I felt myself catapulted into the air then landing with a dull thud, sideways in a clump of switch grass. Off in the distance my father was still yelling, "Whoa! Easy, now!"

My mother's frantic cries trumped those of my dad though, as I struggled to my feet. When I stepped down, my right ankle throbbed and my body shivered. As I adjusted my weight onto my left foot, I felt a wet ribbon of blood trickle down the side of my face that burned as if it were on fire. My eyes filled with tears, but I fought them back, brushing the dirt and debris from my jacket sleeve and pants leg.

I stood there for a minute, too afraid to move, paralyzed by what had happened. I heard my father's voice, calmer now, and it comforted me as it did the horses. "Good! Good." he said. "Easy now."

The moment the commotion came to a halt, my mother swooped down like a bird and smothered me with her cries.

Relieved to be in her arms, I let my own tears flow as her voice soothed me. "Jake, my baby," she murmured as she wiped the blood from my face with her kerchief, and for a moment I allowed myself to be comforted.

"Mama," I said, "what happened?"

"It was a trophy buck for sure. Big as I've ever seen," she said trembling as she held me. "Shot out of the darkness right into our path.

But for the grace of God, son, you weren't killed. I just lost another baby less than a month ago, and now this!" She clutched me so hard it made me even more determined to convince her that I was not hurt.

"I'm fine, Mama."

I wiped my eyes wincing at the sting of the cuts on my cheek, and my ankle was throbbing, but I didn't want to upset her anymore, so I kept quiet about it.

"Mama, please don't cry. Really, I'm okay."

But she couldn't answer me for the great gulps of air and tears that consumed her. My father hurried to join us and determine for himself the extent of my injuries. "Dad …" I said. "I'm not hurt, except for maybe my ankle and some scratches, but Mama …"

"Are you sure, Jake?" My father examined the blood already clotting on my forehead. He asked me to take a few steps to be sure my ankle wasn't broken so I hobbled forward, trying hard not to wince from the pain. "You'll be fine," he said. "Just a sprain, I'd say. Stay off it for a couple of days and you'll be outrunning the prairie dogs in no time."

He then turned his attention to my mother. "Come on now, Sarah." He drew her up by the shoulders and gave her a deep hug. "Nobody got hurt. Just a few scrapes is all."

"It came out of nowhere, Albert. Jake could have been killed!"

"But he's okay, Sarah. Nothing to worry about. Now let's get on home before it gets too dark to see." My father curved his arm around my back and I leaned into him as we followed my mother toward the wagon.

He lifted me into the seat next to my mother, who pulled me into herself, and I surrendered to the mothering she insisted on heaping on me. Back at the house, she checked me from limb to limb as she heated up a washtub of water for my bath while my father headed out to the pasture to herd in the milk cows. After rubbing ointment on the scrapes on my face and head, she wrapped my ankle with a towel filled with ice and tucked me into bed. "Jake … Jake, my poor baby." She dropped her face down close to mine, and I felt her lips as soft as petals on my eyelids.

My mother's dark visions of what could have happened to me kept her awake half the night, and by the time I rubbed my eyes awake the following morning she had convinced herself that she'd been much too permissive with me, and that things around our house would have to change.

"Let me see your forehead," she said, brushing my hair away. "We're lucky you're still alive. If you'd been driving that wagon, it might have been much worse."

I winced as her cold fingertips touched my bruised face. "Mama, I'm fine."

"I wouldn't be surprised if you end up with a real shiner." She studied me with a critical eye. "My God, we were so lucky."

I gave her a wary look and sat up as she pulled back the quilt to check the condition of my ankle. My foot was sore when I moved it, but I didn't let on. I was relieved to see that the swelling had gone down a bit, but my mother didn't seem to notice. "It's best to stay off this foot, son. I'm keeping you home from school this week."

"A week? No! I'm good mama. See!" I slid up off the bed and took a few steps to prove how well I could walk, struggling to ignore the sharp pain that emanated up my leg. "Henry's riding his pony to school today and he said he'd let me ride too."

"I don't want you fooling with any ponies or driving horses from now on," my mother said, directing me back into bed. "There's plenty of time for all of that when you're older."

"Mama, please?"

"No, Jake. And that's final." She turned her back and walked to the door, then faced me again. "A pony can spook as easily as a horse and be just as dangerous. I can't breathe for the terror of the thought. Now don't give me any lip. You lie right still and I'll be back in a few minutes with your breakfast."

She left the door open wide so that she'd be able to hear me from the kitchen.

I pulled the covers up to my chin and sulked in anger and frustration, having no idea at that moment of how deep the seeds of her fear were set and how powerfully it would prove to strangle my life.

CHAPTER THREE

"ALBERT, STOP," MY MOTHER DEMANDED when my father, still foggy from a long, drawn-out church sermon, hoisted me into the driver's seat the following Sunday. She aimed her voice high in the thin, fast wind. "I don't want you encouraging him to do such dangerous things anymore. He's much too young. I don't know why I let him take those reins in the first place. I must have been out of my mind." She shook her head, and her eyes narrowed. "I'll not risk losing my only child to some silly accident."

"He's fine, Sarah. Look at him. Besides, he's driven the wagon with me countless times and that incident was the only time anything out of the ordinary has ever happened." Standing alongside the wagon, my father did his best to convince her. "It's hardly enough to warrant stopping the whole parade!"

But my mother ignored him. Without missing a beat, she bristled. "Jake, get over here."

"I can do it, Mama," I shot back at her, meeting my father's eyes in desperation. "I'm not a baby."

"Don't sass me, Jake." She lashed out again, her voice louder than what I was used to. "You'll not be driving those horses anymore."

Humiliation colored my cheeks as I recognized many of the people fanning out into the churchyard and throwing quizzical looks our way. I remained defiant in the seat though, my eyes set straight out over the backs of the horses and the reins limp in my hands.

Angered by my belligerence, my mother's insistence only escalated. She stood up, towering over me. "Slide over here right now young man, and I mean it."

She reached out and caught me by the arm and I had no choice but to let myself be pulled across the wagon seat, knowing that my best friend, Henry, and some of the other boys had gathered in a semi-circle nearby to watch. "Dad," I cried in misery, but my father just shook his head, hooked his hands onto the side of the wagon frame, climbed in and urged the horses forward, as anxious as I was to be anywhere but there.

I spent my days working the routine chores: feeding oats to the horses and leftovers to the pigs, mucking out the stalls and hoeing vegetables, knowing full well that the other boys were riding horses and fishing in the creek when their chores were done, as I used to do. Sometimes they even went hunting and were allowed to drive the truck with their fathers and older brothers sitting on the seat beside them. As a victim of my mother's iron will, however, I was always left behind. With my father caught up in the spring planting and my mother determined to keep me out of danger at all costs, there wasn't a whole lot going on that excited me. I kept my frustration to myself though, hopeful that over time, perhaps in the slower days of summer, my mother would forget her worries and loosen up.

✫ ✫ ✫

"Jake," my mother called to me one day when school was out and every hour felt as dull and boring as sitting still in church. My father had stopped by the house mid-morning for a fresh horse, and I was fast on his heels as he made his way toward the closet at the end of the hallway in search of his straw hat.

"Take me with you, Dad?" I pleaded as I watched him digging through the shelves. I was desperate to be in the field with him and pretended I hadn't heard my mother as I waited for his answer.

"Your mother's calling you, Jake," my father admonished without turning his head. "Don't ignore her."

I stubbed at the floor with an angry shoe as I ambled back toward the kitchen.

Greeting me with the familiar knot on her brow, my mother turned from the sink with a damp dish towel wringing in her hands. "Don't be going behind my back young man. You've got no business around those horses and plows. Are you listening?"

I grumbled a tight-lipped, "yes, ma'am" and turned my back to leave.

"You're too young, and it's too dangerous," she called after me, determined to drive her point. "You hear me, son? There's enough needs getting done right here with me. In fact, you can gather up the eggs as I'm talking. Basket's by the door."

"That's baby's work!" I cried as I slammed the door behind me. When I returned, I landed the basket on the counter so hard that two of the eggs cracked. She eyed me, but let it pass. My mother had no problem allowing me to stew in my anger as she puttered about. After lunch she thrust jars of coffee at me and sandwiches wrapped in paper to carry to my father in the field. My frustration was compounded by the fact that I was pretty sure Henry was out there with his brothers, working with the men, doing what he could to help. It took everything I had to contain my envy. When I arrived, as I suspected, I found him relaxing with his older brothers and the other men under a large shade tree. Some of them were digging into the food they'd packed from home. My father hopped to his feet, and Henry waved when they saw me coming.

"Appreciate it, son" said my father as I handed him the bag. "Come on over and join us for awhile. Shade tree's the best spot when the sun shows no mercy."

"Looks like you got most of the field turned over," I said, glancing around. I dropped down beside Henry. "How hard is it?"

"It's tough work, that's for sure." Henry unscrewed the lid on a Mason jar half-filled with fresh lemonade. "But it's fun too. Here, have a swig. My mom put extra sugar in it, just the way I like it."

"Thanks," I said, throwing back a long swallow.

"My favorite thing is at the end of the day when I climb into the tractor seat with my dad and we take her to the edge of the road. I get to steer the whole way." Henry laughed. "By that time I'm all tired out, but I feel as if I'd plowed the whole field myself. When's your mama gonna let you come here with us anyway?"

"Ah, I don't know. Hey ..." I wanted to switch the subject. "You wanna' go fishing on Sunday? My dad said he'd take us down to the river in the afternoon. I can dig some worms before we go."

"Let's go Saturday instead. We can climb trees down there too. I know some really good ones."

"Naw. I've got to stick with my dad."

"I'll come by after lunch then. You ever tried corn? The fish really like it."

"No, but I got a jar of bugs I can bring."

When some of the men began to pick themselves up and turn their attention back to work, I stood up. My body boiled with fury and my eyes welled up as I made my way down the hill. When I turned into the farmyard, I ran straight to the barn and dove into the hayloft, bawling out a mountain of frustration to the barn cats.

Whenever my father sensed that my mother might be softening, he pleaded with her to change her mind and loosen her grip on me, but over time it was clear that nothing would persuade her. It was as if her personal troubles exaggerated her already prickly nature, and every heart-wrenching miscarriage left her feeling less and less in control. I was the one child she had successfully brought into this world, and she seemed to be hell-bent on keeping in full control of me any way she could.

☆ ☆ ☆

Late into the fall, following my ninth birthday, my parents shared the news that my mother was expecting another baby. I remember her soft soprano voice filling the walls of the farmhouse as she went about wiping down windows and baking fruit pies. She began in the morning as she gathered up the breakfast dishes, then continued on past lunch and into the long stretch of afternoon when she busied herself preparing dinner. "Lord of all hopefulness, Lord of all joy," she sang in her best Sunday voice, peeling potatoes into the big white sink. Sometimes she hummed instead, a never-ending litany that continued from morning 'til night. After the supper dishes were washed and shelved, the counters wiped and the floor swept, she sank deep into the big parlor chair. Then, lifting her yarn basket to her side, she knitted up more booties and soft wool sweaters than one baby could ever need. When she wasn't carrying on the Lord's praises, she was squeezing my shoulders, oftentimes averting her eyes from things that used to warrant a slap on the wrist, or worse yet a scolding, like when I'd reach across the table for the last dinner roll or pick the walnuts out of her freshly baked banana bread. The promise of a new baby was making my mother so giddy that even my father rolled his eyes at times, but he did so with a wry smile and a wink at me, as grateful as we both were for her upbeat mood.

"We are so blessed," she said to him one evening, with the air of a prize-winner. She rubbed her hand over the roundness that curved out from under her housedress. "Oh, Albert." She reached over then and threw her arms around him, startling him with a peck on the side of his cheek. "It's hard to contain my happiness."

My father returned her embrace and grinned broadly. "It's a blessing alright," he said. "This baby's sure been a long time coming."

She gathered up her knitting and my father laid aside the Farm Journal he'd been reading as she began to reminisce. "Jake," she said eyeing me as she settled into the arm chair. "I know you never knew my mama, your grandmother, but you would have taken to her. Grandma Claudia died shortly before you came along, and Grandpa Roy was alone here on the farm, all my sisters having married and gone off with their husbands. We'd only been husband and wife a day, but we moved in to help Grandpa run things. Weren't even here a year when we had ourselves a new baby. You were so anxious to come into the world that you came nearly a month early but, praise God, you were healthy and strong. Grandpa Roy loved taking you for walks in the garden and playing hide 'n seek with you between the rows of vegetables. You remember any 'a that, Jake?"

"Maybe a little, Mama," I replied. I lay spread out on the floor close to her chair, struck by the tenderness in her voice that had been missing for so long.

"You were only a tot. Hard to remember much when you're that young." She knitted for a bit before changing the topic to the more immediate business of our growing family. "Jake, we've been settling on names now, and we're partial to Mary Claudia for a girl or Joseph Royal for a boy, after Grandma and Grandpa, that is."

"Those are nice names, Mama," I said. I'd never heard the name Royal before, and thought it a strange name for a baby, but I didn't want to say anything disagreeable that might alter her mood.

She rambled on: "Grandpa's name was Royal, though everyone between here and Coon Rapids called him Roy. When this baby is born I want to honor one of them with a naming. After all, we already named you after Grandpa Frye."

Before I could respond, she called me over as excited as I'd ever seen her.

"Come here, son. Be quick now!"

I hurried over and she reached for my hand and placed it on her protruding belly. "You feel that?" she said, studying my face with eagerness. "That's the baby kicking." Holding my hand over the small flutters under her skin, she smiled. It took me a moment to make the connection, but then suddenly the baby inside of her became real for me and my face lit up. "If you put your ear down you might even be able to hear the heartbeat." I laid my head against her hard, round belly. The regular "thump, thump, thump," mesmerized me and I leaned in even closer. "Yes, I hear it, Mama. Imagine that."

She ran her hand through my hair and touched my cheek. "It sure does make me happy that soon you'll have a brother or a sister, Jake. Lord knows it's about time, as long as we've waited and as big as you're getting."

"I love you, son," she said, wiping a smudge of flour from the side of my face with her thumb.

"I love you too, Mama."

CHAPTER FOUR

"JAKE!" MY MOTHER'S PANIC REACHED across the yard one hot day as I poked around the barn loft for stray eggs. "Jake, help me!" Just minutes before, she'd been tossing feed to a knot of chickens pecking at the ground under her skirt. Now, as I swung open the loft door, she was sprawled in the dirt twisting in a lot of pain. Shoving a pitch fork out of the way, I tore across the yard. My mother moaned, and I felt my heart drumming against the walls of my chest as I slid down next to her. "Mama, what happened? What's wrong?"

Panting in the fevered sun, it was only the two of us stuck in the debris of feathers and chicken feed and the pestering sounds of animals distracted from their regular business.

"You have to help me, Jake!"

"What is it, Mama?"

I was terrified to see her this way, unable to stand, her face contorted in pain, her eyes so full of fear. She looked as gray as the cold ashes she had me scrape up out of the living room fireplace. "What do you want me to do, Mama?" I stammered.

"The baby's ... coming ... now ..." Her voice was breaking as she tried to catch her breath, clutching at her protruding belly. I got behind her with my arms and threw my weight against her shoulders to lift her, but her head rolled back and she dropped heavily to the ground.

"Mama!" I flopped down beside her, fighting back tears and struggling to stay strong. "Mama, what should I do?"

"Run ... get your ... daddy, Jake." Her face twisted into a frightening grimace. "Now, Jake. Hurry!"

I raced across the dirt road at the end of our driveway, up and over the hill, nearly tumbling down into the field where I spotted my father's straw cowboy hat near the hay wagon. Screaming his name over and over, I pushed forward, my desperation getting the better of me as tears rolled down my cheeks. Wheeling around, he hurried to meet me. "Jake, what's wrong?"

"Dad! Mama needs you real bad!" I panted, stumbling into his open arms and choking back sobs. "Come quick."

I was wailing hard then as I pictured my mother lying helpless on the ground and twisting in agony. My father bent down on one knee and took me by the shoulders. "Calm down, Jake. What's happened, son? Tell me."

"I was in the hay loft when she hollered for help, Dad. She's in the barnyard in a bad way … crying … there's a lot of pain. I couldn't get her up!"

"What happened, Jake? Is she bleeding?"

"She said the baby's coming. Is she going to die, Dad? I think she's gonna die."

"No, Jake. I'm sure she'll be okay." But his face had turned from concern to fear and I knew I was right to be worried. My father jumped on a saddle horse hitched to a nearby tree and called over his shoulder: "Tell Mr. Stivers what's happened and I'll see you at home." He galloped up the wide sloping hill then down toward the farmhouse.

There he found my mother lying in the dirt just as I'd left her, still fighting the contractions and unable to pull herself to her feet.

"Sarah," he called out, dropping to his knees on the ground beside her.

"Albert," she sobbed. "The baby …"

"Let me get you out of here." Gathering her into his arms, he carried her into the house and placed her as gently as he could on their bed before ringing the wall phone for Doc Blumenthal.

When I told Henry's father what had happened he motioned me into the seat of his old pickup and we rattled up to the front porch of the farmhouse. He was fast on my heels as I banged through the screen door. The familiar scent of my mother's apple pie lingered in the kitchen and her cries tumbled down the hallway from the recesses of their room.

I poked my head around the open door of my parent's bedroom and found my father sitting beside my mother on the bed, his work shirt open at the neck, a glass of cool water ready in his hand.

"Is she gonna be okay, Dad?"

"I'm sure she will be, Jake. Doc's on his way. Would you do us a favor and go to the front porch and watch for him?"

"Okay, Dad. And Dad, Mr. Stivers is here too."

"What more can I do, Albert?" said Oscar.

"It's more or less a waitin' game until the doc shows up. I appreciate you seein' Jake home. That was a big help."

"I'm going to swing by the house and let Minnie know what's going on here. She can pack up some food for supper."

"That would be real nice. I promise to ring you when the doc's come and gone."

Oscar strode past me on his way out the door. "I'll be by later to see how things are going," he said, giving my shoulder a quick pat. "You take care now."

I stared down our long driveway that led to the main road, my mother crying out at intervals when she could not bear the pain. Sitting on the top step, I pull my jackknife out of my pocket and stripped twig after twig of their bark, jumping up at the faintest sound. What was taking so long? Finally, I caught sight of Doc Blumenthal's black Chevy motoring down the road in a circle of dust, and I raced into the driveway with both arms waving high above my head.

Doc Blumenthal pulled up short alongside me, grabbed his leather satchel out of the back and slammed the car door behind him. "Hey, Jake," he said. The fact that his white shirt was crumpled and the arms were rolled up past his elbows belied the fact that he had come quickly.

"Hurry, Doc," I stammered. He swept past me up the steps of the porch, and I hustled to keep up. "They're in the bedroom. Please don't let anything bad happen to my mom." He handed me his cowboy hat, turned into the hallway then disappeared inside my parents' room.

I stood with my ear against the closed door. The conversation between the doc and my dad was muffled, but my mother's cries of pain came through loud and clear. Slumping down along the wall, I pulled my knees up tight to my chest. "Please, God," I prayed, "let my mother be alright."

I sat there as the voices inside the room floated in and out of range like an old radio that could not be tuned in. After awhile, I got frustrated and as I stood up and stretched my legs, I heard my mother's voice loud and clear.

"Why?" she cried. "Why does this happen to me?"

I understood then what had taken place and I couldn't bear to hear anymore. Every fiber of my body was set with my mother's weeping, and I cried too for the loss of this baby who had become real for me that evening by the fire.

Making my way into the parlor room, I dropped like a stone onto the davenport. It seemed like forever until I heard the bedroom door open and I bolted upright almost spilling the tears I'd been holding in. Doc Blumenthal clutched his black bag with one hand and cradled something wrapped in a towel in the other. "Is my mother going to be okay, Doc?" I blurted out.

"You mother's going to be fine, Jake," he said, as he accepted his hat from my outstretched hand. He looked worn out, like my father did when he came home late from a hard day in the fields. "But she's had a baby today, and God saw fit to call him home before he could take his first breath. I'm sorry, son."

"But she's okay, right?"

"Yes, she'll be on her feet in a week or so. You can count on that. I'll come around tomorrow. Try and help your father now, okay?"

"Yes, sir. I sure will."

My mother cried relentlessly after Doc Blumenthal had gone, and she peppered my dad with questions that tormented her. "Why me? What did I do, Albert? Why do my babies always die?" I slowly pushed open the bedroom door but she barely noticed me, distraught as she was, clutching the edge of the quilt to her chin, her brown eyes wet and shiny. "I just want to know why." She leaned up from her pillow as she spoke, twisting the thin gold band on her left hand. When she caught my eye, she reached out and I went running over. "Mama," I said, relieved to be in her arms at last.

My father pulled over a chair and lifted me onto his knee, switching on the table lamp that cast a warm glow about the room. I held onto him while he soothed us both and shushed my mother as if she were herself a small child.

Two days later it was all thunder and lightning - pouring rain outside. We dipped our fingers in the holy water and crossed ourselves as we entered St. Margaret's for the simple funeral. The sight of the tiny white casket in front of the altar started my mother crying all over again, and my father comforted her in his arms as we made our way down the aisle to the first pew.

When the mass was over, we opened umbrellas in the now drizzling sky and followed the casket outside to the small fenced-off cemetery next to the church where a temporary grave marker was placed on the small mound of dirt. My mother stood quietly throughout the ceremony, then dropped to her knees and rendered deep exhalations of grief when Father Waller closed his prayer book and pronounced his final "Amen."

Minnie Stivers, Henry's mother, had plenty to do caring for her own large family, but she came around every afternoon and picked up the slack at our house too, where she wiped down the kitchen floor and left casseroles and homemade buns on the stovetop. She also ordered Henry and me to pick the ripe tomatoes, scatter the chicken feed, fetch onions and jars of pickles from the root cellar, and tend to the endless number of other chores that needed doing. I was grateful to be busy and out in the farmyard feeling useful. Father Waller stopped by on several occasions as well, and I could hear repetitions of the "Hail Mary" resonating as he and my mother prayed the rosary together. Afraid of disturbing her endless naps and the hours she sat in the big parlor chair immersed in her Bible oblivious to our needs, my father and I tip-toed around the house. One morning she showed up unexpectedly at the breakfast table with her Bible tucked halfway inside a front pocket of her apron.

"I guess you can't live on toast and jelly alone," she said bluntly. "I'll just fry up some eggs and a side or two of Minnie's ham."

My father smiled in my direction and nodded. "We'd sure appreciate that, Sarah. There's nothing we love more than your cooking. You know that."

Following the accident, there was an ever-lengthening list of forbidden activities. In addition to her original edict of no driving the horse team or the tractor and no hunting or shooting with the Stivers' boys, now I was also forbidden to hang out with my friends at the railroad tracks or the river, the woods, or anywhere near the county road, where the cars "travel too fast." My father scratched his head at the standoff between us and tried to sort it out, jumping into the ring now and then, but getting nowhere. I knew I couldn't change her mind, but the urge to break out of the straightjacket was so powerful that one day, when Henry told me he was going target shooting with his eldest brother who'd received a field rifle for his birthday, I couldn't stand it any longer. "Hey, Henry, mind if I come along?"

He looked at me, somewhat incredulous. "Yeah, but are you sure?" he said. "You could get in trouble."

"Yeah, no doubt," I answered, "but I don't care. I'm sick of doing nothing but chores. Come on, let's hurry before it gets too late."

I watched Henry and his brother fire off round after round, and then Henry's brother cocked the gun up for me, showing me how to line my eye in the peep sight, and allowed me to fire off a few rounds on my own. I was in heaven!

Predictably, there was hell to pay when I found my mother at our usual meeting place halfway through the Stiver's pasture that ran between our property and the schoolhouse. As I drew up, there she stood, puffing like the dragon I'd seen in a cartoon, smokeless, with arms akimbo. When I defiantly admitted what I'd been up to, she grew even more furious, yanking my collar with a stiff arm and marching me home. Later, I made it clear that scolding me and sending me to bed with no supper was worth the price of shooting a loaded gun.

"I don't care," I screamed as I slammed the door to my bedroom so hard that the portraits on the hallway wall skewed in the wake. "I'd fire that gun again a thousand times." Before she could respond, I added: "Someday you won't be able to stop me from doing anything!"

"We'll see about that, young man. Maybe I'll just keep you home and school you myself," my mother fired back, pressing her cheek flat against the door as she pounded out her reply.

"Hold on you two," said my father, stepping into the hallway, the sweat of a hard day's work still fresh on his brow.

"What's going on, Sarah?" he said, tugging her away from the door.

"Our son was off shooting guns with those Stivers boys. Nothing I gave him permission for."

"Would you give the boy a break, Sarah?" He squared her shoulders, so that he could meet her eyes. "He only wants to do what the other boys do. You've got to let him grow up. Let me teach him to shoot. He's going to learn sooner or later."

"But he's my only child!" Her voice broke as she smudged tear tracks across her cheeks. Wisps of curly, dark hair loosened around her face as she shoved him off. "I don't know how I'd live if something happened to him. You should understand. Why don't you care, too? That's what I can't figure out."

And so she would have none of it, and my father moved quietly away, feeling sorry for the ache in his wife's heart for every baby she had lost. He knew her mothering stifled me, and yet he couldn't bear to see her anymore unhappy than she already was.

Truth is, he couldn't argue that our lives weren't full of danger. Reports of horrific accidents buzzed through the party lines on a regular basis: clothing and limbs tangled in farm equipment, necks broken falling off horses, deadly lightning strikes on men working the fields, friends killed by bullets meant for a deer. Just three months ago my friend Theo, along with Henry and two other boys, had gone out frog hunting. The story that came out later was that they had lugged two tractor-tire inner tubes through the tall grasses that surrounded the wet banks of a nearby pond and then launched them into the murky water. The weather that day was hot and sticky after a hard rain, and the swollen waters were overrun with noisy frogs. Theo and Henry jumped on one of the tubes and the two other boys clung to the second. Each tube had a gunny sack roped around it and the game was to see who could catch the most frogs. Using their hands as paddles to rustle the reeds and pussy willows, the boys bumped along the muddy banks and chased after the frogs as they escaped into deeper waters. It wasn't long before horseplay ensued with each team racing, rocking, splashing and carrying on until one of the tubes flipped over, and Theo went under. When he reappeared several feet away, everyone shouted and paddled frantically toward him, but Theo went down struggling a second time, and then a third, until eventually the water went still.

Word of the tragedy spread like wildfire through our tight farming community, and the blood drained from my mother's face upon hearing the news.

"It's the grace of God that gives me the sense not to let you do such foolish things," she'd said.

She had been too upset to attend the funeral, but she made sure my father took me, and on the way home from the service he seemed to have adopted her attitude. "Jake, kids do a lot of foolish things in the name of play. Promise me you won't be taking off and doing anything you know your mother wouldn't approve of."

I muttered a "Yes, sir," knowing this episode would only fortify the endless silent barrier between my mother and I that would continue to define our relationship.

CHAPTER FIVE

TALK OF BABIES DWINDLED TO nothing as the seasons on the farm ticked by one after the other, but when my mother's belly pushed timidly out underneath her apron in the late summer as I turned eleven, she allowed herself once again to feel a glimmer of hope. I knew something was up when she started up her church singing again, something she hadn't done since she was last hopeful about a pregnancy. When we arrived home from the Labor Day picnic, my father tapped his spoon on a water glass and winked at me. "A new baby is on its way, son," he said, confirming my suspicion. "Doc Blumenthal's going to put your mother on bed rest when she gets a little further along. Looks like you're gonna be a big brother after all, God willing."

I'd witnessed enough of my mother's woes through the years to build up my own apprehension regarding such an announcement, but I was glad to see a smile on my mother's face and grateful for the return of her softer tone and lighter mood.

"If you say so, Dad," I answered. "This time'll be different, I'm sure."

☆   ☆   ☆

Three months later my mother took to her bed and my old Aunt Liddy, never married and with no children of her own to tie her down, rode the train up from Kansas City to help ease the situation. "Growing fast as a weed, Jake," Liddy gushed as she pulled me into her ample talc-scented bosom. "Almost as tall as me already. Why, I remember giving you a bottle and rocking you to sleep when you were just a little thing.

But it's your mama needs the looking after now. You help with the chores and stay out from under my feet and I'll be able to do just that."

With the long, drawn out pregnancy landing my mother flat on her back, impinged by a belly so large she couldn't see her toes, my mother had no choice but to loosen her grip on me. And with real freedom for the first time in my life, after working my chores and checking in on her, I spent every free moment on the Stiver's farm where I ran wild with Henry, scaring up rabbits with the .22, and playing countless games of Hide-and-Seek. I even managed to twice steal a kiss from Henry's twin sister, Jess, as we both hid from Henry in the hayloft. Some days Henry and I would set traplines on the river for muskrat and mink, or hike into town where we'd fill up on penny candy and spend hours jumping on and off slow moving freight trains as their massive engines rolled them through town. Even just dealing a hand or two of racehorse rummy in the barn loft with Henry and Jess was better than anything that went on at my house where Aunt Liddy kept things as quiet as a church.

I pushed my new found freedom to unimagined limits, nearly freezing to death one Saturday after chores when Henry talked me into trying our luck at ice fishing.

"Chop the hole right here, Jake," Henry said, sliding out onto the frozen river on two inches of powdery snow. "Me and Titus caught three crappies here last year."

We had borrowed a pick ax from the barn, and as I let the ax fall where Henry marked the spot, a wedge of ice that was weakened by the current below gave way and the swift moving water soaked us to the skin. Scrambling toward shore, we dragged the heavy ax behind us, our pants legs stiffening into stove pipes by the time we hobbled, half frozen, into Aunt Liddy's kitchen.

"Shush, boys. Mama's taking a nap," she whispered as we tumbled in through the porch door. Handing us blankets and dry clothes, Aunt Liddy demanded to know what had happened. She tisked loudly when we told her and muttered something about 'boys being boys,' but when the expected punishment wasn't forthcoming, I uttered a prayer of thanks that she obviously hadn't told my mother. When I couldn't stop shivering at supper that night though, my father, who had caught wind of the incident, sent me to bed early. Still energized from the day's adventure, I lay awake most of the night day-dreaming about all of the things Henry and I planned to do in the coming months. I feared my mother's heavy hand would return after the baby was born, but I pushed aside the thoughts and returned to my daydreams, just as powerful those days as the anger and frustration that had gripped me these last few years.

For two months I drifted into the mainstream of boyhood, distracted from the goings on at home. Over at the Stiver's farm, an extra mouth at the table of ten was accepted without a word. I loved sitting next to Jess on cold evenings when I was allowed to stay for dinner. Mrs. Stivers hailed from the south and at least once a week she'd cook up a big black pot of chili along with skillet cornbread, a dish that was unfamiliar at my house, but that I grew to crave. Between homework, chores and time spent at the Stivers, I was plenty busy.

It's no wonder I wasn't expecting it when one day I tramped home from school to learn that I had finally become a big brother. It was my father, instead of Aunt Liddy, who greeted me at the door that day looking happier and more excited than I'd ever seen him. "Your mother had a baby today, son," he said, his face glowing. "Come see your new brother."

"A boy!" I shouted. Secretly I'd always hoped for a brother, but I'd never shared that with anyone knowing that the proper response when asked, was, "Oh, it doesn't really matter so long as it's healthy." I tugged off my mittens and undid the muffler around my neck. My father reached over and held the sleeves of my coat so I could pull my arms out. "A little brother, huh?"

"Yes, son," he said, hanging my chilled coat on a wall hook. "He's healthy and strong and looks a lot like you did when you were born. Even has the same cry."

I followed my father toward the back bedroom. "What's his name?" I asked. I realized then that no names had been mentioned for this new baby, so I had no idea what it could be.

"Well, your mother has a name in mind but I'm sure she wants to be the one to tell you."

I hurried to my mother's bedside and stared at the small wrinkled infant in her arms. "What do you think, Jake?" Smiling broadly, she nudged the blanket away from the baby's chin so that I could get a better look. "Isn't he something?"

"Wow! He's so tiny!" I leaned in. The baby had his eyes closed and his hands were curled in round little fists. "What are we going to name him?"

"Edwin," my mother said. "And his middle name is Michael-Royal, after the strongest angel in heaven and your grandpa Roy."

"I like that name a lot, Mama."

My mother gave her best smile and patted the spot next to her, inviting me to come closer. Gingerly, I climbed up on the bed, fearful of disturbing the baby. My father pulled the corner chair up next to me, and we stayed there like that, the four of us, just basking in the wonder of this miracle that we'd waited for, for so long.

✫ ✫ ✫

The tranquility of the first week did not last. Edwin was so colicky and fussy that the exhausted adults had to take shifts to comfort him. After Aunt Liddy headed back to Kansas three months later, my mother, overwhelmed with the duties of the farm and her demanding infant, tried half-heartedly to keep tabs on me. It took more energy than she had to spare though, and her focus on Edwin allowed me even more license to do as I pleased. Elated by my ever increasing freedom, I begged my father to allow me to help with the spring planting. When he silently went about his business without so much as even a small rebuke, I knew that he had agreed. The following morning I rode out in the wagon with him, heady with the realization that at last I would spend my days alongside my friends and our fathers.

In spite of my mother's reluctant leniency, it was clear that she was not happy, and it wasn't long before she started up again one night when she thought I'd gone off to my room. "There's plenty of chores to do around here," she told my father for the umpteenth time. "He should wait until the harvest begins, then go back to working in the barn loft." I was frozen up against the wall in the hallway listening in on the conversation. "He can spread out the hay loads as you bring them in. Why, that's a job in itself."

"Don't worry, Sarah," my father said, and I could tell by his tone that he was frustrated that the uneasiness in her heart still lingered. She had scrubbed the kitchen, bathed Edwin and was sitting in a rocking chair in the parlor catching the evening breeze near a propped open window. My baby brother fidgeted on her lap.

"I'll keep a good eye on him," my father reassured her. "You've got to let Jake grow up, Sarah. It's time he came full-out with the men and did his fair share. It looks bad that he doesn't pull his weight in the fields being as old as he is."

"Go on then," she relented, shrugging her shoulders in resignation. I could easily imagine the old "nothing better happen to that boy" look on her face as she added, "but I don't want to learn down the road that I was right. You hear me, Albert?"

Listening to my mother's words sent a shock of panic into the pit of my stomach. All of my old fears came flooding back and I understood at that moment what a fragile position I was in and how fast things could change. Why did she have to bring this up again? Her robust nature had been chipped away by the difficulties of her failed pregnancies and the harsh realities of life as a farmer's wife, and it worried my father. I remembered overhearing my father talking with Oscar Stivers about it. The men had been resting against the side of one of the wagons, sharing a jar of iced tea during a break. They didn't know that Henry and I were within earshot. My father spoke up first.

"I'm really worried about Sarah," he said. She's having a difficult time since losing another baby. My Aunt Elga, lost her youngest child to scarlet fever, and to this day, as far as I know, she lives a lonely life in some old rambling farmhouse. Rarely ventures out. Last I heard she couldn't even be coaxed to church on Sundays."

"It happens," Oscar had agreed.

"I never thought a wife of mine would suffer from something like that, but lately I'm beginning to wonder."

"Well, you never know which way things are gonna go in these situations."

"Oh, I know. I just hope and pray that the good Lord and time will provide some healing, and that as the children grow she'll regain the pleasant disposition of the woman I married more than ten years ago now."

"She's a strong woman, Albert. I'm sure it'll all work out. I'd bet on it."

"Well, thanks for the kind words. I sure do hope so."

Henry just looked at me. He'd been around my family long enough to know the undercurrent that most days kept my father and me walking a tightrope, never quite sure anymore what was going to shake my mother's fragile resolve and send her spiraling down.

CHAPTER SIX

B
Y THE TIME I MANAGED to get another harvest under my belt, I almost felt as much a man as anyone out there. Luck had shifted circumstances in my favor and my mother didn't say a word anymore as I rode out with my father in the light of dawn, taking my proper place in the fields. The only thing holding me back was her stalwart refusal to allow me to drive the horses.

It was no wonder I picked up my head in surprise at the end of one blistering August day when my father swung his sweat-stained body into the passenger side of the rack wagon, nudged me over and slapped me the reins. "Steady in the hand now," he said, smiling my way as he poked back his hat and wiped his forehead with his bandana. "Remember now, you've got to show you're in control. These horses are smart. They can tell when a man's slacking. Cut your eyes across their backs and let's giddy-up this load to the barn. Your mama's more than likely got supper on the table."

"Really, dad? Are you sure? Won't mom be angry?"

"Only if you tell her, son."

"Let's go!" I shouted, clucking my tongue. "Giddy-up now!" I snapped the reins, causing the horses to lurch forward before they settled into an easy walk. Justice was on the left and Noah on the right. The horses were new, a pair of gray Percheron geldings, heavily muscled with thick legs and necks. Their round hips moved in sync as they sauntered down a straightaway to the edge of the field and onto the farm road, their powerful hooves clomping up ground dust. They sensed a feeding and needed little prompting to move along. The husky scent of cut alfalfa clung to my cotton shirt in the afternoon heat, and sweat mingled with wisps of hay that felt prickly on my skin. A hot breeze was kicked up by the wagon as it rattled along, but the air brought little relief. Perched high in the driver's seat, however, the heat didn't bother me. I was a man now, of that I felt sure, and a sense of worthiness barreled over me as I held my head up high and steadied the team toward home.

After settling the horses into their stalls, my father tapped my arm. "Son, I have something to say, and I need you to listen up." I knew then that he meant business since he only spoke to me that way when he was reprimanding me or when he was intent on teaching me a lesson. "You're doing a fine job, Jake, but I want you to promise me you won't be getting any crazy ideas about taking the wagon-team out by yourself. These horses are kind of skittish, not all broke in yet either. Got to take things slow, ease your mama in now that she's feeling better."

"Sure, dad."

"Now, what did I say?"

"That I won't take 'em out without you."

"Your word?"

"Yes, sir," I promised in my most grown-up voice.

"Good. Now let's go eat. Your mama's got a sixth sense, so I know she'll sniff it out soon enough, but for now let's keep this just between us." He winked at me as he threw his arm around my shoulders.

"I wasn't going to say anything, Dad," I said, flashing him a smile.

We trudged in from the barn, and the smell of onion bread hung in the warmth of our squared-off kitchen. Edwin toddled past my father and bee-lined toward me on chubby bowed legs, his little bare feet slapping the floor. Welcoming him with open arms, I snatched him up and twisted him into the air where he giggled and arched his back like a tiny acrobat. At first I'd had mixed feelings about this small creature who seemed only to spit up, fuss, and stink up the house. But lately he was grinning baby teeth all over the place and I found myself relishing the sweetness of the bond that was growing between us.

"He sure does favor you, son," said my father stepping around to the sink to kiss my mother hello. "Smells mighty good in here, Sarah."

I belly-laughed my baby brother, landing him on the ground and giving him a go, but instead of waddling over to my parents Edwin teetered into my legs and clung to my pants with his tight, pudgy fists.

"Hey, you," I said, patting his thatch of wiry brown hair. "Let me see how big you are today."

I hefted him up. He felt soft and bulky, and a surge of affection for him ran through me, even with the dried milk and orange pieces caked on his overalls.

"You don't cry much anymore," I said, reveling in what had become his good nature. I indulged him with another toss in the air before initiating our now familiar game of hide-and-seek. "Come find me, Edwin," I said as I ran and hid behind the wall of the small vestibule where we'd hung our hats. Edwin giggled and chased in my direction. As he rounded the corner, I jumped out, caught him up, spun him and tickled his belly before running toward the living room to hide again.

"Boys, stop your horsing around and go wash up!" my mother ordered, scowling after us and pulling the roaster out of the oven. "That child took a long nap for once and freed me to prepare a proper meal, and I don't need to set it on the table cold."

When my father and I had scrubbed the grime from our faces, dug the dirt out from under our fingernails, and pulled our chairs to the table, we made the sign of the cross and bowed our heads as my father lead the prayer.

"Bless us, Oh Lord, for these Thy gifts, which we are about to receive from Thy bounty, through Christ our Lord. Amen."

The three of us barely had time to echo the final "Amen" when my mother started in.

"I saw you driving that wagon home, Jake," she snapped as she propped Edwin up in his highchair and turned again to the table. She didn't miss a beat as she zeroed a spoonful of dumpling into Edwin's open waiting mouth. "Don't think I didn't see you, and I'll tell you what … it scares me to death." She pushed on, letting her voice rise to a pitch that made me cringe and set Edwin to howling. "I've enough on my plate these days raising this baby and running this house without having to worry about you and some spooked horses."

My father and I shared a knowing glance as he passed me the plate of bread. My mother clacked the kitchen knife against the porcelain plate as she chopped up meat for Edwin, with an anger she'd not shown since before he was born. I kept my head down, unwilling to meet her fury face to face.

I looked again to my father for support, but he held his tongue and we ate the rest of the meal in an uncomfortable silence until my mother's mood blessedly lifted as she stood to gather the dishes.

"How are the plans coming for the haymaking party, Sarah? I know the men are looking forward to the celebration after all their hard work. A couple of them have even asked me if you'd be making you apple cake again this year. Sure was a big hit!"

"Well," my mother said plugging the drain and filling the sink with water. "Minnie Stivers stopped by this morning on her way to town. The women have divided up the cooking among themselves and will be ready to go by Saturday, if the weather holds. I'll be bringing my apple cake and then some."

"Seems like this season has gone on forever," said my father, pushing up from his chair to help, grateful for the change of subject. Though the harvest has been sketchy for some, we've plenty to celebrate. Jake, you can help me set up the horseshoes. Oscar won the championship last year as I recall, and I intend to take him on."

Relieved that the tension had dissipated, I scooped up Edwin and jiggled him on my lap. I held his hands and leaned him back between my legs then pulled him up fast, eliciting a round of squeals.

"Of course you should, Dad," I said, keeping my focus on balancing the baby. "Luck was with Mr. Stivers last year, but you're sure to take him this time."

The week passed without another mention of my mother's worries, and by Saturday we were all caught up in the excitement of the day. At noon, fathers and sons from the surrounding families hauled long tables into the grove near the field access, while the mothers and daughters worked up bucket-sized bowls of potato salad, heaped trays with fried chicken, stacked plates with corn and bread, and filled crocks to overflowing with dill pickles, carrots and relish. Then they gathered the platters of pies, cakes and fruit kuchen that had been arriving all morning.

In time, Seth Klein pulled an accordion to his knee and whirled up a polka. The older boys wrestled and played tug-of-war and later, under my mother's watchful eye, I took Edwin by the hand and introduced him to Henry's new puppy, "Ba-Ba" - a collie mix that dug around the tree roots and gnawed on a small red ball.

Suddenly, Edwin spotted the ball that slipped from the puppy's mouth and went after it.

"Mine!" Edwin cried, stretching his arms into the air as the puppy pounced on the ball and trotted away with it in his mouth. "Mine!"

Edwin took off after the dog, but I snatched him up, swinging him back and forth between my legs as his squeals of protest soon turned to laughter and got us going all over again. "No, Edwin, that's Ba-Ba's ball," I said. "You stay here with us."

But the second I set him down he took off again, and I was fast on his heels. We went back and forth like this for several rounds, until I caught him up one last time and tried to settled him down by circling my arms around him in my lap.

"He's fast," said Henry who'd been watching us play as he leaned against a tree where he could keep an eye on his puppy as well.

"Oh yeah," I replied, with pride. "He can get almost anywhere now. We play hide-and-seek and you should see him opening closet doors and scooting under the bed. Yesterday, I found him sitting in Mama's laundry basket and when he caught my eye, he burrowed under the clothes."

"That's funny," Henry laughed.

"Having a brother's okay," I paused. "At first I wasn't sure, but now I can't imagine life without him."

When the picnic ended, my mother shooed my father and I home to attend to the chores, while she stayed behind with Edwin who had nodded off and freed her to help the other women gather leftovers and clean up after the festivities. As we strode along, taking a shortcut through an open pasture, I matched strides with my father.

"Remember when I was small and used to sit between your legs and hold the reins?" I reminisced. "I always felt like a million bucks."

"Oh, I remember it well," said my father with a short laugh. "You were hell-bent even then on getting behind those horses."

"Well, I feel like that now when I take the reins," I said as we continued on.

"I'm mighty proud of you, son." My father rested his arm around my shoulders. "You're proving yourself in the field too, like I always knew you would."

"Thanks, Dad," I said, and I knew that he understood how much a compliment like that meant to me.

CHAPTER SEVEN

AT DAYBREAK THE NEXT MORNING a salmon-blue haze whispered across the open land beneath the fading night sky. Somewhere off in the distance, a rooster rallied his harem and a calf bawled low for it's mother. As my father and I rounded up Justice and Noah from the pasture, our work boots and the edges of our pants grew quickly wet with dew. We walked the horses to the barn, fed and watered them and then harnessed them up for the day of labor that lay before us.

"Go ahead and start milking the cows, Jake, and I'll fill the mangers." We worked the chores together like a well-tuned engine, and in short order returned to the farmhouse and sat down to plates of bacon, eggs and warm bread. When our bellies were full, I offered to finish feeding Edwin.

"I'll do it, Mama," I said, pulling up my chair to the front of the high chair. "We'll be in the field most of the day so I won't see much of him 'til supper." Edwin giggled with delight when I took the spoon of oatmeal from my mother and zoomed it, airplane style, high over his head.

"Stop now, Jake," my mother scolded. "You got him used to this kind of play and then he expects me to do the same. I've not got time for such things. You're spoiling that child left and right."

"Let me have another cup of your hot coffee, Sarah," said my father, deflecting her attention. "Then we'll be on our way."

I finished feeding Edwin then plunked his bowl and spoon into the sink about the same time my father took his last sip of coffee. After we'd washed up and said our goodbye's, we made our way back to the barn and the waiting horses. I took my time steering the wagon out into the field where we met Oscar, Henry and three of his brothers. There were still several windrows of hay to gather, and the Stivers had offered to help. I was thrilled that Henry was already there to see me pull up, riding tall in the driver's seat. When I hopped down he greeted me with his new rifle crooked under his arm.

"I spotted a deer along the edge of the tree grove yesterday," Henry said. "I thought we should be prepared."

"Yeah, I've seen him too," I said. "He's been around here for a day or two now."

"Well, let's say the first one who spots him takes the shot," said Henry. "Whichever way it goes, if one of us gets a hit, our families can share the meat."

"Sounds good," I said, still not quite believing all of my new found freedoms. I'd long given up being jealous over Henry's rifle. He was aware of my predicament and always more than willing to pull me into the action whenever the opportunity arose. As we carried on about who would nab the buck, we spread the pitched hay across the wagon bed. We had almost lost track of time working and spying for the buck, when, in the early afternoon, my father waved me over.

"Jake," he said, "would you run down to the house and pick up the lunch your mama's prepared? I know she's wondering why we haven't called for it yet, so you'd best get a move on."

"Sure, Dad. No, problem. I didn't realize how late it was."

I ran off, taking a shortcut over a small hill that sloped down to the driveway of the farmhouse. Leaping the steps of the porch two at a time, I threw open the screen door. "Hey mom," I said as Edwin toddled toward me. "Dad sent me in for the food."

"Well, you're lucky I'm running late myself today otherwise you'd be eating some soggy sandwiches. I've just about got everything ready to go." She added apples and napkins to the bags and reached for the coffee pot that was sitting on the stove.

I grabbed Edwin's hand and walked him out onto the porch. Wondering if I enjoyed my little brother even more than my mother did, I pointed out the large cow grazing close to the fence along the side of the yard. Back inside the house I handed Edwin off to her and headed back to the field with a paper bag stuffed with sandwiches and a jar of sloshing coffee.

Lost in a daydream of bagging the buck myself and all the glory that would come with it, I was about to cross the road to the hill and the field beyond when I heard several shots ricochet through the grove of trees where just yesterday we were all pitching horseshoes and drinking lemonade. I froze as I watched a driverless Justice and Noah, spooked by the shots and traveling fast, bolt the stacked wagon to the top of the hill and rear up, splaying half the loaded hay across the ground. My heart pounded hard in my chest. The horses were stationary for the moment, but I'd been around horses long enough to know they could easily spook again. Glancing back in the direction of the gunshot, I saw no one.

I sucked in my breath. A large flock of birds had set off in a line at the sound of the shot, whipping back and forth like the tail of a kite. In the distance I spotted my mother, who had come to the screen door to see what the commotion was about. Holding open the door with Edwin in her free arm, she sighted me making my way toward the driverless wagon. In a panic, she set Edwin on the porch and ran toward me, her arms stretched and swaying high above her head. I knew she was calling me even as I turned toward the wagon and forged ahead.

"No … No … Jake!" She gestured and cried repeatedly, the same way I'd witnessed a million times before, until, I knew, her mouth was as dry as paper, her throat as parched as sand. "Leave that wagon alone. You hear me?"

I could have heard her in my sleep, but I knew what I had to do. The horses could take off again and next time somebody could get hurt. Finally, I could prove to her that I was a man. I ignored her order and moved steadily toward the wagon, vaulting myself into the driver's seat and taking up the reins. "Giddy-up!" Assuming another round of fire would follow the first, I cracked the leather straps across the horses' backs and pushed the team over the weeds and rubble that littered the hillside, then steered them down in the direction of the farmyard to get them further out of earshot. I managed to hold steady off the incline and was about to cross the road that ran perpendicular to the driveway when another gunshot echoed from near the grove causing the horses to whinny and side-step. I pulled back tighter on the reins to regain control just at the moment when Justice pranced down on a nest of hornets hidden in a thatch of scrub grass. The yellow-jackets burst up in a dangerous cloud, stinging the horse's legs and underbellies. Rearing their massive bodies high above the ground, they exploded like thunderbolts, searing straight down the driveway and rocketing toward the barn. "Whoah!" I screamed in desperation, and though I pulled back with all I had, the reins burned through my hands, leaving me clinging to the seat rail in terror. The horses, wild and driverless now, stormed into the entrance of the farmyard. My mother turned frantically toward the porch, desperate to reach Edwin before he could put himself in harm's way. Before she could reach him though, my little brother, a mess of snot and tears had inched down the creaky steps and was stumbling toward her.

Feeling the beat of the horses gaining speed as they drew closer, my mother veered out of their path and ran along the barbed wire fence that separated the driveway from a small pasture, with no other thought but to get to her child.

"Edwin, get back!" my mother screamed, but her warning was lost in the deafening wake as the horses burst into the farmyard and roared past her.

When they finally dead-ended at the barn, I lay shocked and bruised on the splintered seat, my heart pounding inside my chest. Slivers of hay and barnyard grime clung to my hair and clouded my eyes. The reins had peeled the skin off my hands, and my mouth, bleeding where I had bitten through my lip, stung with salty tears. Trumping all of these sensations though, were the anguished cries of my mother that sent shockwaves through my body. "My baby!" she screamed. "Please, God, don't take my baby!"

Alerted by the neighing of the traumatized horses, my father, along with Oscar and his boys, ran from the grove where'd they'd gone chasing after the buck. They descended on the scene seconds later, just in time to witness what had transpired. At the sound of the others I slowly raised my head from the seat. Then my eyes locked on the sight of my father, clinging to my mother wailing in the dirt with Edwin limp in her arms.

"No ... no. Oh god!" I shrieked from where I lay prostrate on the wagon seat. "No, not Edwin ... no!" Oscar and his sons rushed to the wagon. The boys hurriedly tethered the horses while Oscar half-lifted me from the seat and walked me, his arm encircling my shoulder, toward the house.

He tried to comfort me with a soft low voice. "There, there, now, boy. It was an accident. You did the best you could. No one can control a spooked horse." I was inconsolable in my sobs and even as he spoke the words, I was sure he knew they were falling on deaf ears.

✫   ✫   ✫

The following days were a blur as mourners filled the farmhouse. Spinning in my own private hell, I kept to my room though no one seemed to notice my absence, and for that I was grateful. The funeral was held on Saturday at St. Margaret's. My mother, in her one black dress, with a faint smear of lipstick on her grim mouth, had gone ahead, keeping her distance from me and my father as she had since the accident. Twenty minutes later, my father and I shuffled into the candlelit church and approached the front pew where my mother was praying, fixated on the diminutive casket that had been placed before the altar and draped with a white pall. Slowly we side-stepped into the pew, startling her out of her trance, and when I glanced my mother's way she turned and glared at me with a look that told me she didn't want me anywhere near her. Desperate to be alone with the shame that coursed through my body, I pushed my way back through the stream of people filling the aisles, ignoring their stares and the murmurs that trailed in my wake.

From behind a broken pew in the back of the church, I watched Father Waller enter. He was dressed in his vestments and flanked by two altar boys, bearing a large wooden cross. The choir sang the "Ave Maria" as the small procession moved slowly toward the altar. The older of the boys swung a censer of incense, and the fragrant smoke filled the church with puffy gray clouds as the priest made the sign of the cross and turned to greet the congregation.

"The grace of our Lord Jesus Christ and the love of God and the fellowship of the Holy Spirit be with you all," he began as he sprinkled holy water on the casket.

I peered out over the dozens of friends and neighbors who had gathered to pay their last respects to a child who, because of me, was gone forever. From the shadows of the old church I could hear my mother's sobs over the prayers of the priest and the mumbled responses of the congregation. When the final "Amen" was sounded to the crowd, Father Waller led the procession, with Oscar Stivers and Seth Klein as pallbearers. My father and mother paced close behind them as they moved the down the aisle. I ducked into the shadowy recesses of the choir balcony and cried, unable to witness any more of my mother's tears.

I did not move even after the last of the attendants had filed out. Minutes later, when I was sure that everyone was long gone and had forgotten me, I heard the bulky church door swing open and the familiar sound of my father's footsteps echoed across the worn out floor.

"Son, where are you?" My father's voice was clear and distinct, though I could tell by its raspy sound that he'd been crying, too. "Come on out, Jake. I know how bad you feel, but it was an accident. No one blames you." As my father passed the spot where I hid, I stood up and took a few tentative steps toward him. He turned to me and opened his arms. "Come here, son. It's gonna be alright. There's some things in life that can't be understood, and this here's one of them. Come on now. Be with your mama and me. We can get through this together. It's the only way."

I allowed my father to wrap his arms around me.

"Thanks, Dad," I said, breathing all of him in with a deep sigh. I slid my arm around my father's waist and walked out of the church and into the sectioned-off yard of the cemetery. My mother stood alone, fiddling with a balled-up hanky, her dog-eared Bible tucked way up tight under her arm.

Buoyed by my father's support, I turned to face her as I took my place next to her. "Mama, I'm sor ...," but before I could finish she shushed me with a finger to her lips, and we watched in silence as the men lowered the body of my little brother into the freshly dug ground.

CHAPTER EIGHT

TIME DID NOT STOP ON the farm even for the tragic death of a child, but rather moved inexorably toward the future as everyone struggled to absorb the blow of Edwin's death. Though blame was rarely mentioned outright, it stood between my mother and me like a sheet of rain across an open plain. Contrary to the assurances of my father, it was clear to me that my mother would forever hold me responsible for the death of the precious baby she had waited so long for.

My mother coped by turning to God in a way that left room for little else. Preferring to keep her nose in the Bible, she refused to look me in the eye and sometimes started supper so late that by the time it was half-prepared my father would be dead-out snoring with his boots hanging off the edge of the couch, our food long forgotten. On the days when she did manage to put together a simple meal, she would serve us while she wiped up the kitchen and fussed over a small canary she kept perched in a cage by the window, lost to us inside herself.

Only once did she pull up her chair and sit down with us, breaking the deadly silence that hung over our house like a threatening cloud. Without warning, she leaned forward and took hold of my arm, her face frighteningly close to mine. "You never did listen, Jake. Why couldn't you just heed my warnings?"

She spit out her words in a voice hoarse from crying, clearly drawing satisfaction from the pain she knew she was inflicting.

"Accidents happen, Sarah," said my father, firm but gentle. "It wasn't the boy's fault. We shouldn't have gone off after that buck either, leaving the horses unattended and free to spook."

"I'm sorry, Mama," I uttered in the direction of my plate, unwilling to face the full blast of her anger. However, even as I spoke the words I knew they would never change her judgment of me.

Ignoring us both, she lunged forward and unleashed a rage that stunned us both to silence. "If you had both listened like I told you nobody would be talking sorry. It's too late for sorry and sorry won't bring my baby back!" Then, stepping back to face us both, she spit out the final words of her tirade. "Sorry won't fix promises not kept!" She turned then and stormed away to the privacy of the bedroom, slamming the door behind her.

The days passed in a haze of silence. Anger and grief seeped into every crevice of life in the old farmhouse and left me feeling more numb and alone than ever. A month or so later, when I could stand it no longer, I stuffed a gunny sack with a few pieces of clothing, tied it with a rope and hid it behind the barn. Later that night, I waited until I heard my father's muffled sleep before creeping down the hall into the kitchen. Splashing its light wide and washing the room in an opalescent glow, the moon beamed in through the filmy window panes and the bird slept hushed inside its covered cage.

"*I can't live here anymore,*" I scribbled nervously on a scrap of paper. "*I'm sorry. I wish I had died that day, but Edwin is gone and nothing can bring him back. My being in the house just makes things worse. I hope someday you can forgive me.*"

I poked the note on a nail where the dishtowel embroidered with my baby brother's name in bold letters dangled loosely. My mother had hung it there when she returned from Edwin's funeral and it had remained there untouched ever since. I felt tears well up remembering her working on those dishtowels when she was laid up in bed the months prior to Edwin's birth. She had worked up several sets for every day of the week, and then decided to embroider names on two more: Edwin for a boy, Claudia for a girl. One day, in a voice more energetic than I'd heard in awhile, she had called me into the bedroom and waved one of the towels as if it were a flag.

"Look what was tucked away in the bottom of that old chest." Motioning me to sit beside her, her arm reached out as I drew near, and she scooted aside on the bed. "Your father found this when I had him digging through it last night. I stitched this towel when I was pregnant with you. I had forgotten I had it." She'd smiled wanly, tucking a loose curl behind her ear and showing me that she had stitched one with my name on it as well many years before.

"That's nice, Mama," I said and for a moment, I was struck by the beauty of her face, her translucent skin as pale as milk, her soft, brown eyes, the dark wisps of hair always slipping out around her face. She took my hand, already as big as hers, and I let myself be pulled into the confined space of the bed that was now her world. For the first time, I was aware of the sacrifice she was making, lying by herself like that so much of the time, alone in the amber lit room, with only her thoughts to keep her company. I had never imagined her as anything other than headstrong and confident before, and it shook me to see her so vulnerable, her body at the mercy of this unborn baby.

It had been one of her better days, and she drew herself up with an air of attentiveness when I came near, revealing a sliver of her old self. Setting her stitching aside, she picked up a glass on her nightstand and held it out to me. "Here, son," she said. "Would you do your mama a favor and water my geranium plant on the windowsill? Poor thing's dying of thirst."

I filled the glass in the kitchen faucet and when I returned, her eyes followed me as I watered the gangly plant. The stem of the plant had bent reaching for the window light, and I turned it now so that its single red blossom faced my mother on the bed.

"The plant was full of blossoms when your father gave it to me," she said in a languid tone, her voice raspy and dry, "but long after the blooms had dropped off that one bud hung on, shut tight for so long that it seemed as if it would never open." She took a sip from her own glass on the nightstand. "I was about ready to toss it out, but I woke up this morning, and lo' and behold, there's a flower. I know it's been real hard on you, Jake, me being laid up and all," she said, shifting her position to face me directly. You're too young to have to deal with any of this and be so much on your own."

"It's okay, Mama. I'm not too young." I threw her a hesitating glance from the window.

"It's my job as your mother to keep you from harm, Jake."

"Yes, Mama," I said as my heart filled up. There was so much I wanted to say to her, but I hesitated. I was afraid of not finding the right words. Instead, I picked up the empty glass and quietly left her room.

☆ ☆ ☆

Alone there in the tidy, bleak kitchen, the house around me slept. The scent of yeast in rising dough hung in the dark silence flooding me with memories of happier times, and I drew my breath in slowly, grief and despair seeping in to poison those reflections. As always, vivid, disjointed scenes raced through my mind: the baby-like white casket, chasing Edwin in the yard, my mother's sobs of grief, the horses racing out of control, the sight of Edwin's body limp in my mother's arms. When the canary fluttered inside its cage interrupting my memories, I scooped up the dishtowel with Edwin's name on it, stuffed it into my coat pocket and eased open the door.

PART II

"Life is not measured by the number of breaths you take, but by the moments that take our breath away."

--- anonymous

CHAPTER NINE

Heading west, 1937

I T WAS MORE THAN AN hour before I came to the edge of town where I crouched among the tumbleweeds stuck along the Great Northern track, and longer still before my ears picked up the faint but recognizable rumble of the train. The long string of railway cars slowed as they passed on their way into the station, the engine's loud decompressing brakes screeching to a final halt that set my heart to pounding. I ran several yards down, then ducked away into the brush again, pausing and listening breathlessly as the massive engine glowed in the moonlight, both of us panting like hard run horses. I was still a long way down the line of boxcars, but I hesitated to leap onto the ladder, in spite of the fact that Henry and I had done it dozens of times before just for the sheer fun of it. This time, I knew, was different. This was no joy ride, and I'd not be coming back on the next train. The magnitude of the decision weighed on me something fierce, but when the engine suddenly came alive in a burst of oily soot and the cars began to roll forward, I willed myself from my hiding spot, grabbed the third rung, swung myself up, and scrambled to the catwalk. I hung on tight, my mouth hanging open as if I'd been sucker-punched under the full weight of my decision. Within minutes the old train wheeled up to speed and slithered westward into the deep, black night.

Petrified, I lay flat, too afraid to even look at the star-filled sky. About a half hour later, when we slowed to a crawl around a narrow bend in a river, I mustered the courage to hop several cars up the line and swing myself into the warmth of an open-door boxcar. When my feet touched down, I was startled by at least a dozen pairs of eyes that stared out at me like ghosts through the darkness of the dingy space. A shock of fear grabbed hard at my insides. The fact was, I would come to learn, thousands of young men and boys had taken to the rails over the past few years, running from the poverty of the depression and situations where they too were not wanted. At least a handful of them were there now. Several mumbled unintelligible greetings to me as I joined them. Though frightened and wary, I sensed a comforting camaraderie in spite of their varied ages, and my fear eased when two of the men shifted together to make a space for me against one of the walls. Taking in my new surroundings, I sat myself down and leaned back. As my eyes adjusted further to the dimness, I could make out the allotment of dirty faces, rag-tag clothes and hollow looks of hunger and neglect. It was only minutes though, before I felt a part of them as some of the older men used the opportunity to spin stories and share lessons of survival they had acquired on their journeys. As the train rolled on, I paid close attention, mustering up the courage to ask a question now and then. "Where do you go when the train stops?" It was clear that there was a lot I needed to learn about life on the rails.

"There's 'jungles' out there," one of the men said. He told me the jungles were really camps where I could find others to shelter with along the routes and, if I was lucky, find food as well. The jungles were essential to survival on the road. No matter how bad things got, wherever I landed, as long as there was a camp, I would more than likely not starve to death.

"That's if you make it past the 'yard bulls'," a timid voice piped up from the darkest corner of the boxcar.

"What?"

"Guards," the first man replied. "They come and go. Sometimes they're on the tracks looking for riders like us. Depends on the station. If you see one, just run like hell."

As lonely as I felt beginning this journey, and as haunted as I was by the nagging fear that had tagged me like a shadow ever since I'd closed the kitchen door behind me, I found consolation in the fact that there were hundreds of others just like me also trying to eek out an existence as best they could.

When the train finally pulled into Great Falls, Montana two days later, I was strung out, but heartened by the information I'd gathered and by the easy parlance of the men who had welcomed me. Desperate to breathe fresh air, stretch my cramped legs and fill my long-empty belly, I followed the others to a jungle that had sprung up on the outskirts of town. There I met another kid who could have passed for Henry's brother. He had the same sandy curled hair and blue-green eyes, but he spoke with a more determined clip. "Franz Mueller," he said, offering me a shake and a half-stick of gum. Turned out he'd never been out of North Platte, Nebraska until he'd jumped a long freighter moving west, same as me, three days ago. "Hog farm failed and the old man lost his job," Franz told me right off. "Don't need a hired hand if there's no hogs to tend. Then he took sick with the gout, and now he ain't good for nothing, 'cept he's still saddled with my ma and eight hungry mouths to feed. I got mighty sick of eating watery potato soup for every meal. My ma was so worn out I couldn't stand looking at her anymore. She got so thin it scared me to close my eyes at night. I was just one more burden they didn't need. I'm wantin' to head somewhere where I can find work and not starve to death."

When Franz asked me my reason for leaving home, I hesitated. "I just felt like traveling." I wasn't about to discuss my situation with anyone, let alone a stranger. I quickly changed the subject to information I'd gathered from the more seasoned riders about life on the road.

"We should stick to the warmer climates," I told him. I tried to sound as authoritative as I could, hoping to appear sure of myself and a lot more knowledgeable than I felt. "I hear that's where the work is. They say the picking season's late this year, so when we hit Portland I plan to head south into California for the fruit, then back up north for fall berries before it gets too cold."

"I heard that too. Think we got maybe two months," said Franz. "Don't reckon we'd starve out there. I grew up watching the Union Pacific roll through the acres of tracks in Bailey Yard not more than a mile from my house and there sure weren't many empties coming out of California."

I was inclined to listen to my gut. That's what my father had taught me to do, and that's what I did now as I sized up Franz. We'd been blown together like a couple of tumbleweeds stuck in a barbed wire fence, and he seemed friendly enough, but I was skeptical. He held an air of confidence about him I'd never encountered before in a kid, who I figured, was about my age. "I plan to keep heading west." I threw it out there.

"Me too," said Franz. He studied my face and clothes. They were half-clean but in better shape than the tattered jacket with missing buttons and rolled up sleeves that he wore. "We got to watch out for the yard 'bulls' though." Hearing these bulls mentioned for the second time and Franz's cautionary tone got my attention full-out. "Believe me, I seen enough of that growing up next to the biggest rail yard in the country. There were miles and miles of tracks and mean-ass bulls patrolling every which way."

"Ever run into any of those bulls yourself?"

"My friends and I seen plenty of them going after the hobos, clobbering them over the head with thick flashlights or the butt of a loaded gun. We used to watch from a hill above one of the main switching tracks. A bull could threaten, steal your money, haul your butt to jail, or if you was lucky, just chase you off, but more than likely beat the snot outta' you … you just never knew. We saw one old guy get kicked so hard he looked like nothing but a sack of flour when they were done with him."

"Steal your money?" I asked.

"You got any, they can take it. They'll say it's to pay for the ride, but you know that ain't true. That money goes right into their own pockets."

Franz's revelation about the yard bulls left me more than a little uneasy. It felt natural to me that a note of caution was mandatory for a life on the road since a man never knew what he might cannonball into. But Franz's advice went beyond a note of caution. It was a full-out, life-or-death warning, and it scared me more than I cared to admit.

We traveled the same lines in the coming weeks as we scrounged for food and shelter.

Franz came off as the more street-smart. He'd had Bailey Yard as his playground and had come face-to-face with many of the dangers surrounding the rail yards. I listened, unsure at times and wondering if he might be exaggerating, but I didn't want to take any chances either. The truth was, out in the wild we weren't much more than two lonely, hard-luck boys that life had consigned to one another. We hadn't chosen the circumstances that led us here, but we were together now, and over time I began to rely on him to lead the way.

Franz's story about the bulls had struck me with fear and I knew that I never wanted to encounter them. But I didn't want to stoop to their level either. "Let's make a pact, Franz," I said, "that we won't sink to being thieves, no matter what comes our way. My parents were real strict about that."

"Sure, man. I feel the same way. Whatever we do, we'll be honest about it."

CHAPTER TEN

AFTER TWO NIGHTS HUDDLED IN the jungle camp in Great Falls, we were itching to head out. Franz was more adept at jumping aboard the trains and had been quick to teach me how to haul up on a boxcar going fifteen miles an hour. "You've got be able to outrun the train at the moment of the hop, otherwise you won't make it," he explained with great confidence.

The lessons didn't stop there however, and I soon discovered there was a big streak of the wild in him too. Within days of traveling together, Franz was also instructing me how to run along the top of a train as it sped to the next destination, leaping over the spaces between the boxcars "with a rhythm of step," he emphasized. "The same on every car." Whooping it up in the clear September air, we spread our arms and let the wind steal our laughter as we skipped a long line of boxcars, dropping to our knees well before the caboose. "You got to watch it though, Jake," Franz warned me as we caught our breath. "I once seen a group a kids goofin' off, running on top of a line of cars pulling out of the yard. They got their rhythm going, same steps every time, same leap, until one time someone must'a changed out a boxcar and the distance between the cars spread - not much, I'm telling you, but they weren't paying attention, and it was enough to throw 'em off. One kid went down between two boxcars and never saw the light of day again. The engineer didn't even know it'd happened, just kept rolling right on out of town. I went running down there with three other boys, and I never saw such a mangled mess in my whole life. Something you don't ever wanna' see."

"You're telling me that now, after I just ran twenty cars? Hell, Franz, we could have been killed."

"Well, I knew the cars were lined up and spaced all the same." Franz laughed. He flashed his wide grin that was a big part of his charm. "Checked them out myself before we pulled out, but I'm warning you now. You got to be careful if you ever try it on your own."

I shook my head and punched Franz's shoulder, shouting a high "whoop" at the top of my lungs as we ran back the way we'd come, leaping the spaces between the moving cars. For the first time in my life I felt as if I were drunk on the sheer freedom of it all, and for several amazing moments we weren't anything more than two carefree, wet-nosed kids.

Our friendship grew stronger with every passing day and by the time we journeyed through the undulating hills of Oregon, our connection felt as natural to me as breathing. Moving closer and closer to our destination, we prayed that we could count on the mild weather of California to stretch well into the fall.

That night when darkness fell, in the blackness of the unlit boxcar we hunkered down half-suffocating on the stale air laced with pine tar and creosote. The only fresh air we'd breathed that day had been hours earlier when Franz had us recklessly pounding down the tops of the moving freight cars.

"I can't get my breath in here, air's so thick," he said. Neither one of us was able to sleep, and he toed my leg to rouse me up. Franz yanked down the bandana he had tied across his nose and mouth. "I'm goin' to go hang on the ladder outside for awhile and get some fresh air."

"I can't sleep worth a damn either" I mumbled. "I'm right behind you." I followed close behind in the darkness as we felt our way out of the foul smelling car. The rush of the night air, amplified by the speed of the train, blew frigid against our lightly clad bodies and a long cold shiver rolled down my arms and back. We climbed into the space between the boxcars, looping our arms through the middle rung of the ladders and sucking in the fresh air as it smacked us in the face. We hung there, planted on two separate cars, lulled somewhat by the rhythmic vibration of the train and the constant drum of the rumble on the track, and I drifted into a sleepy reverie as my mind wandered. I couldn't say how long we rode that way, maybe an hour, maybe more, but when I felt the line slowing to a crawl, I startled to attention. "Are we stopping?" I shouted to Franz. "We're in the middle of nowhere."

"Dunno."

Without even a hint at another warning, the boxcars lurched forward, shaking us with earthquake force. "Help!" I cried out as my feet gave way and I began to slip down one rung after the other like a slow motion movie. "Franz!" Terrified, my arm flailed, but I managed to catch hold of the ladder as my legs dangled inches away from the wheels that sparked metal on metal as the engine again picked up speed. I felt Franz grip the shoulder of my jacket, splitting the worn fabric as he yanked me toward him.

"Pull up!" Franz screamed over the deafening clatter of the now speeding train. "Pull up, damn it!"

Desperately, I wrestled to get some kind of a foothold. Finally, I managed to raise myself up enough to twist a leg through the lowest rung and climb to safety. Franz grabbed me and we clung to each other, hearts pounding in our throats, stranded on a single ladder between the moving cars. When we finally caught our breath, Franz unbuckled his belt and slipped it through the loops of his pants.

"Give me your belt," he yelled. "It's too slippery to try and make it back inside."

My fingers were near numb, but I managed to un-loop my belt and hand it over. Franz buckled them end-to-end, then wrapped it like a rope around us and secured us to the ladder. "Don't know why we didn't do this first thing," he said. "I seen guys strap themselves on like this before. I should have known better. The iron rungs pick up moisture in the night air and become as slick as a frozen pond."

We rode that way in the remaining hours of darkness, fueled by fear and adrenaline and clinging to each other for warmth and what little safety the improvised rope-belt provided.

Worn down and trembling when the train mercifully wound to a stop the following morning, we struggled to open the belt buckles with stiff, aching fingers. Climbing down the ladder wasn't easy, but there was no time to indulge our wobbly legs. We had just managed to set our shoes on the ground though, when a bull appeared like a phantom out of nowhere. He moved down the side of the long line of cars with a barking German Shepherd at his side and a loaded gun in his hand. We watched in silence as he pulled open every boxcar door to root out freeloaders and at the moment he stepped inside one of the cars, Franz wordlessly motioned for me to follow him. Terrified, I started after him as he took off down the line with me huffing at his heels. Within minutes the bull spotted us as we raced into a woodsy area that ran alongside the tracks.

"Stop or I'll shoot!" he bellowed.

The dog threw a vicious snarl in our direction as he strained against the leash and we shot ahead, darting in and out of the trees as bullets whizzed past our heads. In the distance, the dog's bark echoed, spurring us on, and we pounded down the narrow path for what felt like a mile before slowing to a walk, lungs aching, hearts drumming in our ears. Confident we were no longer being chased, we sucked in the moist air and scrounged around before settling for what looked like a safe spot in a thicket of trees on the backside of a sloping hill.

"Damn, Franz. We almost died back there!"

"Yeah, those two meant business," he said, dropping to the ground. "Those were more than warning shots." The sun had shifted on the horizon, softening the turning colors in the fall landscape and promising warmth.

"I can't believe they'd just shoot at us like that. Shoot two boys cold dead."

"You can never figure what they're up to. They know that if they dragged our bodies into the woods and left us, no one would ever know. Probably the only reason he didn't come after us was because he had his hands full rounding up some of the others." A small ground squirrel sounded and bolted into the trees and both of us startled.

Franz pulled himself to his knees and began mounding a pile of leaves into a makeshift bed. "The bulls are the most dangerous things out here by far. They'd just as soon see a man dead as round him up."

I sank down beside him and gathered my own nest close to his, oddly comforted by the scent of the dying leaves. "I sure didn't see it coming."

"Well," Franz went on, "getting stuck on those ladders was bad luck, and running into those bulls made it even worse. We've got to be more careful. That's all there is to it. As long as we stay clear and stick together we should be okay, though!"

"I hope you're right."

"Hey look, we're still here. There's no use worrying over something that didn't happen."

"I suppose," I said.

In time, our exhaustion overcame us, and we slept away the day, waking only to wander off and relieve ourselves in the woods before drifting back into a deep sleep, the kind reserved for the most weary and depleted. As the hours ticked by, the sun stole its light and warmth behind the dense Oregon hills, and the raw, cold air shivered me awake. I glanced toward Franz who looked as if he'd been drugged, his eyes closed tight, his mouth gaping open. Lying there I fingered the jackknife my father had gifted me one Christmas, and let my mind wander back home to my parents and my warm, comfortable bed. I remembered how, early as the first frost, my mother would sew yards of soft flannel into sheets and fit them to my mattress. The sheets were soothing and smelled of the light, fragrant soap she always used. How nice it would be to lay down on them now, my head on a freshly stuffed pillow, my belly full. We would not have full bellies tonight though, of that I was certain. Back in Great Falls we'd spent our loose change on two sandwiches. Now they were sitting in the bottom of our rope sacks in the boxcar we'd just abandoned, long gone by now. "I hope some hungry rider finds them," was all I could think.

Come daylight, stomach's growling, we wound our way back to the grassy edges of the tracks. Surrounded by the hopeful colors of the morning sky, we sat with our knees bent, watching and waiting like hunters for our next opportunity, praying that the next ride would be a good one - a long bull-less train with many empty cars. After a bit, Franz interrupted his own daydream.

"I used to have so much fun with my pa," he said. "When I was real little he used to swoop me up and balance me on his open palms so high I near hit the ceiling." He paused, pinching off strands of tall grass and blowing on them between his thumbs to make a whistle. Years of experience insured a strong, loud sound. "My ma'd be screaming at him to stop," he laughed. "She was so worried I'd fall and break my neck or something. I loved that he got her to thinking that way, like he was playing with both of us. I never did fall though … and even if I had, I knew he'd catch me."

"My mama worried too," I said, "especially when I used to swing my baby brother around or toss him in the air." I glanced Franz's way, cursing myself silently as soon as the words were out of my mouth and bracing for the inevitable question.

"I didn't know you had a brother, Jake. How old is he?"

I stared straight ahead and answered with a silence that told Franz he'd crossed that invisible boundary between friendship and a guy's private nightmares. Respectfully, he met my silence with his own, watching as I gazed out across the tracks from where we had planted ourselves. A broad line of trees swayed in the distant wind. One of the trees was freshly uprooted and lay sideways in the crook of a stronger tree's limbs. Its leaves were prematurely turning, yellow, ochre, rust, and I felt the changing of the seasons in my bones. I knew my father was about finished with the harvest, and I wished I could have been there with him to see it to the end. I picked up a stick and started chipping the bark with my jackknife. I leaned back on my elbows and shifted the direction of our conversation. "For as long as I can remember my father would sit me between his legs and let me drive the horses. I know I was not much more than four or five, but in my mind I was so big. I was like a king sitting there. I felt I could do anything. But my mama …" The hollow whistle of a train pushing its way over a bridge interrupted my musings as it moved toward a wide curve in the track. The now familiar sound of the long drawn-out cry reverberated through my body and I felt my heart racing inside my chest. There were so many unknowns in the minutes before the train was upon us. I felt I'd never get used to it. Would we make a successful jump? Would there be bulls waiting at the other end?

When the engine was upon us and had slowed to a reasonable pace, Franz held us back for a middle car. There were several to choose from. Just as we'd hoped, the train was on its way south to reload and we found it to be a perfect ride - a long line with lots of empty boxcars. At last, Franz gave the call: "Bodies on," he yelled, taking the lead as he always did while we trotted alongside the train as it wheeled its way down the track.

We leaped on. It seemed like no time before we were enjoying the long anticipated view of California's trundled fields and orchards, some harvested, some still heavy with fruit. It was late in the afternoon when we emptied out just south of San Jose in the verdant town of Santa Clara.

CHAPTER ELEVEN

IT FELT GREAT TO SET our feet on the ground after the long uncomfortable ride. The mountains that surrounded the flat low-lying valley we pulled into were outlined in the distance and shadowed by a sky swollen with storm clouds. A late season heat spell rendered the air so thick with moisture that we could almost taste the rain, and although the impending storm clashed with our vision of sunny California, we were excited to be there. California was still an illusion to us, unlike other more jaded travelers who had ventured west seeking a fortune in gold or an easy life near the beach. To us, hungry as we were, it looked as if free food was hanging from every tree, and even an impending storm could not dampen our mood.

"Looks like it's gonna to pour," I said. I cast my eyes upwards studying the situation. "We've got to find some cover."

"Food, first," said Franz. "I'm damn near starving to death."

Before we'd even hit town, we found ourselves on the edge of an apricot orchard, an endless maze of trees all cut and pruned in similar fashion, their branches bending under the weight of golden fruit. The orchard workers had quit for the day, and we scrounged around for the apricots that had been left behind on the ground. Anxious to fill our long-empty bellies, we missed the intensifying warning of the smell of electricity in the air, and were just beginning to bite into the apricots when the black clouds rumbled and tracks of lightening flashed high above our heads. Seconds later, a burst of thunder cracked, and the sky shouted a final warning before the clouds let loose. We raced across an apron of gravel that edged the orchard and then a road potholed from a sleuth of summer storms. Pausing under a large sycamore tree, we caught our breath even as we knew it was one of the worst places to be in a lightning storm. Through the downpour, in the distance, Franz spotted a smattering of one room shacks at the edge of a large irrigation ditch now pooled with rain and thick with mud.

"Look! Over there," he said.

The primitive structures, some little more than lean-tos, some with sagging center-pitched roofs and stove pipes, looked to be part of a migrant compound. A rope that was drooping under the weight of soaked clothes was strung between two of the shacks. Large open tubs of water were perched atop now extinguished fires situated around the camp. Candlelight could be seen flickering through several small openings that looked as if they were hacked into thin wooden walls, and in the eerie storm light we watched some of the cook-pipes smoking, a reliable signal of a presence within. As we tried to figure out where in this shanty town we might seek shelter, the heavy rain abated as quickly as it had begun, and the aroma of frying food came wafting our way. So intense was the attraction of the powerful scent that we both took off slogging through the mud. Franz knocked on the door of the shack where the smell was coming from, our pride taking a backseat to the fantasy of filling our bellies with a savory meal. Almost immediately, as if he somehow was expecting us, a Mexican man cracked the door. "Que? Ah ... Que pasa," he said.

"Please," said Franz. "Me and my friend are starving. Do you have anything you could share with us? Some bread ... anything?"

The man looked us over and smiled a fatherly grin. "Come in," he said, widening the door. He turned and spoke in Spanish to his wife who had come to the door too, but who now stood back hugging a fussy baby to her hip. She pushed a strand of long, black hair out of her eyes and inclined her head in our direction, a shy smile flickering across her face, as the man reached around for a pair of tattered Mexican blankets that he handed to us. Two other children peered out from a dark corner. The family watched silently as we dried ourselves off and wrapped the woven blankets around our shoulders.

"Thanks so much," we said in unison, nodding our gratitude to the man and the woman.

"Have a seat," he said, pointing to some overturned fruit crates that were set around a low, square table that took up most of the space in the one-room shanty. The woman sat the baby on a bare mattress near the other children and began dicing peppers into a cast iron skillet over a one burner flame. There didn't seem to be any running water, or electricity, and the rough-hewn floor was cracked and split. Though the shack was clean, I wondered how this family of five slept on one small mattress, now doubling as a couch. The man's body looked strong and fit, but his face bore the deep lines of the sun and his rough calloused hands betrayed a life of hard, physical labor. His wife was shy and slim, and she worked over the skillet with one eye on the children, tossing in a handful of diced onions that simmered into the intoxicating aroma we had smelled outside.

"I'm Angel," said the man with a heavy Mexican accent, "and this is my wife, Manuela. He spoke to Manuela in Spanish who then piled two tin plates high with rolled tortillas and set them before us. We smiled our thank-you's and dug in like starving dogs, mindless of the manners our parents had worked so hard to ingrain in us.

As we cleaned our plates, Angel stepped outside and returned with a brightly painted pitcher filled to the brim with rain water. "The water is fresh from the storm," he said. He slid the pitcher on the table and pushed a couple of jars toward us, then filled them up. "When you're done you can put these on." He pulled worn-out pants and shirts from a cloth sack stashed behind the mattress and handed them to us. "Your clothes can hang in the sun tomorrow, but tonight you can borrow these. Manuela will turn her head and then you can change."

"You are very kind," I said. When Angel spoke to Manuela, she scooped up the baby and turned to gaze out one of the only two openings carved into the side of the shack. "Thank you, thank you. We haven't eaten in two days and haven't had a home-cooked meal since we left home a couple of months ago. Please tell your wife how grateful we are."

"Si, si," said Angel, translating for Manuela before joining us at the table when we had pulled ourselves into the dry clothes. Manuela stepped away from the window and handed Angel the fidgeting baby before turning to attend to the other two children.

When we had eaten our fill and could focus beyond primal needs, we began to talk about why we were there. "We are looking for work," said Franz. "Do you know of any place around here that's looking to hire?"

"You can find work here," Angel told us, jiggling his infant son in his arms. "You're lucky because the weather has made the picking late this year. The apricots are ripe only now, and they must be picked quickly before they go bad. The storm will have knocked a lot of them down so we will have to clean up tomorrow." He stood his son on his knees and kissed his cheek. "A few miles down the road," Angel went on, "is another orchard for plums, and we can work there when the apricots are done. After the plums there are pears. Even though it's almost the end of September, the work will last through October, maybe November. After that, everyone here will travel to the south where, God willing, we will find more work."

"That's great," Franz chimed in. "That's what we were hoping for: some steady work."

I exhaled more fully than I had in weeks and my shoulders relaxed. It looked as if what we'd been fantasizing about was finally coming true. If ever there was such a place as the promised land, California, I decided, surely must be it.

"Unfortunately, you're too late for the housing," Angel said, anticipating our next question as the baby coughed and broke into a loud wail. "Manuela," he started, but before he could say another word, she turned and reached for the baby, replacing him on her hip. "There are already eight or more people in many of these shacks."

I leaned forward on my elbows as my tension returned. "Is there really nowhere for us to go?" Angel's news about the housing situation made me desperate at the thought of spending the next few months with no shelter.

"Well, come to think of it," said Angel, "there is one place I know. Manuela and I had to stay there once some years ago when we found ourselves here too late also. It's a cave not too far up in the hills, and you could shelter there if you want, if no one else has claimed it yet."

"How do we get there?" said Franz. "Is it far from here?"

I could tell Franz felt as nervous as I did. We'd been so sure that we would find work in California that the subject of where'd we'd live hadn't even come up. I guess both of us just assumed that there would be some sort of housing for the workers.

"Not too far," Angel replied. "I will have to take you there myself, however, otherwise you will never find it."

When the clouds had passed and the sky lightened, we took the generously offered blankets and a stack of tortillas that Manuela wrapped up for us along with several bruised apricots. Angel loaded a picking basket with a good amount of firewood and drove us in his rickety truck to the foot of the mountain range that turned out to be farther off than it looked.

On the ride over, he opened up. "We're from Matamoros," Angel told us, "across the Rio Bravo from Texas. There is no work for me there though, and now we have babies to feed. As much as I wanted to stay in Mexico, the work is here and so we came."

"I guess it's tough everywhere," Franz said. "My pa broke down when the work dried up. I don't know where he could've gone with eight kids anyway. That's why I jumped the rails. One less mouth to feed is the way I figured it."

"I was lucky I had a choice," said Angel. "I know that there are many who don't, but a man must do what he can to feed his family."

I felt like I should share something about my own life, and I considered what to say, but thankfully just then Angel pulled the truck to a stop well off the main road. He led us to a primitive path that was soggy from the downpour and we began winding our way up into the foothills. "Watch your step," said Angel as a rattlesnake slithered across our path into the woody scrub sage that dotted the gentle slope. "They won't bother you if you don't bother them, but keep an eye out."

The light was fading and the air, cooled by the short storm, gave relief to the hot day. We drank in the wonderful rain smell of the desert as we hiked along several yards beyond a rocky ledge where a small cave came into view. Angel paused at the entrance to the cave and stuck his head inside. "It looks like no one's here now. Tomorrow you can ride with me and I'll point you in the direction of the boss. When the sun breaks over the hills, follow the path to the road and I'll pick you up on my way."

☆ ☆ ☆

The following morning Angel rattled us to the orchard where we were hired on with few questions asked. At the end of our first day, as beat as either of us had ever been, we slumped together in the front seat for the ride back to the migrant camp. Thankfully, Angel had invited us home to get some food and a much needed washing. As we rolled into the compound, Angel slowed his truck to a crawl. He pointed to two men who looked to be making a sweep through the center yard. Turning the wheels and inching behind a shanty close to the latrine, he killed the engine.

"It's best to keep your distance from them," said Angel. He rested his forearms on the steering wheel and focused his gaze on the officers.

"Who are they?" I asked.

"Security officers from the fruit packing company. They march by to let you know they are in charge. Sometimes they hassle the drunks, but you never know who they might turn on. They don't need a reason. Being Mexican seems to be enough." Through the open truck windows we could make out bits of the officers' conversation.

"Damn, this place smells so bad," said the stocky, fat one. "Makes me almost gag. I don't know how they live here."

Angel chuckled under his breath. "Well, we had a choice between here and some fancy mansion with electricity and running water, but we really prefer this place!"

"It's that greasy food they cook all day, all those rice and beans," said the taller, tough-looking guy with a pock-marked face. "Should be happy they've got cold water'n lots of fresh air, all free, and they pay damn near nothin' for a roof over their heads. Give 'em somethin' better, hell, they'd smell that up too."

"Maybe if they had fewer kids … one or two of 'em might get ahead."

"Yeah. They let 'em run like street urchins. Look what's behind us." The officer turned and flipped a shiny new penny into a group of children who had gathered in their wake and descended on the coin like a flock of birds on a crust of bread.

"Always underfoot for a handout," the other one added. And with that he lunged at them with his hands open like claws and yelled: "BOO!", causing the squealing children to scatter in all directions.

"See what I mean." Angel looked at us.

"That's horrible," I said.

When the officers were out of sight, Angel revved up the engine and pulled the truck up closer to where he lived. A gray trail of smoke rose from the metal stove pipe in the roof and the air was savory, a sure sign that Manuela was busy preparing supper.

"Who do those men think would do the field work if it wasn't for the migrants?" said Franz.

"Or people like us who're down on their luck," I added. I felt angry at the ugly tone of the conversation we'd overheard. "It's like they hate for no other reason than that people are Mexican or poor."

"That's the way it is, Se'nor," said Angel. "It won't change. We hear talk like this all the time. We've just learned to stay out of their way."

☆ ☆ ☆

Every morning, with a reliable distant rooster as our alarm clock, we made our way down to the road to wait for Angel. Each day it was the same scene: Angel's old truck shaking its way through the morning mist at a good clip, then pulling up short at our feet. Angel was always there for us, always cheerful and ready for the day. He'd hand us each a breakfast taco and a jar of coffee with sweet scalded milk to share and off we'd go.

As grateful as we were for the steady pay, the picking was backbreaking work just as we'd been warned it would be. Climbing ten and twenty foot ladders, we shifted from tree to tree, stretching to reach the ripe fruit. The ladders were heavy and cumbersome, but we'd yell, "need a move-on," when they needed to be shifted, and the Mexican laborers would lend us a hand as much as they helped each other. The trees formed a dizzying network that seemed to stretch on forever with no end in sight. Even the strongest body wore down under the strain of the constant bending, reaching, climbing, hands all roughed up and stained orange by the end of the tiresome days. Most nights, Franz and I would ride home with Angel to wash away the grime under the communal shower at the camp, and Manuela made sure there was always an extra plate of rice and beans or a thick burrito to fill us up. Other nights we were too beat to do anything other than climb the winding hill to our cave and fall into the deepest of sleep before rising with the sun and repeating the monotonous routine all over the following day. The only break we ever got was on Sunday, when the orchard shut down and church bells tolled somewhere below the distant hills as we slept on, too tired to heed the call. We hung in there though, grateful for the steady work and the feel of a few dollars rolled in our pockets and buoyed up by the warmth and generosity of Angel and his wife.

CHAPTER TWELVE

A T THE END OF THE long season, when the trees were picked bare, the first cold front crept in, and the foreman ordered us to move on. As concerned as I was about where we'd next find work, I wasn't ready to leave the sunshine, the friendship and most of all, the steady food that California supplied.

"Things are about wrapped up 'round here," the foreman told us. "Won't be anything left to clean up by the end of the week. You boys can come back next year though, if you're still on the circuit. You're good workers and I'd be happy to hire you again."

"Thank you, sir," Franz replied. "We'd appreciate that."

"They don't want migrants hanging around much after the work's done," Angel explained after we'd collected our final wages. "We're heading to Brownsville in the morning. We'll cross over into Mexico and visit our families in Matamoros before making our way back to the cotton fields in Texas. The winter is mild there, and the people are kind. It's a good place for work."

Early the next day we hitch-hiked to the migrant camp and stopped by Angel and Manuela's shack to say goodbye. Manuela was sweeping out the floor one last time, and Angel was busy loading their belongings onto the back of his pickup truck. The mattress had been pulled from the dark corner of the shanty and placed under the rear cab window for the two oldest children.

"Amigos," Angel waved, smiling when he saw us. "I'm afraid this is adios."

"We have so much to thank you and Manuela for, Angel." I nodded my head toward Manuela who had leaned her broom against the wall and was watching us from the doorway. "Gracias, Manuela."

She smiled shyly and then took up her sweeping again, leaving us to have our parting conversation with Angel. I started pulling the Mexican blankets they had given us that first day out of a rope sack we had brought with us. "Thank you for the use of the blankets, Angel."

"Keep them. You'll need them." Angel waved me away.

Franz pulled five one dollar bills from his pocket. "This is from both of us, Angel. Gracias … for everything." He grinned, reaching out with the money. "See that, you've even got us talking Spanish."

"No, no, please." Angel held up his hands, refusing anything to do with the much-needed cash.

"Buy something pretty for Manuela," Franz said. "Please take it." He stuffed the bills into Angel's shirt pocket. "Jake and I insist."

I watched the interchange thinking that I wouldn't have expected any other kind of reaction from a man like Angel, and I realized how much I was going to miss him and his family. "It's the least we can do for all that you've done for us," I added.

Angel smiled and lifted the last of the worn out fruit crates into the open body of the truck and helped his children climb in. He tied up the back with multiple tight knots. "Gracias," he said, turning back to face us. "And good luck to you both."

"I don't know what we would have done if we hadn't run into you, Angel. Probably would have starved to death."

Angel laughed. "We were happy to help. I figure if we can't all help each other what are we here for? There's plenty of cotton to pick in Texas. We'll be there after a brief stay with our families. It's a big state but, who knows, maybe we'll see you there. If you decide to come, head for the panhandle. Just ask around. Word on the street will lead you to the fields that are hiring. It doesn't take long for word to get out."

"That would be great," I said. "Not sure where we'll end up, but you never know."

"Neither one of us has ever laid eyes on an ocean," said Franz. "I'd like to head toward the water, see what life is like on the beach."

"Yeah," I agreed. "The ocean's not something I'm familiar with, that's for sure. It's hard to picture a body of water that great. Franz has got me all curious about it though. I'd like to see it, I'm just not sure what we'll do for food and shelter. I know it won't take long for our money to run out if we're not careful."

"I'm afraid I can't help you there. "Pickin's the only work I know." Angel smiled as he watch Manuela climb into the cab of the truck with the baby on her lap. Hoisting himself in the driver's seat, he leaned out the window. "Take care of each other," he said. And with waves of goodbye from the whole family, we watched them drive off down the road.

☆ ☆ ☆

Franz and I set out again, now with a little money in our pockets. We thumbed a ride to the beaches in Monterey that we'd heard so much about. The ocean turned out to be more magnificent than anything we could have imagined. The sheer beauty of the open water and the power of the waves as they pounded against the rocky black coastline left us shaking our heads in awe. We spent hours walking the rough shores and taking in the billowing sailboats far off in the water. We pointed out pelicans floating near the wharf pilings and the giant gulls that spread their wings and swooped overhead squawking like angry hens. But the weather had cooled there too, and the nights left us shivering in the sand as we huddled together on the beach in Monterey Bay. Finally, we splurged and spend a chunk of our hard-earned cash for two nights in a cheap motel room, but that, along with shelling out dollars for burgers and chowder at the local Beach Shack, grew worrisome. Our supply of money would not last forever, and no one was hiring. With employment at a standstill, after a week, we decided to heed Angel's advice and head to Texas to take our chances in the cotton fields.

Securing a ride down the Pacific Coast Highway with a disgruntled trucker started out easy enough. Our thumbs were barely out when we spied him down the road already pulled over and checking a broken tail light. "You got any cash?" he said, waving us forward. "I don't take charity cases."

"All we got is what's in our pockets," Franz lied.

"Well, hand over five bucks and, I'll take you as far as Los Angeles. That's my last stop."

We pulled some crumpled ones from our pockets and handed them over.

"Wait for me inside," said the man. "I'm about done here."

We walked to the front of the truck and climbed into the cab that reeked of smoke and spoiled food. A cigarette stub was still burning in the ashtray. I shoved an old pillow and blanket out of the way to make more room, and once we got situated, Franz said: "This guy gives me the creeps."

"What do you mean, Franz? Is something wrong?"

"Nothing that I can say for sure. Only a feeling."

"Should we skip the ride?"

"No, I guess not. We already gave him five big ones. Besides, I'm tired of walking."

The run along the ocean was scenic, but Franz kept an uneasy eye on the driver. I wasn't sure what about the man was bothering Franz so much. The trucker didn't look any different to me from men I'd seen on the trains with his day-old beard and dirty hands. "There's hidden beaches around here," the driver said pulling a fresh cigarette from his shirt pocket. He picked up the smoldering butt from the ashtray and used it to light up. "You can't see 'em from the road. I used to pull over and drink a little whiskey down there on my way out of town. Not much anymore, though. Too many stray bums."

It was already past sunset when we stopped at a street light in Malibu and were distracted by a caravan of painted wagons that had encamped in a small circle across the road. Most of the wooden structures had their doors thrown open with lanterns strung around the entrances and signs tacked up: "Palm Reader," or "Tarot Cards." It was an intriguing window into a world that we knew nothing about and could only imagine. Colorful lanterns dangled between the wagons that formed a kind of courtyard, where dozens of people danced to a makeshift band dominated by guitars and banjos. I could tell by the look in Franz's eyes that he was ready to pounce.

"Hey, that looks like fun," he said, "What is it? Some kind of carnival?"

"Gypsies," the truck driver answered. He was quick to pick up on Franz's enthusiasm. "Wanderers and vagabonds who never stay in one spot long enough to give a crap … no town, no place to call home. Some of them rely on fortune-telling or even the con to keep food in their mouths. Take a good look, but be wary. I've tasted their women before. They'll find a way to get you to part with your money if you're not careful."

"I don't know," Franz said, never one to shy away from a new adventure. "I say we get out here and have ourselves a little fun."

"Wait a minute, Franz." I couldn't tell if he really wanted to join the party or if he was using the gypsies as an excuse to escape the creepy driver and the confines of the truck. I could see L.A. all lit up and shimmering in the distance from where we were, and I just wanted to get there as quickly as we could.

"Aw, come on, Jake. After all we've been through? Don't you think we deserve it?"

"Didn't you hear what the man just told us?"

"He's not listening," said the truck driver, flicking his cigarette out the window. "He's too busy watching that girl with the flashing eyes twirling her skirts."

Franz put his hand on the door handle as if he were going to bolt, but I pulled his arm and held him back.

"I don't like it Franz. It makes no sense," I said. "We're almost to L.A."

When the light turned green, the truck driver revved the engine and we inched forward. "Back off the door, son" he said. "It's a bad idea. Let's keep rollin'."

Franz sulked in silence with his nose pressed against the glass, his hand still ready to spring the door.

"If I didn't think I'd get conned, I'd go over there and introduce you to the gypsies myself, but why take the chance? If it's a party you're looking for, I can rent us a nice motel room after I check in with my rig. I got plenty of whiskey with me." The driver turned his head to both of us. "Hell, I'll even throw in a hot meal."

We rode on to the next light. "I don't know," said Franz. "It looks pretty nice around here, and from what I've learned, one of those beaches you've been mentioning is not too far back. We could shelter there, and find our own dinner. Come on, Jake. The tracks are nothing to get to in the morning." It was always hard to argue with Franz but this was against my better judgment. Before I could put my foot down though, he turned his head to the driver and said: "Appreciate the ride mister, but I'm outta' here." And with that, he cracked the door and I had no choice but to tumble out after him, uttering a hasty goodbye to a man who didn't deserve much more.

"That guy made my skin crawl," said Franz as we trudged across the highway and made our way onto the beach.

"I know, I know," I said, more nervous at this point about what lay ahead than what we'd just left behind. A few yards down was a ridge of drifted sand, and while I wandered off to relieve myself in the tall grasses, Franz hid our rope sacks among a small group of rocks. When I returned, we crossed the road again and soon found ourselves engulfed in a haze of jasmine incense. Two young women with soft brown shoulders and jewelry that jingled when they moved, welcomed us like old friends and ushered us into the middle of the party. Another woman handed us a couple of rum drinks. "Come on, take a sip, Jake," said Franz. "Now this is my kind of party."

I'd never had a grownup drink all to myself before. I hesitated, turning my face away. But Franz kept insisting I try it, and I finally gave in and took a swig. The drink tasted sweet, nothing at all like the occasional sip of brandy from my father's glass. It went down easy and filled me with a warm flush.

"You like it?" said Franz.

"It's good."

We were standing off to the side watching the large ring of dancers who were having a ball. Remembering the truck driver's warning, I felt uneasy but there was no time to indulge myself. Halfway into our second drink, the girls pulled us into the circle. I was more than a little uncomfortable and apprehensive but felt I had little choice at that point but to just go with it. Within what felt like a few minutes, I was swaying, caught up in the seduction of the rhythms and rum drinks that kept flowing freely through the crowd. Holding a real live woman so close heightened the intoxication. Dancing until our foreheads glowed with sweat, the band finally took a break and the girls pointed to some old mismatched chairs that had been set off to the side. They promised to return shortly and strode away, streaming pieces of bright gauzy fabric behind them. "Can you believe we almost missed this?" said Franz, taking a seat. "You have to admit you're having a great time."

"Yes, yes," I answered. "It's a lot of fun." Some of the skepticism I'd had about the gypsies had left me with the second round of drinks. Everyone had been so welcoming and nobody even mentioned our age. We were only thirteen, but there seemed to be no rules for anything in this gypsy camp other than to have a good time.

"Stay here and wait for me, Jake. I'll be right back."

Ten minutes later Franz returned with the girls, a bottle of Mexican tequila, some limes and a shot glass that he filled to the brim. "I just learned how to do this," he grinned. "Come on, Jake, hand me that jack-knife of yours."

I dug the knife out of my pocket and handed it over. "Careful with that," I warned. "That knife means a lot to me."

The women smiled sweetly as if they understood, and we watched him slice a section of the lime and bite into it before downing a shot. "Aaaarrrgghh!" he said, slamming the glass down on one of the chairs. "Next up!"

We took turns with the shots, the second easier to knock back than the first. The young lady I'd been dancing with called herself Catarina, and I sensed that she was several years older than me. She kept playing with the silver necklaces that fell near the top of her breasts, and I felt a strong physical response like nothing I'd ever felt before. When I looked up, the light of the lanterns that hung from every low-hanging branch shadowed the soft curve of her bare shoulder and glinted in the mane of black hair and only added to her allure. She leaned over and kissed me hard, but before I could return her advance, the musicians returned and kicked up a vigorous tune. Catarina reached for my hand, and I stumbled as she pulled me after her onto the dance floor. As we twirled and laughed in the frenzied music, things suddenly began to spin out of control.

The next thing I remembered was opening my eyes on the beach with the sun beating down on my face. My head was throbbing, and I turned on my side and realized my jack-knife was folded into my right hand. I glanced over to see Franz lying next to me. Our old Mexican blankets had been bunched under our heads and tossed over us, but our rope sacks had been pulled from the rocks and emptied; our pockets were turned inside out. All of our money was gone.

"Franz!" I screamed. I reached over and pulled the blanket away, jabbing him full-force in the ribs. "Wake up, man! We've been robbed!"

Franz groaned and rolled over on his back, squinting in the glaring rays as he pushed up on his elbows. "Where are we?"

"We're on the beach, damnit! Every penny we had is gone! There's nothing left." I was ready to blow as I paced back and forth in the sand. "This is all your fault." I yelled. "You and your stupid ideas. I never should have listened to you! I knew one of these days you'd get us into trouble. Goddamn you!" I kicked a load of sand at him and in an instant Franz was on me, and we were scuffling ... pulling, pushing, yelling ... blaming each other for the nightmare before us.

"I didn't force you into anything." Franz shoved me away, making his escape into the sand and plunking himself down, laughing. "You walked into that camp on your own, buddy. Last time I looked, you looked pretty cozy with that girl. You looked happy as hell, I recall. I had nothing to do with this."

"What the hell are you laughing about, Franz. Are you crazy? Everything we've saved is gone, I tell you. Everything! You can never just be, Franz. You're always looking for something out there that's better than what you've got. It's like the present isn't ever good enough."

"That's not it at all! We've been working our asses off for months now. I don't see how you can blame a guy for wanting to have a little fun. Maybe if you weren't so uptight all the time ..."

"Shut up, Franz. All those backaches, all that scrimping and saving we did ... disappears into thin air in one night ... because you saw some gypsy girl that looked hot-to-trot." I paused. "Can't believe that they didn't take my knife. I'd probably have to kill you if that was gone."

"What makes you think it was the gypsies who did this?" he said, laughing again. Hell, it could have been anybody."

"You know they did it! There was nobody else and you know it. What the hell is wrong with you? Are you still drunk? What could possibly be funny about us losing everything?"

Franz sauntered casually over to where our rope sacks had been stashed. I could hear him pulling at the rocks, rolling them over. He returned with a sly grin as he held out two wads of cash still rolled in rubber bands. "Here's your precious cash," he said, tossing one of the bundles to me. "I didn't want to take any chances, so I took the money out of our duffle bags and buried it deep in the sand under the rocks."

"What the …? If you did this yourself then why did you let me carry on like that? It scared the hell out of me and you knew it."

"Sorry, buddy. I just couldn't resist. Guess I was just looking for a little more levity in our lives. Come on, you gotta admit last night was fun."

"Okay, yeah, I'll admit it, but damn, Franz! You really had me going!"

"I know, man. Sorry. I just thought that if someone stumbled upon our bags, like say those bums the trucker had mentioned, at least they wouldn't get our cash. No hard feelings?"

"No hard feelings," I said tucking my money deep into the bottom of my bag.

✻ ✻ ✻

We hopped a train out of Los Angeles the following morning and journeyed east into the deserts of Arizona and New Mexico through uninhabited land and small silent towns. Every now and then for entertainment, we waved a hand at the stragglers who'd come out to watch the trains wheel through. I wondered what had brought them there to such isolated places, what they did and how they lived. Evenings, we sat at the open door of the boxcar watching sunsets that raged with color, our own thoughts running like quiet prayers through our heads.

We switched trains in Albuquerque, veering further east before jumping off near Dalhart, a plain and dusty town in the northwest corner of the Texas Panhandle. Hiking in from an outlying road, we passed a smattering of modest houses with sloping roofs, each set on its own patch of land, most with a small corral for livestock or a vegetable garden out back. Unsure of what our next move was, we decided to stop and consider our options. We perched ourselves on a split-rail fence that sectioned off a cow field and rested. The early night sky was clear and already decorated with stars.

"See that up there?" Franz said tipping his head back. "That's the Big Dipper constellation, and right over there, close by, that's the Little Dipper. Oh, and that massive one over there is the Milky Way."

"How do you know all that?" I asked.

"My father used to point them out to me. He loved to look at the stars. Said that's where he did all his dreaming."

We discussed our options going forward for a bit and had pretty much decided on continuing deeper into the panhandle. A small bungalow situated on an incline not too far from where we sat caught my attention. The lights were on, and I could see a woman arranging plates on a table through a window that dominated the left side of the house.

"Look at that," I said. I touched Franz's shoulder to shift his focus back to earth. "I used to help my mama set the table sometimes. Sure does make me homesick."

"Yeah, look at the corn wreath on the door," said Franz, joining my mood. "Must be near Thanksgiving. Ever since I was seven I'd go on a turkey hunt with my pa this time 'a year. It was the best! Caught one every time and it always made me feel kind of proud when I saw that turkey in the center of the Thanksgiving table. I never took to pumpkin pie, but my ma made sure there was apple too in the years before my pa got sick. If times were good, she'd whip up some cream to go with it."

My own memories of Thanksgiving flooded in, and I could hardly breathe for the tears that stuck in my throat. When my reverie got the best of me though, I was unable hold them back, and I quickly brushed them off with the sleeve of my jacket before they betrayed what my dad had always called "sissy stuff." The similarities between this scene we were witnessing and my own childhood were startling: same warm setting, same family table, a mother busy preparing supper in the kitchen, maybe all of them gathering around the fire after dinner. Still, it surprised me how fast I'd choked up.

"I remember it so well," I said. "I used to get mad at my mother for always bothering me, but now I'd give anything to be fussed over."

The murmur of a light wind swayed the tops of the nearby cottonwood trees. Franz hung there with me on the fence, harboring his own feelings about the lives we'd given up, both of us afraid that if we jumped down we might never see anything like it again, might never experience this tranquility that our recollections had kindled.

"I had a wooden fort," I said quietly. "My father built it for me with cowboy and Indian figurines he carved that flanked the opening. He loved to whittle, even carved us a whole manger scene for Christmas one year: Mary, Joseph, the baby Jesus, three Wise Men and all kinds of animals. When I was ten, he came into my room on Christmas and handed me this jackknife. He winked and told me to keep it hidden from my mother. Every chance he got after that he'd teach me how to whittle. I loved that knife so much I used to run up to my room just to finger it some, even if I had no wood. I can't believe I still got it."

"You're lucky, Jake," said Franz. "We never got toys at Christmas time, but there was always a piece of chocolate and a new pair of mittens or socks. My ma made certain of that. She sure did love us. Leaving her was the hardest thing of all."

"Yeah, well, I never did see eye-to-eye with my mama. We were always fighting about something. There were times when I wondered if she loved me at all. I guess I wasn't an easy kid to love though, always arguing, always wanting more and more freedom. I just wish I could go back now and relive my whole childhood."

"Yeah, I know what you mean. If we could redo our lives though, I guess we wouldn't be friends sitting here right now." Then he added, "But ya know, if we had any horse sense at all we wouldn't be letting our memories get the best of us, we'd be knocking on that door for something to kill these hunger pangs. I bet anything the lady inside is a darn good cook, and maybe, if we're lucky, full of the holiday spirit."

"Worth a try, I guess," I said, hopping down off the fence. "I gotta' say, I never thought my life would become one hungry mile after another."

"Me either!"

The well-lit house held its own on a road that was forged on the outskirts of the town. We wandered toward it as we combed our fingers through our straggly hair and brushed off our clothes. Franz stepped ahead of me and gave the door a hard knock. A woman answered with two young children crowded in behind her, their curiosity trumped only by shyness.

"We're sorry to bother you, ma'am," said Franz, enjoying a wave of heat from inside the toasty house. "I know it's coming up on a holiday time and all, but we're mighty hungry and sure would appreciate anything you could spare. We'd be more than happy to do some chores for you in return."

"Just the two of you?" she asked, peering beyond Franz's shoulder to get a good look at me.

"Yes, Ma'am," he answered. "Just me and my friend, Jake, here. We're kind of between jobs and we haven't eaten for a couple of days. We're not fussy, though. Just hungry. Like I said, we'd be happy to work in exchange for food."

The woman had a plain but kind face, and I sensed her trepidation at finding two tumbledown boys at her door.

"The chores are done, but if you wait here I'll fix you something you can take with you," she said. She stepped back with her children hiding their faces in her housedress and clinging to her every motion. "Won't be but a few minutes."

"Thank you, Ma'am," we chimed. "Thanks so much."

Pacing around the yard with our hands dug deep inside our pockets, we waited, eager for the promise of food - something home-cooked if we were lucky. In a short time, the woman cracked the door, and we hurried over. She handed Franz a paper sack, then wiped her hands with the edge of her apron. "There's a cooked pheasant in there," she said. "My husband's a good hunter so we always got plenty 'a that. I cut it up with some bread, sandwich like, so it'd be easier to eat. There's cornbread too, and black beans in a coffee can, and two jars 'a hot coffee." She bent down to listen to a small blonde girl who was tugging on her skirt. "Oh, and a molasses stick. My children insisted. Happy Thanksgiving. And boys, if you don't mind, please keep this to yourselves."

We thanked her with a gratitude familiar to hungry people fed by the kindness of others, and then, after she closed the door, cracked the molasses stick in half and shoved it into our mouths. "Can you believe this?" I said, relishing the taste that the unspoken memories inspired. "Did we get lucky or what?"

"You can say that again."

We hitched ourselves back up on the fence rail and tore into the feast, savoring the seasoned meat between the thick slices of bread, and washing down the beans with the hot coffee.

"Best meal I ever ate." Franz pushed off the fence and ran a final swallow of coffee down his throat.

"These days every meal we eat tastes like the best," I laughed. "As we sucked on our fingers for the last lick of flavor we noticed that the cluster of town lights in the distance had grown brighter and, curious to see what the small town had to offer, we struck out in that direction.

The town itself was unremarkable with it's simple unadorned buildings, the exception being the "La Rita Theatre" set smack in the center, whose marquee was lit up in bright-red neon letters. A movie called "Duck Soup" was well underway and the ticket booth had been shut down. As we turned to leave, I caught site of a side door between the two buildings propped open with a large rock.

Without a word, Franz crouched down and stuck his head into the opening. "Come on," he mouthed the words, motioning me over. "Back row's empty."

The movie was a little less than half way over, and by a stroke of luck no one kicked us out. The movie was side-splitting and we were still laughing when the final credits rolled and we joined the rush of people out the side exit. Easing ourselves away from the group, we made our way toward the railroad tracks we knew to be heading south. A couple of hours later we were sacked out on a freight train traveling deeper into the Texas Panhandle as it passed through Amarillo and on into Plainview, a small treeless town surrounded by wide open cattle ranches and plenty of high-yielding cotton fields.

CHAPTER THIRTEEN

W E EMPTIED OUT AROUND NOON and camped out on the steps of the feed store on the main street, debating where to head next. Before we could catch our breath though, a foreman who was in town rounding up supplies stuck a boot up on the step and gave us a once-over.

"You boys lookin' for work?" the foreman said as he dusted off his cowboy hat. He'd no doubt seen the likes of us before.

"Yes, we're looking," Franz answered. "Whatcha got?"

"Cotton picking. You boys ever pick cotton before?"

"No, sir," I answered, "we only just …"

"We only just do 'bout everything, sir," Franz said, nearly pushing me behind him. "We're about the fastest learners you'll ever find. We can promise you no one has ever regretted hiring us!" He added for emphasis.

"Okay, well if what you say is true, we're lookin' to hire.

"Oh, it is, sir," I said. "What about pay and food?"

"Pay's by the pound, every two weeks. There's a bunk house too, and a camp cook. You take your meals in the mess house with the rest of the workers. It'll cost you two dollars a week, docked from your pay. It ain't your mama's fried chicken, but guaranteed it'll hold ya."

"Where's the camp?"

"Due east." The foreman pointed an arm. "Look, you boys mull it over, and I'll meet you back here in an hour or so if you're interested. I got business at the bank and I'm late grabbin' a bite. If you're still here when I'm ready to cut out, you can load up on the back of my truck."

"Oh, we'll be here," I said.

"Thank you, sir and like I said, you won't regret it," Franz added.

The foreman replaced his hat and stepped around us, eager to go about his business.

"Well, that was quick," I laughed. "We didn't even have to ask."

"Yeah, no kidding," Franz agreed. "Guess it's our lucky day."

The foreman returned awhile later just as he had promised. "Hungry?" he said, tossing us each a ham sandwich.

"Gee, thanks!" we said.

We bunched together in the open end of his pickup for the twenty-five mile drive east where we hired on at the Barton spread with its impressive miles of cotton fields sown in neat rows out across the land. There was always something that needed getting done on Joe Barton's well-tended acreage, and extra hands were always welcomed it turned out, in addition to the regular flock of migrant workers that showed up every year.

The harvest got a late start here too, and was in full swing. The weather had been uncooperative, we learned, and cotton bolls are inclined to bloom when they want to, troubling the strongest of prognosticators and forcing even the Farmer's Almanac to take a bow. At night we bunked barracks-style with the Okies, or "poor white trash" as they were known in these parts, that wandered over from Oklahoma to try their luck close to home before uprooting their families to the bigger promise of gold in California. As we chose our bunks and settled in, we inquired about the boss's temperament and the nature of the work. "Barton's a fair man," a thin man with a slow nasal drawl told us. "You will work hard but the pay's 'bout average and you won't go hungry. He makes sure there's no scrimpin' on the food."

At dawn, when the sun filled the big Texas sky with enough light to see, we trekked out to the fields with the others, staking our weighing baskets at the head of a cotton row and strapping our picking bags around our necks as we saw the more experienced men do. We spent the morning tugging at the stubborn plants, struggling alongside the Okies and a group of Mexican migrants that bantered back and forth in Spanish as they picked their way through the long line. After awhile, damp and sweaty from the labor, when the boredom of the repetitious work set in, I took comfort in their soft yammering.

"I keep thinking of Angel," I said. We'd picked to the end of a long row and I let my bag drop to the ground. "I wonder if he's anywhere near here."

Franz loosened a strap to even out the weight of his load. "Yeah, I sure would like to run into him."

"Me too. He made it sound like finding him here was a possibility, but I don't see how."

"He was right about the work though. Seems there's plenty to do here. I've never seen fields this big in my life. Didn't know one man could own so much land."

I smiled. "Come on, let's finish off this row. I'm luggin' way too much weight here."

I hefted up my bag and started back down the row, anxious for the day to end. "You comin'?" I said.

When our cotton bags were stuffed full, we spilled them into larger weighing baskets before traipsing back and beginning the same tedious effort all over again. Once our baskets got to brimming, we weighed in and they got dumped onto a wagon bound for the gin house. At the end of the long grueling day, when the last of the baskets had been emptied, we heaved a sigh of relief and headed to the mess house with the others. Grateful as I was for the work and the meal that awaited us, as I traipsed back to the barracks with Franz I couldn't help but wonder how long we'd be able to keep up this grind, and if this was as good as it was ever going to get for us.

"I hear the chef doesn't mind doling out seconds either and that suits me more than anything." I said as I pushed back my hat and wiped a handful of sweat from my brow.

"Yeah, well he may change his tune when he sees how much we can pack away. But you're right, the food's worth about everything by itself."

By noon of the second day my back got to throbbing so bad I thought I'd never stand up straight again. The cotton was dirty with seeds and twigs and burrs and thorny sheaths at the end of every boll that left our fingers pricked raw and our hands scratched and bleeding worse than if we'd been trying to stake a barbed wire fence without gloves. We didn't complain, though. None of the pickers complained.

To keep motivated, we focused on the prospect of honest money jingling in our pockets, and that, along with the assurance of regular meals, was enough to keep us going. We discovered that our bunkmate's comment about Joe Barton rang true.

Barton did everything he could to run a smooth operation, and even with the exhausting work our bodies grew strong with three squares a day for the first time since we'd left California. Having a son of his own who worked alongside him, the farmer held a softness toward youth and charged Franz and I less than the others for room and board, provided we kept our mouths shut about it. It was backbreaking labor, but we stuck it out, hitching a ride into Plainview on Saturday nights and parting with some of our hard-earned cash on a motion picture show and a drink at the bar. As long as we could slap our money down on the polished mesquite top, not a man in town would question our age, and we could count on Sundays to sleep it off and be up at the crack of dawn for the start of another hard-earned week.

☆ ☆ ☆

When work at the Barton spread slowed to a trickle, the camp chef hit the road, and the rest of the crew, including us, followed suit. Jumping the first freight train out of town was easy enough, but crashing in flop houses and cheap motels was expensive, and we spent most of our money just finding shelter. Sometimes, on the lucky days, we'd stumble across an occasional soup kitchen. On other days, we'd beg at back café doors along the way which made us realize once again what a gift it had been to have steady work and regular meals. It was already April when we found ourselves in a jungle camp outside of Pueblo, Colorado. We shook our heads in disgust when an early spring blast of snow caught everyone off guard, and we decided to ride the extra miles into Colorado Springs where we'd heard we might find a "Salvation Army" or "Volunteers of America" to dish us out a hot meal.

The wind was gusting when we piled after two hobos under a late gray sky into what looked like an easy ride in a low-sided, open boxcar car already layered with several inches of snow. No sooner had our feet hit the steel bottom of the car, however, when the train hiccupped with the same slack action that had stranded us on the ladder months before, pitching us like bundles of straw against the opposite wall. As the train gathered speed, we hunched down alongside the strangers and sheltered that way, bent over and shivering with only our lightweight jackets to warm us all the way into Colorado Springs. We were halfway frozen by the time the great iron horse pumped down its brakes, and we were able to lift our heads and look around.

Our travel mates were poised to clamber like prison escapees over the side of the open car. "We heard there was a soup kitchen around here." Franz was the first to speak. "You know where that might be?"

"Don't know," one of the guys answered, a large black man, "but there's a jungle about two miles in. Follow us if you want." With the train still inching forward, he and his side-kick took a leap over the top of the car and headed toward a loosely defined trail that veered off into an overgrown thicket. We waited until the wheels ground to a final stop before following suit, grabbing our packs and scrambling up and over as the other men had done. No sooner had we set foot on the ground, however, than the sound of heavy boots crunched in the snow behind us and my blood ran cold.

"Stop, or I'll shoot!" a bull shouted with a megaphone held to his mouth. He was already gaining on us as we bolted after the older men who had ducked into the thicket and disappeared. We raced ahead, veering after them down the path, searching desperately for somewhere to hide, when I stumbled on a tree root and almost landed face-down. In the minute that it took to regain my footing from the shot of pain, the bull was on me, attacking with a powerful kick that knocked me to my knees. "Stay put, damnit, or I'll stomp you out right here on the ground."

Up ahead, Franz was in trouble too. The bull turned his attention to the direction of the comment where several yards away Franz had tripped up in the dead brambles of an overgrown blackberry bush. His rope sack, strung around his back, was caught up in the prickly scrub and he was wrestling with cold, stiff fingers to free himself. "Leave him alone you bastard!" he screamed.

As if in slow motion, I watched in horror as the bull aimed his gun in Franz's direction and let a shot fire over his head before pointing the barrel back on me. "You move once more and I'll blow your little shit-brained head clean off." He waved another threatening motion in the air with his gun then took off after Franz.

"No!" I cried. "Franz, run!" I was terrified of the violent attack that I was certain Franz would suffer. "Leave him alone!"

Within seconds, the bull was upon Franz, knocking the wind out of him as he yanked him free from the brambles and threw him to the ground. As Franz gasped for air, the bull jerked up Franz's leg and trawled him, spitting and fighting, through the snow and brush. By the time he was heaved like a bag of trash onto me, Franz's clothes were shredded, his face scratched bloody, his hands and forearms imbedded with short, fat thorns.

The bull prodded us cruelly with the toe of his hard-heeled boot. "What the hell do you think you're doing on my train?" Looming over us and moving in tighter, he poked his gun back and forth in our faces as if we posed some huge threat to his life.

"Nothing, sir." I said, sputtering and desperate to somehow appease him. "We were just hitching a ride, looking for work. That's all."

"Work? Work is for men, not snot nosed free-loaders like you who don't know crap about nothing 'cept maybe how to steal or get yourselves killed."

The bull spit twice, hitting us each square in the face before hammering on. "Now you get outta' here before I beat you to death and don't you never come back, or I'll sure as hell shoot you both clean through. Now, git. Go!"

Franz snatched his rope sack from the brambles as we ran past, and we took off wavering after one another down the path. We kept moving, me stumbling along behind Franz, until the searing pain in my ankle finally took me down.

"Wait-up, Franz. I can't run anymore."

Franz stopped in his tracks, bending down to help me up, but the pain was too much. "Franz, I can't … I can't go any further. I'm sorry, but it hurts like hell."

"No problem, Jake. That overgrown bastard is history. We might just as well sit here for awhile anyway and figure what to do next."

"Wonder how far down the trail that camp is those other guys were talking about."

"No telling. Hopefully, not too far."

Then, as if on cue, the two older hobos who had managed to hide when they heard the bulls shouting, stepped into the clearing. The black man, as big as a prize fighter, his face ravaged by weather-beat, moved close. "We heard the shots and knew you might be in trouble," he said, loosening a piece of twine that held a cloth pack together. He pulled out a ragged blanket which he handed off to Franz who looked the sorrier with blood on his hands and face. "Wrap those cuts up with this," he orderd, in a no-nonsense voice, before bending down to check out my ankle. He wiggled my foot back and forth then stood up when he was satisfied that it wasn't broken.

"I told him," I said, clutching my throbbing leg, "we were only hitching to look for work. Don't mean no harm to nobody."

"You should know better than to try talkin' sense to a bull. Ain't no such thing. "You boys is the worse kind 'a tenderfoot."

"That was the meanest son-of-a-bitch I ever run across in my life," said Franz. "He almost killed us back there."

The man reached deep into his pack and came up with a jar of white lightening. "Yeah, well you're lucky he didn't. I'm sure he thought about it. When you know you're caught like that, you just keep still and take your lickin'. You hear me? Opening your trap only gives 'em more reason to beat the tar outta' you." After pausing for emphasis, he softened his attitude: "Here, take a swig." He unscrewed the lid of the jar and held it to Franz's mouth. After Franz swallowed deep, the man pulled out a tattered hanky and dipped it in the lightening before handing the jar off to me. He got to work dabbing the scratches on Franz's face with the alcohol.

"Damn, that stings!"

"Hold still! 'Sposed to clean a wound right away."

As the man worked, I kept my eyes fixed on him, leery as I was with all that had transpired. Truth is, I was in awe of such a formidable presence.

"What you gawking at boy?" he said. "You never seen a black man before?"

Ashamed to be caught staring, I shook my head and averted my eyes, drew my jacket in tighter and then took my turn with a gulp of the lightning that burned down my throat and set me to a fit of coughing. I gagged and spit in the snow, wiping my mouth with the sleeve of my coat.

"Ain't there black men wherever y'all are from?"

"No," I stated somewhat apologetically. "I've seen them working in the fields with the Mexicans, off in the distance, but you're the first close up. I only saw you just now - on the train."

"Well, lucky me. Now stop gawkin' before your eyes fall outta' your head. I ain't gonna' bite. I'm as much flesh'n blood as you are. Name's Moses. Mo, for short."

"Sorry, sir. I didn't mean to stare. I'm Jake and this here's Franz," I said, passing the bottle back to Moses.

"Sir? No "sirs" 'round here, that's for sure. Name's Mo, like I said. You boys is damn lucky. You gotta' lot to learn about life on the rails."

"I was just hoping he'd go easy on us."

"It ain't his job to go easy on you. You're nothing' to him 'cept a couple of free-loading boys. It's his job to keep you off the trains and he don't much care what he has to do to keep that from happening."

"Well, I thought …."

"That's what I mean … thinkin' too much and talkin' too much. Hell, it ain't worth wasting your breath." I handed him back the bottle and he tucked it carefully into the safety of his bag. "Honestly, I can't think of why he didn't beat you more than he did. I seen kids younger than you killed right on the spot. You got lucky. You'd best follow us over near Fountain Creek where a good jungle's always planted. Our luck holds, there'll be a fire, maybe food. Come on now, before we all freeze to death out here."

"I'm not sure how far I can walk," I said. "My ankle's all swolled up."

"Hop on, then," said Mo, squatting down.

I hadn't been hoisted on anyone's back since my dad had given me piggyback rides when I was Edwin's age. I hesitated, but Mo was right. There appeared to be no other way for me to keep up.

"Mo'll keep your long lost mamas' smiling in their dreams at least for one more night." Mo glanced at Franz and pointed to the other hobo who had not uttered a word. "Follow up behind Deadfoot over there."

With Franz's wounds cleaned up, he loaded up my rope sack, and we pushed on. Mo led the way, tramping down the path that looped through the underbrush of a small forest. It felt like we'd been trudging for nearly an hour when the glimmer of a campfire caught my eye coming up at the edge of a large creek bed still half snowed over. As we moved closer, I could see about a dozen men hunkered down under pieces of cardboard and old blankets, all huddled around a large crackling fire. The circle shifted reluctantly to make room, and we settled ourselves, nodding our greetings to the others as a loaf of stale bread was passed our way. Breaking the bread in half, we were more than grateful to dip the pieces into cans of a weak mulligan stew: an over-sized black kettle of murky water littered with food scraps that the men had managed to scrounge up.

We squatted close to the flames, reaching out our hands for warmth and the stash of beef jerky and shelled pecans that Mo sent in our direction before passing them along. Sitting there like this for the better part of an hour, we listened to the small talk and kept a look-out for other bits of food that might be making the go-around. One man, aged and ragged, stumbled our way and jiggled a near empty bottle of whiskey at us.

Mo waved his arm, shooing him away. "Get on outta' here now, before you fall on your dumb ass and burn up in this fire." As the man wobbled off, Mo muttered under his breath: "Damn bum. Only thing worse than a tramp is a bum, and that one is pure bum."

"What's the difference?" I asked, wrapping myself in one of the Mexican blankets I had stowed in my rope sack. I hunched as close to the fire as I dared, nursing my ankle with a melting snow pack that Mo had improvised.

"There's a saying on the road: 'A hobo, he just work and wander, the tramp, he drink and wander, and the bum, well, he just drink.' A bum don't give a rat's ass about working or wandering, only drinking."

"Don't say," I said. "I've never thought of myself as any one of those."

"I never thought about it either," said Franz. "I know one thing for certain, I sure don't feel like a man. Don't know if I want to be one either if it's this hard just being a kid."

"Oh, you'll know when you're a man," said Mo. He hunched his big frame forward, soaking up as much of the fire as he could. "You're a man when you got yo'self some 'sponsibilities and you can handle 'em. Like when you got a woman and a couple 'a babies depending on you. Ain't nothing better, as long as you can handle it. But if something should happen, you lose your work and you can't even buy food 'cause the money's dried up and there ain't no jobs, then your manhood goes down the swamp. You feel like nothing. Oh, you still got the wife, and the babies ain't going anywhere, but you ain't no man in the 'spectable sense, anymore. The world done strip you of that."

"Yeah," said Franz. He inched up closer to catch more of the fire glow. "That's what happened to my pa the very day he lost his job. After that, he just sat and brooded at the kitchen table from morning 'til long after we'd all gone off to bed. Saddest thing I'd ever seen."

"It's one of the worst things can happen to a man," agreed Mo, "and you can't do a damn thing to stop it. You wanna' work but there ain't nothing to do. Like Deadfoot over there. He got his'self a wife and five pretty little girls down in Georgia, not far from where I was raised. Power plant shut down and jobs just dried up. Watching his babies come down with everything from rickets to scarlet fever, he almost went crazy in the head. Set out to take his chances on the road. Froze the toes off his left foot first year out stuck in a mountain pass right here in Colorado. Surprised he can walk as good as he does. Nicknamed him 'Deadfoot' myself. He don't look much like it, but he's still a man 'cause he sends money home whenever he can."

"Well, if you lose something big like that, I mean if you're a kid and you lose your parents or a brother or sister, what does that make you?" I asked, hanging on every word.

"You a hobo, like me, 'cause all you can do is work and wander. But you still trying to be a man, see ... and that's the difference."

CHAPTER FOURTEEN

EARLY THE FOLLOWING MORNING THE camp emptied out and all of us, save a few too jittery to travel, crouched in the brush along the rail yard track, eyeing a long train as it readied itself to head north toward Denver. When the engine churned to life, one of the hobos eased out of the shadows, slid open an empty boxcar door and quickly climbed in. The other men traipsed after him like cat burglars, one at a time so as not to draw attention. The car was half-way full when Mo' hefted me aboard with Franz and Deadfoot slipping in behind us. The swelling in my ankle was down somewhat, but still plenty painful to step on. Franz and I were more than a little reluctant from the terrifying drama of the day before, and I said as much to Mo, but he egged us on anyway. "I know," he said. "Once bitten, twice shy, but you got to get back in the saddle. What choice you got? Sit here and freeze your feet off or starve to death? It's alright. We got a crowd here this morning. With so many ridin' and with Denver bein' a big city station it'll be easier to avoid the bulls and get lost in the shuffle."

The engine hadn't even fired up completely though before the boxcar door was thrown open and the same bull that had beaten us so badly the previous day stuck his gun in Mo's face. "Everybody out unless you want to eat a bullet!" Mo scooped me up and jumped down as the other men followed suit, all but trampling one another, pushing and shoving to escape the bull's wrath they knew was sure to escalate.

True to form, the bull threw back his head and streamed a long tobacco spit into the snow. "You're like cock roaches. You just keep multiplying!" He waved his pistol over the group, then lowered it when he recognized me. The bull lunged forward and grabbed me by the scuff of my collar with his free hand. "You again?" He shook me hard then dropped me as if I were on fire. "You didn't learn jack-shit yesterday, did you?" He back-handed my face hard. "I'd beat the crap out of you, but I've already done that. Seems all that's left is to just shoot ya." Keeping his gun aimed at me, he faced the crowd. "I could fire a round into your dirty asses too, or haul you to jail unless you wanna' pay proper fare like civilized folk." The bull cocked his head to work up more saliva, then blew another gritty wad into the snow.

The group inched back, but Mo had had enough. He stepped forward, the sculpted muscles in his face flexed with anger. "You gonna' pick on a young boy?" His voice boomed from somewhere deep within.

"Watch your mouth, nigger. You're next."

But Mo would not be intimidated. "Well, go ahead and shoot then. I guess you could kill six of us dead as flies, right off. But what you think's gonna happen to your ass when those bullets run out?" Mo stood rooted in the ground, not twelve inches from the bull's face with his arms wrapped tight around his massive chest. He paused to let the truth of his words sink in before he continued. "Thirty hungry men gonna' eat you alive, that's what's gonna' happen." He was nearly shouting now, more determined than ever to intimidate the bull. "That is, after we beat the life out of you. So shoot, fool. Go ahead. Take your chances."

The bull froze and the brakeman, who had been hanging off a side ladder, watching the scene unfold, stepped in. "Hey, Merle! We clear? This ain't the "East Wind" luxury liner to New York, you know. Got to get this train to Denver by two o'clock. You've done your job, now let's move it."

The bull grabbed the shoulder of my coat and shoved me into Mo's legs. "You're not gonna be so lucky the next time around I promise you that!" He grunted, cussing and waving a clenched fist high into the air as he stomped off. "Go ahead," he barked at the brakeman. Then turning back he waved his gun menacingly one more time. "Get 'outta here, I said and watch your backs 'cuz next time I'll be sure I'm packin' five pistols!"

As the train began to push forward, the men crowded around Mo, slapping him on the back and laughing. "You sure did shut him down, Mo! Think I saw tears in his eyes." one said.

"Yeah, well his pants looked kind of wet in front too, I think," another guffawed. Deeply relieved, we followed closely as the band began to scatter back into the thicket of pine trees not too far off the line of tracks. After hiking a safe distance, we rested there lounging on a thick, wide bed of pine needles.

"I'm riding the next train," said Mo. "I'm not waitin' for him to come back with his pistols."

One of the men sitting with us, a young guy who never ventured further east than Colorado spoke up: "That's a good idea. There'll be a train through here around noon and my guess is that bull's had enough excitement for one day. I doubt he'll show up so soon."

"We'll wander back later," said Mo. "In the meantime we can just hang here and get some rest."

"We were told there'd be a good soup kitchen in Colorado Springs, but there was nothing … only trouble," I said.

"You were told wrong," replied the hobo. "And as far as trouble goes, well that could be anywhere. The kitchen's in Denver."

"Are you sure?"

"Ate there myself about a month ago. Volunteers of America."

"That settles it," said Mo. "I'll be the first one in line. You can count on it."

When the sun came up high above our heads, Mo stood up and pulled me to my feet. "Time to get a move on. Come on now, boy. You can make it."

We all rose up and took our time wandering back to the edge of the rail yard to wait for the train. Watching patiently, we checked for signs of trouble but it was quiet and there were no bulls in sight. At the last minute before the wheels began to roll, Mo hefted me into the last empty boxcar then pulled himself in after me followed by Franz, Deadfoot and the other two hobos who wasted no time in sliding the door shut behind us. The engine belched an all too familiar sigh, advancing beyond the rail yard at a moderate, jerky pace before picking up speed and spinning into Denver just as dusk set in and shadowed the sky purple.

That night we camped in the relative safety of a jungle that was staked out along the banks of the South Platte Rive, but first thing the next morning I limped after Franz and the others into downtown Denver where a Volunteers of America soup kitchen, as promised, served up better fare than we'd seen since the Barton ranch. There were warm sweet rolls for breakfast, and at noon several young girls surrendered their lunch hours at school to volunteer alongside their mothers, dishing up homemade soup. Franz flirted shamelessly, earning him second helpings which he shared with me. Dinner was more soup with bread, a slice of meatloaf or a mashed bean sandwich, Jello, and even a wedge of cake or a cookie for dessert with plenty of hot black coffee to wash it all down. Both of us had lost the extra pounds we'd gained in Texas, and my clothes hung on me like a garden scarecrow, my hair having grown well past my ears. We knew we needed to keep moving toward the work, as our money had all but run dry, but Denver was turning out to be a nice place, and we were suckers for regular, close-to-home-cooked meals. We were desperate to find experiences that memories of our old lives beckoned us to seek out.

Warning us of bad weather ahead, Mo and Deadfoot hit the trail after just four days. "I ain't interested in no snow," Mo said, pulling us close in a fatherly hug. "Just point me south and show me the peaches. I strongly suggest you boys do the same."

"We'll see, Mo," Franz said. "Jake's foot is still bothering him."

Truth was too, the weather seemed far from ominous and we had other inclinations. A touch of homesickness had crept in, and we agreed that somewhere in the Midwest was where we wanted to be. My injury was as good an excuse as any though, and we lingered in Denver for another week reluctant to leave the steady, hot food and pretty girls. We couldn't rely on handouts forever though, and work was scarce there, so finally we too decamped and set out. By then spring was fulfilling its promise of warmer days ahead and work was foremost on our minds. We chose not to follow Mo's advice and head south, but set our sights instead on the sugar beet fields that we'd heard blanketed the fertile Red River Valley near Fargo, North Dakota.

By the time our train hit the mountains of Wyoming we were starving again, only this time, in the town of Cheyenne where we chose to disembark, there was no soup kitchen to turn to. We spent over a week burning through the last of our hard earned cash and when it ran out, we were left to rifle through trash cans for food with a small group of men who camped along the banks of Crow Creek. To make matters worse, we discovered that more snow was expected, not to mention that we had misjudged the migrant season in North Dakota which apparently wasn't to yield work for another three weeks or more. Discouraged and driven by hunger, we begged for food on the windy streets, splitting up to increase our chances. The town was small though, suffering it's own scarcity, and the cowboys threw unfriendly, intolerant looks our way. After a few days, it was clear that heading out was the only option we had left.

"I got a tip today," said Franz, one morning when we hadn't been able to pinch so much as an apple from the scrap barrel of the only grocery store in town. "Some say there's construction work in Ohio building a bridge, and the pay's better than farm-handing, too. Maybe we outta' go further east and give it a try. Heck, if that doesn't work out, it's a straight shot south to Georgia like Mo said and we can try our luck getting work picking peaches."

"Ohio sounds promising, but I'm thinking if we end up having to head to Georgia the peach picking jobs may well be filled by then." I said.

"Well, we won't live long if we stick around here. I say we go where the money is."

"I know, you're probably right. I guess Ohio's got plenty of fields too, if the bridge doesn't work out."

By now we were both fed up with our lack of opportunities in Cheyenne, and the information Franz had stumbled upon made a lot of sense. All it took was one more night without a meal to convince us to set off once again to try our luck somewhere else.

☆ ☆ ☆

Energized once again by a plan and renewed hope, we laid in wait for a freight car that would journey through Kansas on its way to Ohio. While dozing in the side brush not too far past the rail yard, the sharp, high whistle of a train off in the distance startled us awake, and

I felt a quickening in the pit of my stomach that came on every time I heard the familiar long, drawn-out cry. All that we'd been through had more than fueled my fears about not being able to make the hop without slipping under the wheels to my death, or the threat of some bull appearing out of nowhere, leaving me dead in some unknown neck of the woods. I knew better than ever now the risk we were taking every time we jumped a train, and I was getting tired of the constant undercurrent of fear and the desperate search for work and food that had come to define our days. I ached for stability, a routine, a place to eat and sleep, something I could count on. But tortured by thoughts of all that had happened and that had caused me to leave home in the first place, I resigned myself once again to this life of hunger and fear and travel and uncertainty, knowing that there was really no way out, at least nothing that I could foresee.

On the outskirts of Topeka, late the following day, we huddled with ten other men in a jungle where a now familiar black, cast-iron pot bubbled over an open campfire into which men emptied their pockets: a grimy onion dropped in whole, a fistful of worn out kidney beans, a small gutted fish from the river. We slurped at the watery mix, guilty once again about our inability to contribute, but grateful to relieve the ever-present hunger pains and rest our tired bodies for at least one more night. As the fire crackled, we ate and dozed, and my thoughts again drifted toward home. Tomorrow we'd be passing through Kansas City, and I pictured old Aunt Liddy in her kitchen, round as ever, scrubbing potatoes in the sink and frying up chicken. I wondered if she was any more forgetful or if she had aged much since I'd last seen her well over two years ago now. I wanted desperately to knock on her door and feel her familiar embrace, enjoy a meal or two and sleep on a comfortable bed, but I worried that she'd also banished me from her heart and mind as I feared the rest of my family had done. Images of my parents flooded in next, my father laying his Farm Journal aside and taking up his place at the table, while my mother admonished us to eat while the food was still hot. I wondered if her heart had softened, if she missed me at all, or if she'd ever even cared that I'd left.

Franz wandered down to the stream to rinse out his cup, then sat down beside me with a sigh that spoke volumes. "I'll eat about anything to keep from starving," he confided to me in a hushed tone. "But what I wouldn't give for a nice, big helping of Sunday pot roast."

I nodded and stared, fixating my gaze on the flames of the fire. Flies and early mosquitoes buzzed around us as insistent and annoying as the thoughts of home-cooked meals.

"I feel like I'm always hungry," I said after awhile, rubbing my grimy face. "If I ate a whole side of beef I doubt it would be enough." Thinner than I'd been in years, these last few days had wiped out any reserves I had and weakened my body as well as my spirit.

The fire blazed steady through the night, warming those lucky enough to curl up close. An old bum everybody called "Grandpa Jack" blew on a rusty harmonica, whiling away the hours with a sad, slow tune. Periodically, a pile of sticks was tossed onto the fire, and the flames sputtered and jumped before finding their center and burning higher and brighter than before. In time, I fell off into a fitful sleep, but in the dark damp hours of the morning I woke up with the shakes so bad I thought I might never stop. I leaned over and shook Franz awake. When he realized the state I was in, I could see the alarm in his face.

"Hang on, Jake," he said. Franz covered me with the now worn out Mexican blankets we shared, then hopped up and begged a bottle of whiskey in an attempt to warm me, but nothing could chase the tremors from my body, and days passed that I would never remember. Steadfast by my side, Franz wiped my forehead and lifted my head for regular sips of the cool stream water as the men around us wandered in and out like characters in some dramatic outdoor play.

"I give up," I told Franz after three nights of feverish dreams, and sicker than I'd ever felt in my life. "As soon as I get better I think I'm gonna' find my way back home."

"Don't be talking nonsense now," said Franz with a weak laugh. "It's not the time to be thinking about that. Let's just get you through this. There's plenty of time later to head back 'round."

But the fever raged on, and in my dreams I walked for miles down a long familiar road that ran past horses grazing peacefully in the fields before coming upon an old dilapidated farmhouse. The house was going to ruin, and I needed to get out of there. When I turned to leave though, a railroad bull appeared out of nowhere and blocked my path as he tossed a lit torch onto the porch. The house burst into flames and I shrieked and screamed trying to warn everyone to get out, but my cries were silent and no one heard. Beating back the flames with my hands, I was desperate to save the strangers inside. Like in a horror movie, when I glanced down, I watched my hands blacken and shrivel to the size of a child's. I just stood there and sobbed as the house collapsed into burning embers, one room after another.

On the fifth day, my fever broke, and Franz leaned me on his shoulder and walked me down to a nearby stream where we splashed our faces in the clear running water. It was late spring by now, and the temperature had turned mild. Redbud trees filled the empty spaces at the edges of the woodland, their branches laden with colors of raspberry and cherry pink, while showy clumps of blue prairie violets dotted the slopes of the creek valley.

"Looks like some nice weather finally coming through. Mo should stuck with us and given things a chance ... waited before he cut out." Franz leaned back on his elbows in the grass to get a full dose of the sun above our heads. "You had me worried there, buddy."

"Yeah," I said. I moved a few steps to join him on the shallow embankment. "I ached so bad all I could think about was going home."

"Yeah, I know. You still feelin' that way?" "Nah." I let my eyes slide shut, allowing sun to throw splinters of colored light behind my lids like I did when I was a little boy picnicking with my parents. "Guess it was just the sickness talking."

"Yeah, fever can do that." Franz sounded relieved. "I don't know about you, but I'm about ready to head out of here."

I glanced over. "What do you think, another day or two to get to the bridge in Ohio? I hope I'll be strong enough to work by then. Maybe there'll be a hot meal somewhere too."

"Yeah, well, I was going to talk to you about that, Jake. While you were flat on your back, I overheard a conversation. This guy was only in the camp for one night, but he was saying that there's plenty of summer crops in California if you know where to look."

"I thought we were shooting for the bridge, for the money."

"We were, but this guy … he was heading back west 'cause he'd been to Ohio and found out that working the bridge is no longer an option."

"What do you mean?"

"I mean, they weren't hirin' anymore. They were full up. The pay was so good every man that could work wanted to hire on, and they got all the help they needed months ago. He said the bridge was almost done too."

I wasn't sure what to do with this bit of bad news. It was my first day back in the world and all I wanted was some decent food. But we needed to focus on where we were going to head next for work if we were going to survive the upcoming season.

"What about Dakota?" I said. "The timing could be good for the sugar beets now. It'd be almost three weeks by the time we got out there."

"Word is the Mexicans have that covered. And it's a short season. We'd be better off back on the west coast where they need labor well into the fall and we already know the territory. If we rode a straight shot we could be in California in three days. Heck, we could check with the apricot orchard again, and there's more orchards if that doesn't pan out. I know you'll be back on your feet in no time, but I could start out working and you could take it easy for awhile if you need to. The man said there were acres of artichokes, onions, avocados, who knows what else. If we head back now, we can find something. I even remember Angel talking about potato fields not too far from where we picked apricots." He raised up and turned toward me. "At least with the farm work we won't starve to death."

"I do feel like I'm wasting away, Franz, but I'm still shaky from the fever and with me in this condition it'd take us longer than three days to get out there. We'd have to hope for a Salvation Army or a good kitchen 'cause I can't go that long without something thicker than watery soup."

Franz set his eyes out over the creek. "Well, do you think you could make a straight shot to the coast if we had plenty of food with us?"

"Yeah, sure, but I don't believe there'll be any corned beef dinners falling from the sky any time soon."

"Let's just say we had plenty to eat, and that food wasn't a problem. When do you think you'd be ready to go?"

"If we had some decent food I guess I'd be ready now, but like I said, I'm not sure … I want to get a move on too, Franz, but …"

That was all he needed to hear. The impetuous side of Franz had reared up, and there was no use arguing. We were full steam ahead. "Jake, there's a freight train due to pull in this afternoon around four. It won't be stopping so we'd have to catch it as it moves through. Several of the men are planning to ride. They say it's a long line of cars with empties and rumored to be making an almost straight shot to the coast."

"I'm sure I could manage to make the hop Franz, but like I said …"

"I got a plan, Jake. Just get your rope sack and go with the other men to the tracks. I'll meet you there at four."

"But, Franz …"

"This is a good train and it's our only chance of getting out of here right now. Everything's gonna' be okay if you'll just meet me like I said … and be ready to make the jump."

"Alright." I threw up my hands. "I give up. I don't know why you're being so secretive, but I can tell your mind's made up."

"Moving on is our best bet. I'll see you later today when the train pulls in. Come on, let's get back to the jungle, I got things to do before we head out." And with that Franz was up walking me back to the camp where we found that a fight had broken out and most of the men had scattered. Two older guys I'd never seen before had wandered in and were scrounging around for scraps of food and sticks to rebuild the fire. Our rope sacks were still there but one of our blankets was missing. "It's a sign," said Franz. "Time to hit the road." He stuffed the contents of his rope sack into mine and turned to leave. "Four o'clock," he said, waving the empty bag as he wandered off into the woods and disappeared.

Thirty minutes before the train was due I folded up our remaining blanket and shoved it into my rope sack. Three other men and a boy who couldn't have been more than ten years old waited for me tie up and then we followed each other toward the tracks and hid in an alcove underneath a small trestle bridge where several other men were already huddled. Franz was right about many people wanting to ride.

I recognized several faces from the camp. We crouched together with our heads cocked for the familiar howl of the train, and after awhile I began to worry that maybe Franz would not make it on time. When the whistle sounded the others began to clamber up the short bank to the tracks. I trailed slowly behind them, not wanting to miss my chance, but unwilling to leave without my friend. As the engine rumbled past me at a slow, steady pace, my heart pounded. I glanced around, but Franz was nowhere in sight. I knew that there were only minutes to spare. My chest tightened. There was no way I could make the jump without Franz. Then, with the timing of a perfect stage entrance, I heard his voice.

"Jake! Jake!"

Out of nowhere Franz came speeding toward me. "Get ready, Jake. Come on." I shot off like a bullet, but Franz overtook me, heaving his bag into the door of the last open car and jumping in. Reaching out at the last second, we grabbed hands and he pulled me toward him as I made the leap with every ounce of strength I had left. I landed on my knees and rolled on my back with my chest heaving. When I found the courage to glance sideways, Franz was there looking almost as beat as I was. We were the only two people in the boxcar and for a minute, I thought one of us might die from sheer exhaustion. Franz, however, was ecstatic. He turned his head and grinned. "Wait 'til you see what I pulled off, Jake," he said. "You're not going to believe it."

Easing himself into a sitting position, Franz reached for his rope sack and let loose a pirate's bounty. Some of the things I'd never even tasted before like Oreo cookies and bottles of Orange Crush. There were the healthier items too such as apples and cooked ham and a loaf of Wonder Bread, but the real treasure was in his pockets: chewing gum, Life Savers and enough Hershey's bars to satisfy even a ten year old.

I rose to my knees, tore open the ham and began stuffing slices into my mouth. "Where'd you get all this stuff?" I said. The savory meat was about the best thing I'd ever tasted.

"Take it easy, Jake," he said, "I know you're hungry, but remember, this grub's got to last us all the way to California."

"Sorry, man. How did you manage this?"

"I don't know if I should tell you, Jake, 'cause I know we made a pact and I know you'll be mad. But I didn't see any choice this time. I'd a worked if I could, but it was either steal something or risk your gettin' sick again."

"So what did you do? Where'd all this food come from?"

"I must have hit every market in town."

"You mean you just waltzed in and ripped them off?"

"Well ... it wasn't that easy. I stashed my rope sack in the alley ways and snuck whatever I could grab under my coat, a couple of oranges, a pack of cookies."

"Damn, I can't believe you didn't get caught."

"Oh, there were some close calls, like this woman who shook her finger and gave me the stink eye. I tell you, I high-tailed it out of there like a scared rabbit. But then I settled down and somehow, as the day went on, I got bolder."

"I must be getting used to you, Franz, because for whatever reason, this doesn't surprise me. I don' like it, but it doesn't surprise me."

"This place called McKenzie's was so much bigger than the other stores that when I slipped in, I was sure I'd hit pay dirt. I thought no one would notice me. Boy, was I wrong. My eye was on this bag of apples and just as I got it stuffed under my shirt, out of nowhere this man pokes his head around the corner as if he might come at me. 'Whatcha' think you're doing, kid?' he says. I took off so fast, but he must have called the cops because the next thing I know I'm hoofin' it at the edge of the tracks, and I got two policemen on my trail madder'n a couple of wet roosters."

"I can't believe you made it."

"Damn, it was close."

"You're not kidding." I continued to stuff my face with another helping of the ham, this time layered between slices of Wonder bread and chunks of cheese. "A lot of things could have gone wrong. You pulled off a miracle, Franz. We're alive and sitting here instead of dead or in jail. I guess that's all that really matters."

"You mad at me, Jake?"

"Part of me wants to be, I mean, we had an agreement, but I'm too hungry to be mad and I really don't think I could have gone another day without food, depleted as I was. I want to eat as much as my stomach will hold, then lay my head down and sleep until I wake up and can eat some more."

Franz grinned, pleased with himself. "You'll be a new man by tomorrow." He passed me a peeled orange and a small bottle of aspirin. "I should have done this days ago when you needed something nutritious to eat and something for the pain, but I was afraid to leave you. You never know who's gonna' to wander into a jungle, and I didn't want to risk something even worse happening."

"You did everything right," I said. "You're a good friend, Franz. I don't know if I would have made it without you."

"Probably not," he laughed. "But there's not a doubt in my mind that you would have done the same for me."

CHAPTER FIFTEEN

B Y THE TIME OUR FEET touched the ground again in California, I was feeling like my old self. I had done nothing the entire ride but sleep and eat, and it made a huge difference. We quickly learned that the winter there had been warmer than usual, yielding an early crop of apricots and since it was familiar work for us, we were confident that we'd be able to secure steady pay, food and if our luck held, maybe even reconnect with our old friends, Angel and Manuela.

Hitching a ride to the old migrant camp, we were intent on finding our friends and some home cooking if we were lucky. As we strolled into the familiar rundown camp, however, it was apparent right off that things were not the same. The kids playing in the dirt were pale and towheaded, a dramatic change from last year, when dark-haired Mexican children dominated the yard.

"Weird!" Franz met my eyes with a look of confusion that equaled mine. "These white kids are the only ones here. I wonder what's going on."

A bad feeling gathered in the pit of my stomach as we walked toward Angel and Manuela's shack. The reality of the new landscape was beginning to sink in as I rapped on the door. "Angel!" I called. "You in there?"

A thin white man cracked the door open just enough to show his face. "Ain't no Mexicans here, if that's who yer lookin' for."

"What happened? Where'd they all go?"

"They're turnin' 'em back at the border. Some have gotten through, but not many."

"But, why? The Mexicans are hard workers. It makes no sense."

"Gotta' take care of our own first. Most of the folks here now came from Arizona and Oklahoma. Left a bunch of dust for this."

"What ..."

But before I could finish my sentence, he shut the door as he muttered a barely audible, "Sorry, boys."

We turned and wound our way back through the group of boisterous children to the edge of the road shaking our heads in disbelief and sadness at this strange turn of events.

"Wow," I grumbled. "This is horrible! What will they do for work in Mexico? Angel said they came here because there were no jobs there."

"I know. Not only did they work hard, but they were so good to us. I've been thinking about Manuela's tortilla soup for days."

"Damn, Franz. It just won't be the same without them."

"Well, the man did say that a few had made it across the border. Let's keep our fingers crossed that maybe they're some of the few."

"Tomorrow we can ask at the orchard," I said. "Maybe somebody's seen him." In silence, we hitched a ride to the old cave and found it was just the way we'd left it and that in an odd sort of way, it even felt a lot like home.

Early the following morning we hiked down to the road, intending to hitch a ride to the orchard. Wild flowers dotted the path as the rising sun washed the horizon with a soft, velvety glow. After trudging a half mile on the main route with no luck, we came to an intersection where a small group of Mexican men were just hanging out.

"Are you waiting for a ride to the orchards?" I asked, hoping that one of them spoke some English.

"Yes, we come here for a ride to any place there is work." One of them stood up. "If they need us, they send a truck. Sometimes there's hoeing in the fields, but not too much."

"Damn." Franz glanced at me. "I wonder if we'll have any trouble hiring on."

"You won't have any trouble," said the Mexican, unable to hide the bitterness in his voice. "You're white. The jobs are given to the whites first now."

"This is so crazy," I said. "We just heard that migrants are being turned away at the borders."

"That's right. We were already here working when the white families began to show up. At first it was only a few, but soon many more came. Now we get hired only if they need extra labor and most of the time it is not more than a day."

It was the first time in my life I'd ever felt guilty about being white. Here we were younger and less experienced than any of these men and we were the ones most likely to get the job.

"I'm really sorry to hear that," I said. "I guess that may be what happened to a friend of ours we're hoping to find. Any chance you know Angel Sigala? He comes here every year from Matamoros with his family. Ever heard of him?"

"No. But even if he did make it across the border, with all of the Okies pouring in, jobs are scarce. They're deporting people like us too. Any day we could be picked up and sent back or worse. Last week a Mexican man disappeared only to be discovered hanging by his neck from a tree. Rumor says it was five white guys who strung him up."

My stomach turned. Glancing at Franz, I knew he was feeling the same way. "I'm so sorry," I said again. "I had no idea it was this bad."

"Bad and gettin' worse. You best keep hitchin' toward the orchard," said the Mexican. He took a step back shading his eyes with his hand. "Somebody'll pick you up."

"Damn, Jake," Franz said as we headed back down the road. "I can't believe this! I wonder if Angel got stuck at the border."

"Seems like he might be lucky if he did." I threw my thumb out to a pickup truck that blew past us in a cloud of dirt then rattled to the shoulder and stopped. We ran to catch up.

"Where you boys headed?"

"We're looking to pick fruit at the orchard. If they're hiring, that is," Franz replied as we climbed in next to the driver.

"Orchard up ahead's the last stop."

"That'll work."

Dead-ending at the orchard, we waved our thanks and headed to the flat-roofed office where the same foreman we had known from the season before hired us on, but not without some further explaining. "There's a lot that's different around here, but I'm glad to see you boys back. It always helps to have workers who know the ropes."

"Thanks," Franz said. "We sure do appreciate the work."

"Hey, can you tell us what's going on?" I asked. "We understand the Mexicans are being turned away."

The foreman held up a large flyer warning Mexicans about deportation and needing work permits. "It's not good for the migrants these days. There's car loads of whites coming in from all over the place, Oklahoma, Arkansas, Arizona ... saying things is just dried up out there. I've never seen anything like it. Government says we got to hire them on first, then, if there's any work left it'll go to the few Mexicans that are here. I still got a few of the better migrant workers, but it's nothing like before."

"What about Angel Sigala?" Franz asked. "You seen him around at all?"

The foreman cocked his head and rolled up the flyer, swinging at a couple of flies that buzzed around his head. "I sure have," he said. "Good man, good worker. He's one of the few I let slip through. He's picking in the north end of the orchard today. Grab your sacks, and you can start up there if you want. Just remember though, pay's by the pound, and I'm running a business here, not a social club."

We scribbled our names on some papers he slid across his desk, then shook hands and hurried toward the north end of the orchard. "What do you make of all this?" I asked Franz.

"Well, I never expected to find so many white folks come this far west. It makes sense though, as bad as things were when I left home. It's every man's call what to do to survive. I never thought much about the color of my skin 'til now though. As tough as things seem, there's always someone worse off I guess."

"That's for sure," I said. "I'm so glad that Angel's still around."

"Yeah. It wouldn't feel right being here without him."

We found Angel high up on a ladder plucking the delicate apricots from the tree at a faster rate than Franz and I could ever hope to achieve.

"Angel!" we yelled, waving our arms when we spotted him.

"Amigos!" He stuck his hat into the air in response. Angel inched down the narrow ladder, jumping the last three rungs and landing on his feet. "It's wonderful to see you again." He reached for our hands and pulled us close for a warm embrace. "How have you been?"

"Fine, good. We're fine. We looked for you a few times," I said, "but we hadn't realized just how big Texas was. There's no way we could have found you out there in all that land!"

"I don't know what I was thinking back then," Angel laughed. "But we caught up and that's what matters! It sure is good to see you."

After filling each other in, he invited us to stop by their living quarters and say hello to Manuela and the kids. "Why don't you come around on Sunday," he said. "We should be a little rested that day and I can ask Manuela to cook something special."

"Oh, man, you're speakin' my language now," said Franz. "I've had dreams about Manuela's cooking ever since our first meal together."

"She will be flattered to hear that." Angel grinned. "Where are you staying?"

"We're back at the cave," I said. "It was there waiting for us, as if we'd never left."

"What about you, Angel?" Franz jumped in. "Where are you living? It was strange, we stopped by the old place and found only white people there."

"Yeah." I nodded my head. "We can't believe how things have changed."

"It's pretty bad for us now," said Angel. "I guess we made it across the border just in time. Word was that things were toughening up, so we headed back a little early. We had to pitch a camp in a different area though, not too far down the road."

"Good," said Franz.

"That is good news" I said. "Good news for us!"

Angel seemed pleased by our remarks. "I will pick you up Sunday after you hear the noon church bells, as we did before."

Seeing Angel again was almost like reconnecting with home, and I looked forward to spending time in the midst of a real family after so many months on the road.

On Sunday afternoon Angel's truck showed up at our usual spot just as it had those warm misty mornings when we'd first found ourselves in California. Passing the old compound, we arrived at a tented, loosely defined community strewn with colorful Mexican blankets staked to the ground to separate the families, all of whom had young children enlivening the area with their laughter and noise. Angel and Manuela had settled in with their kids in the far end of the grouping to insure more privacy and take advantage of an old walnut tree that provided shade. Same as before, a low table and fruit crates had been arranged in the center of the space with a mattress tucked into the back corner. The two older children, as shy as their mother, were an inch or two taller now, and the baby teetered around on unsteady feet, a sight that awakened painful memories for me. Manuela was smiling when we came in and even uttered a quiet "hi" before turning her attention back to sautéing onions and pieces of chicken that would be used in the tortillas she had fried up earlier. From what I could tell, it looked as if another baby might be on the way.

"I have some news," said Angel. "Something has been brewing since spring." He joined us at the makeshift table with three bottles of Coca-Cola, popping the caps with a metal opener and proudly passing them around. "For special occasions," he smiled as he handed one to each of us.

"Thanks, Angel," Franz replied.

"Yes, thanks," I said, "what's going on?"

"Well, I'm not talking about the situation here with all the white families moving west. I'm talking about something else, and it's not all bad news for us."

"What do you mean? What is it?"

"After we left you at the end of the season, we made our way to Matamoros to visit our families. We had only been there for three days when there was talk in the village about a meeting taking place at the high school across the border in Brownsville. The Mexican President was sending representatives to talk to those of us working and living in America about free land back home. A friend took me to the meeting. It turned out the Government of Mexico was offering free acreage to those willing to clear it, farm cotton and settle their families in Matamoros. I was so excited I wanted to shout my praises to the heavens right there, but I waited and listened to make sure it was true. With all that I have learned about cotton, I was sure I could do this. They signed me up, and once I had scribbled my name on the document, it was official. It was that simple. The government was already working to divide the parcels and build irrigation for the farmers. When it's all done, we can return to Mexico and begin again."

"My God, that's great news, Angel," said Franz. "It's what you've always wanted."

"Yes!" I was excited for Angel too. "This kind of thing never happens. It's like a miracle."

"Thank you, yes. There is no other way to explain it." Angel couldn't stop smiling. "Almost every man I know would prefer to live and work in his own country. I am no different."

"And what could be better than not having to uproot your family every few months just to keep food on the table," I added. "Now you'll have a place to call home."

"Wow, I guess we'll have to travel to Mexico now if we want to see you," said Franz. "We'll sure miss you, Angel, but you know we're happy for you."

Angel's eyes were bright with hope. "Not only will we have our own land, but we'll be living close to our families again. My wife is so happy, she's had a smile on her face ever since I told her the good news."

"That's so exciting," I said, trying to hide my disappointment at the prospect of losing the closest thing we'd come to having a family since we'd been on the road. "What are your plans in the meantime? Will you be here long?"

"Well, as you've heard, it is difficult to get into the states now, but I had a pass to work the apricots, and word had come down that the crop was up early so we decided to make the trip. Come August though, when the work dries up, I'll collect my wages and we'll pack up our belongings one last time. Officials will meet us over the border from Brownsville and take us to our land. For the first time, we will be going home with the chance to build a better future. I am so tired of moving around I don't even care how long it takes to clear the land. I am young, and I know I can do it. God has answered our prayers."

"You deserve it, Angel, you really do." I said.

Angel's eyes met mine. "Maybe your prayers will be answered someday too." And I could tell that he meant it from the deepest part of his soul.

"I hope so, Angel. I didn't realize how much having a home meant until I was out here on the road without one."

"Sometimes," Angel paused, "life can surprise you beyond your dreams. Do you know we're even going to have our own town? 'Valle Hermoso.' It means 'Beautiful Valley.'"

How unbelievable it was that when we'd met Angel and his family they had no future at all and now, not more than a few months later, by the stamp of a politician's hand they were granted a section of land, restoring their hope in life. Though it was hard for me to envision something this exciting for myself, that night I wondered what it would feel like to put down roots with a wife and family of my own. I remembered the innocent kisses I stole on Jess in the barn loft, and I wondered if she ever thought of me. I dismissed the notion as soon as it came into my head though. "Such crazy imaginings." Still, I couldn't picture home anywhere else but the farm in Minnesota, and I knew that if I was ever going to have a place of my own, I'd want to start there.

And so our summer began. Franz and I stuck close to Angel and Manuela, often joining them in their camp on weekends when a neighboring man would heft a Spanish guitar to his lap, joined by an accordion and maracas, serenading a small audience who shouted out requests and danced and clapped their hands in appreciation. No one loved this more than Franz who never turned down the shots of tequila that livened up the festivities and by the end of most nights, he'd be singing "Guantanamera" with all the passion of a native Mexican.

We'd kept our noses clean since we'd almost lost our money back in Malibu, but time had dimmed our memories and mitigated the trauma. Money was once again jingling in our pockets and we felt safe in the familiarity of old friends and the protection of our cave. Most important of all, we had plenty to eat. There'd been a girl who worked at the edge of the orchard where some of the freshly picked apricots were split and pitted, then left on racks to dry before they were shipped out. Franz had taken a liking to her. He flirted with her, showing up around the lunch hour and again at the end of the day when the men climbed down off their ladders and packed it in. The girl seemed interested at first, cutting her pale eyes back and forth, smiling ... but her demeanor changed after she'd slipped and dropped Franz's name to her parents. They hadn't been pleased. The girl's father, an Okie, with a chip on his shoulder had materialized in the orchard the following day and warned Franz to stay away. "I got a daughter at home pregnant already! Don't need another mouth to feed, ya hear? She's only fourteen. You keep away from her."

But Franz was undeterred and he answered the man's warning by picking the girl a bouquet of field flowers and asking her to the movies. "I can't," she said, blushing and shying her head away. Franz lingered around past the break time trying to persuade her, until the supervisor stepped in and asked him to leave.

That Saturday night I began to suspect something when Franz gussied up with a bottle of Old Spice he'd somehow gotten his hands on.

"You planning on meeting someone special tonight at Angel's?"

"Oh," he laughed. "I'm going to meet Darlene at the orchard if she can sneak out."

"Aw, come on, Franz. You know this is a bad idea."

"I'll see you at Angel's place. Just wait for me there."

"Franz ..."

"You worry too much, Jake! Relax, I won't be long. Let me just have this one night, please!"

"That's what you said the night we got almost got robbed, too ..."

"Hey, I thought we'd put that behind us! Look, I told Darlene I'd be there. I can't leave her hanging. I'll be at Angel's later. Look, it's no big deal."

When I showed up at Angel's, I was repeatedly asked where my "sidekick" was. I was uncomfortable talking about Franz with him not around, but it did feel good to know that these people cared. As welcomed as I felt, as time went on I couldn't help but grow more concerned about my friend. Finally, in the middle of a song, Franz arrived leading Darlene by the hand. Throwing a nod in my direction, he put his arm around her and coaxed her to sit down. She seemed comfortable and blended in easily as the evening wore on, but no one was prepared for the rusted old pick-up that squealed up too close for comfort an hour or so later with the driver's door swinging on a loose hinge.

"Darlene get in the truck! Darlene scrambled toward the truck as her father rushed at Franz like a bear, pushing him in the chest with his hands and backing him dangerously close to the fire before closing his fist and side-punching Franz's nose.

The women and children scattered to the safer recesses of the camp, but Franz came back at him with a solid punch to the jaw and it took Angel and two of his friends several minutes to pull them apart. The Okie broke loose, turned and ran to his truck where he pulled out a sawed-off shot gun and recklessly waved it in the air before firing off a shot over the heads of those that were brave enough to still be there. Darlene jumped out of the truck screaming: "No, stop! He'll kill you, Franz. Let it go!"

"If that bastard, or any one of you comes near my daughter again, I'll shoot the whole lot of ya."

"Okay, okay," Franz spoke up, drawing himself tall and stepping forward. "I won't go near her. Jesus! Just leave us alone."

"Yeah, well see that you do. Next time I won't be so nice." And with that he grabbed Darlene by the arm and pulled her back to the truck. She didn't even look back.

Crickets chirping in the background, a hard crackle of the fire, the squeal of the truck's wheels as it sped away on the dry dirt, the mutterings of the group of men left shaking their heads in disbelief as they disbanded and walked away, a child's cry somewhere deep inside the camp - all of this juxtaposed so dramatically with what had just transpired. Rumbles like this weren't uncommon, especially now when tensions were high between the whites and the Latinos, but this put everyone in Angel's circle on edge.

Nursing Franz's bloody nose with an ice pack in his tent, Angel broached the subject of our long term plans for the first time, doling out some fatherly advice. "I know you feel a connection here among us and that is a good thing. We have welcomed you and taken you in but still, it's not the same. I know how it feels to be part of this make-shift community and I know how it feels to be going home. Have you boys ever thought of returning to your families and seeing if a new life could be possible for you too? A lot can change over the years. I never thought I'd be going back to Mexico to be a landowner, Lord knows, but the future doesn't always mirror the past. Just something to think about."

Of course, I had thought about going home off and on since the day I'd set off on my own. But I wasn't ready to explain to Angel how the circumstances that made me leave in the first place made it impossible to simply show up on the front porch. I also understood that Franz's situation was different than mine. He harbored no strong feelings about the place he'd called home so long ago and for him, there was nothing to reconcile. If he ever did return, it would only be for a visit. I assumed this had something to do with Franz's bursts of heedless behavior. He felt he had less to lose. His future was as wide open, raw and as unpredictable as life on the road. My future was open too and uncertain, but I still felt a deep, albeit sad, connection.

When August finally rolled around and the last of the apricots had been weighed in, we once again found ourselves watching Angel settle his two oldest children among the worn out fruit crates in the back of his truck.

"Adios!" They waved their hands and smiled.

"Adios!"

"I remember last time Angel, you told us to keep the blankets," said Franz.

"It's a good thing too," I added, "couldn't have survived without them. We've worn them out. In fact I think we're down to one!"

"Well, there are plenty of blankets where we are headed," said Angel. You'll just have to come to Mexico for more. Goodbye once again my friends." Angel gave us each a hug and a firm shake. Manuela was in the front seat with the toddler on her lap, but she turned and smiled her own farewell.

"Goodbye, Angel," said Franz. "We'll miss you, but we're happy too."

"Yes," I said. "It couldn't be more different this time. You have a real home now."

"It looks that way," Angel agreed. "I am confident that you will find it some day too, both of you. In the mean time, be sure and keep Franz out of trouble, Jake. Don't let the girls go to his head!"

"I'll sure as heck try, Angel" I laughed. "But you know it won't be easy."

"Yeah, good luck!" Franz chimed in. "Girls are my life!"

We laughed and waved as we watched them go, and the wheels of the old truck wobbled down the road as if it were on its last leg which indeed, it was, at least in this country.

Franz and I stayed on after they were gone, laboring in the potato fields, with peppers and sweet onions after that. We'd been fortunate to be able to find work long into the fall season, but by the end of November it was time to hit the road once again.

✫ ✫ ✫

The third winter in we struck out again for Texas with its high, ever-changing plains, sloping mesas and empty country roads. Glowing hot Texas sunsets blasted across the wide open skies, and miles of fields spread themselves lush and thick. It felt good to be back.

"Let's try Joe Barton again," I said. Our train had rumbled its way through the tip of the Panhandle and was heading south toward Amarillo. "He was kinder than most and fed us good."

Franz agreed. "Good idea. Plenty of fields to pick there, so chances are he'll take us on."

Jumping off the train just outside the sleepy town of Flomot, we hitched a ride in the back of a pickup to the Barton spread and found Joe buzzing flies and digging a series of fence posts with two hired-hands. He was a tall, but well-built man with a weathered face etched like a map from too many days in the hot Texas sun. Mr. B. would always rather work than talk, and, since he already knew us the hiring was quick. "Work's already underway. Check with the foreman in the morning and get your assignment. You know the drill."

"Thank you, sir. We sure do appreciate the work." Franz reached out for a handshake and I followed suit.

As we turned to walk the quarter mile or so to the migrant bunkhouse to stash our meager belongings, Joe called us back.

"Hey, boys!"

When I looked over my shoulder he was bow-legging after us and wiping the sweat off his forehead with the sleeve of his shirt. "I got nicer quarters off the barn," said Joe. "My boy liked to sleep out there so he could play his guitar without bothering anyone. Always thoughtful, that one." Mr. B. took a deep breath as if he might choke up, but then he went on: "He went to sea on the USS Enterprise five months ago and the place is empty now. Why don't you boys settle in there. My wife can't sleep she worries so much. Maybe it'll cheer her up tending to y'all with some home cooked meals."

"Gosh, thanks Mr. Barton," I said. "That sure is a kind offer."

Franz reiterated the sentiment. "Yes, thank you. We sure would appreciate that."

Luck seemed to be our constant companion these days. I smiled, and Joe Barton smiled back.

We settled in, sweating hard for the Bartons, grateful for the gift of being able to sleep in the comfort of a bed and have Mrs. B. fuss over us. We were more than willing to be on the receiving end of whatever mothering she had to give. She came to life the first night we bunked down after we'd taken our supper in the mess hall and had just wandered back. There was a soft rapping on our door. "Boys," she said, peeking in. "You got everything you need?"

"Yes, ma'am," we chimed as we jumped up from our beds and widened the door.

"I'm Mrs. Barton," she said with a soft southern accent as she made her entrance, "but you can call me Evelyn if you like. I know you've been here before, but I'd like to welcome you back to Texas."

We nodded our response, unsure of what would be expected of us.

Evelyn got busy moving the washstand and bowl into the corner of our room to make more space. "We always eat supper at six o'clock but I know you'll be hungry earlier as soon as you come in off the fields. Just rap on the side door of the kitchen. There's a table in the corner and you can take your meals there. Your plates will be ready, but I've got to ask that you wash your hands and faces before you come into the house. The pump's right outside your door and there's plenty of water."

She slid a basket that was sitting on the floor away from the wall. "Dirty clothes can go right in here. Tuesday is wash day."

"You don't have to do that," I said.

"Yeah," Franz piped up, as incredulous as I was at such an offer. "We can jump in a lake or something. There's no need to wash our clothes."

Evelyn laughed. "I don't know where you saw the lake around here, son, but you'll have to point it out! Just wash up proper at the pump. And don't worry, it's just the two of us now, and I have help. You're not an imposition."

She was right about our being hungry when we came in off the fields. Starving was more like it. We couldn't pump the water fast enough to clean our grimy faces and head on over to the kitchen. There was a kind Mexican lady who assisted with the housework but when it came to the cooking, Evelyn was hands on. "It keeps me busy," she said, "and I know you boys appreciate it."

She was not the typical farmer's wife with over-washed aprons and pockets full of chicken feed. Mr. B. called her "darlin'" and "Evelyn," and she had trimmed flowers set on every table in the house and a lot of style with her modern dress and soft red hair cut short like a lady in a magazine. Unlike Mr. B., she was chatty too and shared stories of their life with us over dinner. Turns out Mr. B. had lured her there with his money from the big city of Dallas, where she'd held an important company job. She'd had a baby and settled into country life well enough, but now her only son was away at war, and Evelyn was left scrambling with the likes of us as she stood by the stove stirring this or that, checking the oven to see if the roast was done. She also wanted to know where we were from, why we'd left home. During these conversations I never mentioned anything about the accident and why I'd really gone away. I stuck along the lines of Franz's story, keeping it simple and vague … times were tough and I had left.

"Well, things are sure to improve once this war is over," Evelyn said. "I know there are a lot of heart-sick parents, including me, who are anxious to get their boys back."

Of course we were aware that America and its allies were fighting overseas, but our struggle to survive had kept us pretty ignorant of all that. We didn't have access to newspapers or radios and the field workers never mentioned it. They, too, had more immediate things to worry about. We knew we had it good for the moment and that's what mattered most to us. Evelyn treated us like sons and we could hardly wait for Sunday night. The farmhouse had an oversized pantry room off the kitchen and Mr. B. had splurged some of his cotton farming money on a large copper tub for his pretty wife. Every Sunday night, Evelyn had it filled with hot water and left us a bar of soap, fresh towels and a plate of her pecan cookies. We took turns soaking and munching as we listened to the distant sounds of the radio playing in the parlor. Sometimes I closed my eyes and imagined I was home in my own room listening to my parents settled in the parlor, their conversation a quiet comforting hum.

The time flew by in spite of the hard work, but in the waning days of the season when it looked like vultures had picked the cotton fields down to the carcass, Mr. B. rapped on our door one evening with a wrinkled newspaper tucked under his arm.

"Season's 'bout over boys, and I'll have to let you go, but this here's an article about what they're callin' the Civilian Conservation Corps." He rustled the front page of the paper with a thick calloused hand and held it up for us to see. "Looks like Franklin Roosevelt's got these CCC camps set up all over the country to help out young men like yourselves. Signin' up gets you thirty dollars a month. I believe you'd get some job training too. You're good workers, but I'd hate to see you end up migrant laborers your whole lives if you can do better."

"You don't say," I said, accepting the paper from his hands and skimming the article as Franz crowded in to read over my shoulder. "Thanks for the tip. We'll check it out." I didn't know if this could be an answer for us, but it sure did sound promising.

The day we left, we rapped on the front door of the Barton's farmhouse hoping to pay our respects and to thank to Evelyn for the fine cooking and extra care she had provided us. I wasn't sure which I'd miss most, the cornbread smothered in butter or the clean sheets and warm blankets. She held the screen door open. "Hurry on, boys. Don't let the flies in." I could tell by the flavorful scent in the air that she'd been cooking. "I packed some goodies for you to take with you. Can't have my boys goin' hungry now, can we?"

"We can't thank you enough, Mrs. B.," I said. "You've sure been more than kind to us."

"Yeah, never had it so good, Mrs. B.," said Franz. "Thanks for your generosity, all that great food. I'll be dreamin' about your cooking."

"Well, there's not a boy on this planet who doesn't need some good mothering," she said. "I was happy to do it."

"Boy, did we need it," Franz laughed.

"Yeah, you couldn't have picked two better candidates for that than us," I laughed.

"Well, you boys have good luck out there now and keep in touch from time-to-time, too. We're expecting that, you know."

"Sure thing, Mrs. B."

A few minutes later we were settled in the back of the old man's stake bed truck with gunny sacks full of freshly laundered clothes, cold pork chops, hard boiled eggs, and jam cake. It was on the cusp of winter dark when Mr. B. drove us the hundred or so miles to the Amarillo switchyard and pulled over within first view of the red and green signal lights. Climbing out and setting his foot up on the bent-up fender, Mr. B. cracked his knuckles while he waited for us to gather our belongings.

"We don't know how to thank you," I said. I offered him my hand that was showing early signs of toughening up from the hard labor, same as his. "You've been mighty good to us, sir, and we'll never forget it."

Franz held out his hand in gratitude as well. The farmer ignored our outstretched hands though, and pulled us close, one after the other, with an expression of warmth that neither of us had expected or experienced since we'd left home.

"Only did what I'd hope folks would do for my boy." Barton talked over his shoulder as he bent his rangy frame toward the truck. "Y'all take care now, and when you're settled you drop us a line, ya hear? Let us know you're alright."

"That we will," I said. "Soon as we're signed on."

"We're sure gonna miss Mrs. B.'s mothering," Franz shouted after him. "Be sure and tell her again. We'll be remembering all that you both done for us."

"Will do." He tipped his cowboy hat in a final farewell and turned away.

We watched until the taillights of the old man's truck disappeared down the blackened stretch of road, then snuck like thieves into the rail yard, hopeful of a new life to come.

PART III

*"Nature gave us all something to fall back on
and sooner or later we all land flat on it."*

--- *Texas Bix Bender*

Chapter Sixteen

Back 'round, 1942

THE TRIP WAS A LONG two days to the coast with arduous starts and stops, but we were used to such things by now and passed the time dozing and sharing our fears and dreams late into the night, wondering what this new leg of our adventure had in store. Near dusk, the train whistle blasted as we snaked around a bend following the path of a swift flowing river that shifted vistas with every new mile or so.

"I'd love to go to a real dance sometime," said Franz. "Maybe hear an American swing band and meet a pretty girl."

I glanced over. He had let his eyelids close, so he could savor the picture in his head, and I wondered what new shenanigans he might have in store for us next. "If things work out the way we're hoping, you'll likely be able to meet lots of pretty girls," I laughed.

"I'd be happy with one," Franz replied, savoring the fantasy. "But she has to be real good lookin', with red hair like Mrs. B. and legs like that movie actress in the poster. You know the one I mean, Jake? Was it Betty Grable? Oh yeah, and eyes. Eyes that light up when she smiles and laugh when she talks."

"Heck, Darlene didn't look anything like that. Didn't have red hair either. What are you talking about?"

"Forget Darlene. I'm talkin' about my dream girl here. She's a redhead!"

"Sounds like Jess Stivers from back home," I said. "She's not a redhead, but she's about as close to a dream girl as I'd ever want."

Peeling a stick with my jackknife, I was lost in my own daydreams of times long ago. There were many moments these days when I found my mind wandering to thoughts of Jess. I imagined she must be almost a woman by now, and I fantasized about what it would be like to ask her out on a date, hold her hand in a darkened movie theatre, or even better, make out with her in the back row the way Henry said his older brothers used to do with their dates.

"Who's Jess Stivers?"

"My friend, Henry's, twin sister. I snuck a kiss on her once, playing hide-and-seek. She was so surprised, she just took off running. Running and laughing. Jess had those smiling eyes, but her hair was the color of gold. I still dream about her sometimes. Sure do wonder what happened to those people."

"Did you love her?"

"Nah, I was too young for that. Doesn't mean I don't think about her though. I definitely had a crush on her."

"Hell, I never kissed anyone I cared about," Franz admitted. He picked himself up and leaned on the edge of the open boxcar door, staring at the passing rapids and whitecaps that slowed in spaces of great calm when the wind died off. A large bare rock jutted out from the side of the riverbank, but the water just flowed around it, it's power only briefly interrupted.

"There'll be plenty of girls to choose from, Franz, once we get steady jobs and a roof over our heads."

"Man, I hope you're right, Jake. I'm tired of this all work and no play life we've been leading!"

"Our time's coming, I would bet. I'm counting on this Civilian Conservation Corps camp to turn our lives around."

After arriving in Los Angeles, we sought out the CCC camp that was set up in Griffith Park with its thousands of acres of wilderness on the eastern edge of the Santa Monica Mountains. In all our travels, we had never seen anything to rival the beauty of such a landscape spread with California oaks, rocky ledges and waterfalls, and the chaparral with its tall, dense shrubs and the scent of wild sage. The relief camp itself, on the other hand, was stripped bare of any such distractions and was organized like an army barracks. Each rectangle-shaped building had nothing more than rows of beds and a wood stove that provided a minimum of heat. We quickly signed on for a six month hitch and were issued blue denim work clothes as well as a fancier green uniform that we would change into for dinner. When reveille sounded at sunrise we headed outside with the other men for some light calisthenics followed by a hot breakfast in the mess hall. True to the promise of the article Mr. B. had read us, we were put to work straight away spending our first day with a two-man saw, clearing trees for a fire road and a drainage channel that would wind high up into the forested park. The work was strenuous but satisfying and less debilitating than migrant life had been.

Our days at the camp were regimented, but there was a comfort level as akin to home as any we could expect now. After each full day of labor at the worksite, we trucked back to the camp for dinner at five o'clock sharp, a routine we came to appreciate. After dinner, I oftentimes sat outside and whittled, enjoying the solitude and the fresh mountain air. Later on, ping-pong and chess filled the evenings, adding a dimension to our lives we'd almost forgotten. We heard that we were also free to explore L.A., to catch a movie, or hit a bar after KP duty - as long as we were back by ten sharp when, in the dark, blank stillness, the bugle rendered Taps, signaling lights out.

Two weeks in, as the men settled down for the night, several of the other guys started bragging about the hot time they'd had at a place called "Arnie's" across the street from the beach in Santa Monica.

"That place sure is hopping," said a freckled kid from Des Moines. He snapped a hand towel into the air with emphasis to make his point. "I've never seen so many pretty women in one place before. You boys outta' check it out. If I hadn't been in and amongst them myself, I wouldn't believe it." He let the towel fly with another snap into the air.

"Oh, man, you're killing me with that talk," said Franz. He was elbows to his knees on the side of his cot, taking in every word. "How do we get there?"

"Bus comes by every hour down at the entrance to the park. Your friend there," he said, swooping the towel off the floor and swinging it at me, "he's gonna' have to hold you back once you put your head inside that door."

It was all too much for Franz, and he rolled back on his cot in ecstasy, his head swimming with all the beautiful women he was sure he would meet. For the rest of the week, it was all he talked about.

☆ ☆ ☆

The following Saturday, we donned a couple of clean shirts and caught the bus to Santa Monica. Jumping off at a stop a block away from "Arnie's," we paused to stare at a couple of good-looking girls packing up the baskets of their bicycles after a day at the beach. One of them was still wearing her bathing suit and I had to pull Franz by the arm to get him to move along. "Arnie's, Franz," I said. "We're looking for a place called Arnie's, remember?"

Arnie's turned out to be an old speakeasy that had become a full-fledged bar when prohibition ended in '33, and Arnie liked to make sure everyone had a good time, calling for rounds of free pints whenever the spirit moved him. Maroon leather-tufted booths lined the whiskey-stained walls, and white globe lights dimmed by years of grime hung from the ceiling. The centerpiece was a long mahogany bar that shone like a well-polished rifle, and Arnie had lined the paneled wall behind the bar with every kind of liquor imaginable as a tribute to the common man's now legal right to imbibe. The menu included a handful of sandwiches and a few "starters," but the most popular choice, we quickly learned, was the French Dip, a generous half-pound of shaved beef piled high on a hard roll and served with a side of "jus" in a small gold-rimmed bowl. To those who frequented the place, it seemed damn near un-American to stop in at Arnie's and not order a French Dip to accompany your first beer of the night. Best of all, almost every night of the week the joint was packed with working girls and plenty of us CCC camp boys and sailors on leave all crowding in for a bit of levity to take the edge off.

Arnie was smart. He appreciated the steady business of the servicemen and the guys from the relief camp and wanted us to enjoy ourselves, so he made a special effort to entice his female customers to frequent his place. Women's drinks were half price every "Happy Hour" between five and seven and all night on Saturday. A juke box played popular hits by the likes of Glenn Miller, Jimmy Dorsey, and the Andrews Sisters. Groups of guys and gals lingered in the booths, and then, if they were lucky enough to have connected with a kindred spirit, went for a walk on the beach and maybe shared an Eskimo Pie from one of the vendors on the boardwalk. By six o'clock most nights, the place was buzzing with young women who clocked out and came straight from work, filling up the booths, enjoying the affordable drinks and anticipating the throng of men they knew were on the way. We felt like we'd hit pay dirt and entered a world of new possibilities. Things were definitely looking up.

After the first night, Arnie's became our destination of choice, and we gravitated there every chance we could. At the CCC camp we would hustle to shower and button up our dress uniforms, then eat a hasty dinner and bus down to mingle with the working girls who packed into the booths and always seemed to have money for a spare drink. Indulging our never-ending appetites, they were more than eager to share their discounts too, waving over some lucky guy they fancied and offering a cold beer and maybe a split of their sandwich. It was here that I met a friendly, sweet-natured girl who spent her days working as a switchboard operator for the telephone company. I'd been playing eye tag with her for awhile, but she was wedged in the middle of a tight booth flanked by girlfriends, and I'd been reluctant to take on the whole table. When two of them left a short while later though, I decided to make my move.

"Name's Jake Frye," I said. I slid in next to her with my heart racing and catching a trace of her eau de toilette, a fresh cut flower scent I found pleasing. She greeted me with a warm smile, and I was captivated by a special something that was both charming and attractive. Instantly, I wanted to know this girl with the beautiful smile who looked so alluring with her honey color hair bobbed around her face complimenting her emerald eyes, almost luminous in the muted light of the booth.

"Bonnie Turner," she said, maneuvering her shoulders in the cramped space to face me. "Nice to meet you. This is Lucy and that's Delores." They leaned forward and poked their heads around Bonnie.

"Hi," they said in unison, giggling.

"You all look like you're enjoying yourselves tonight. This is my buddy, Franz Mueller." Franz, who'd just picked up a cold draw at the bar, slid seamlessly into the other end of the booth, packing Bonnie's girlfriends even tighter and setting off another bout of giggles.

"Hi, ladies," Franz said, beaming. "How are you all this evening?"

Over the course of the next couple of hours, Franz ordered rounds for the table three times as we all made small talk and took our turns showing off our rusty dance moves with the girls.

By eight o'clock, I'd had enough to drink, but Franz, who'd had more than his fair share, took Lucy and Delores on each arm and left for the "Spotlight," a club down the block that hosted an authentic swing band and boasted a larger-than-most dance floor. A half hour later when the juke box at Arnie's fired up another decibel and the place got rowdy, Bonnie and I decided to join them. "I could use a walk and some fresh air," she said, sliding her empty drink to the center of the table.

We took our time strolling the short way down to the club. The breeze off the water was cool and salty, rustling the tops of the palm trees that lined the road. It was a busy scene with cars driving by, stragglers on the beach, couples and groups of friends trading off between the bars and restaurants that dotted the shoreline. When we arrived at the Spotlight, Franz was easy to pick out on the far side of the dance floor, leaning on the bar face-to-face with a girl whose eyes at half-mast indicated she'd more than matched him in drinks.

He pulled himself up straight when he spotted us and waved us over. "Hey, you two!" he yelled. "It's about time you showed up where the action is. I want you to meet someone. This here's Linae." Franz put his arm around the girl's waist as if he were afraid she might get away. "It was love at first sight, wasn't it, darlin'?" He leaned into her, throwing her off balance in her high-heeled shoes that strapped around her ankles and grabbing her up before she hit the floor. "Ain't she something?" he grinned, planting a big wet kiss on the side of Linae's cheek. "Most gorgeous thing, I ever saw."

Linae's breasts were pushed up so high inside her bra and presented such a sharp contrast to her tiny waist, curvy hips and long, slim legs that it looked as if she might topple over at any second from the sheer imbalance of it all. Her hair demanded attention too, since it was dyed the wildest shade of red I had ever seen, pulled back high in a brassy mound of curls that cascaded down over her forehead. Heavy makeup pan-caked her face, including heavily lined eyes, and dark pink lipstick smudged around the edges of her mouth, undoubtedly from smooching with Franz. Her jade sequined cocktail dress couldn't have been tighter if it had been painted on and was in sharp contrast to Bonnie's more modest attire. I couldn't take my eyes off the two of them, but Linae seemed to relish the scrutiny and laid it on thick with Franz, batting her blue eyes and flirting with him so shamelessly that Franz, who was way beyond enamored by now, acted like he'd died and gone to heaven. The boy who had never kissed a girl he'd cared about seemed determined to make up for it now.

Unabashed and unable to contain himself, Franz grinned and slid his arm around Linae's eighteen inch waist. "We're in love, buddy," he gushed, pulling her close. "This one right here! This one's it. She's my dream girl."

Soaking up the lavish attention, Linae leaned her head on his shoulder and sighed, "Aaahhh, Franzie."

"I mean it, baby," Franz was earnest. "I'm hooked. I don't ever want another woman but you."

"Franzie, stop," Linae said, dropping her chin coyly. "You're making me blush. Now you'll have to excuse me, honey. I'm gonna' have to powder my nose."

"Baby, you don't have to do a thing for me. You're perfect in every way already." Franz threw her a smile. "What do I have to do to make you mine?"

"Keep on adorin' me, sugar. I adore being adored, and no one's ever done it quite like this before." Linae tickled Franz's stomach and giggled before sauntering away and I watched the show unfold with my mouth open.

It didn't surprise me that Franz would fall hard when he finally met a girl that he liked. Linae struck me as different from his previous flirtations though, older and undoubtedly more experienced, but she did have the red hair that Franz claimed he had always dreamed of. And it did appear they were living up to each other's expectations, in spite of the fact that they'd only known each other, by my calculations, just under an hour at the most.

"Hey," said Franz, lifting his hand to the bartender as he watched Linae disappear into the crowd. "We need a Tom Collins. You want a strong one tonight, Jake? This round's on me."

"I've been sticking with beer," I said, "but I think I'm about done for tonight. Don't forget we've got that bus to catch."

"Don't bag out on me now, buddy," Franz said. "Come on, one more. We gotta' toast to the luckiest night of my life. Besides, Linae has a car. She's gonna' drive us back to camp."

Franz ordered two more beers, a Tom Collins for Bonnie and a Sloe Gin Fizz for Linae. When she returned, we all hung out - the women on the bar stools, Franz standing as eager as a spaniel next to Linae, and me sidled up to Bonnie.

"So, what is it that you do, Linae?" I asked.

Accepting her drink from Franz, Linae wiped the side of the wet glass with a cocktail napkin and sucked the sloe gin off the top in one long inhale. "Well, I came to Los Angeles to get my name in lights, 'cause that's what my heart told me I should do. But I'm open. A gal just never knows when she's gonna' catch a break." The glue on one of her false eyelashes had come loose at the edge, but she didn't seem to notice. Linae sighed and rewarded herself with another long slurp before continuing. "Meantime, I'm helping run a boarding house for the old lady who owns it but is too old to jitterbug. It's a big white place over in Venice near the beach." She set her drink down and gave it a good tweak with the swizzle stick. After a vigorous swirl she drew another long sip. "I also sing at Jason's down the block when they let me, though not tonight which meant I was 'sposed to come out 'n meet Franzie here."

"Where are you from, Linae?" Bonnie asked.

Linae paused long enough to blow a kiss Franz's way "I'm an Oklahoma girl, but I outgrew that old dust trap years ago. Gave it all up for the city lights."

"Yeah, she belongs in the "City of Angels." She's gonna' be a big star too," said Franz, nuzzling the side of her neck. "Go ahead, baby, tell 'em."

I was trying to picture the likes of Linae in a small, western town. She was a whole lot of woman for any town, but it was easy to imagine that in a small town she stood out as something special, something glamorous even.

"Oh yeah, I almost forgot to say," Linae said in response to Franz's prompting. "I'm an actress too. And I model. Like I said … I'm open. You just gotta' throw it all out there and see what sticks."

"Why, I know she's got so much talent," said Franz, "I can feel it oozing right outta' her pores." He gave her a light a squeeze.

Bonnie sat up tall and crossed her legs. "Have you been in any productions or movies? she asked, after she'd taken a sip of her own drink. "Anything we might have seen?"

"Not yet, but I did get a call back for a Warner Brother's picture they're callin' 'Lonely Tonight.' It's so secret though, they won't even tell me which big stars have been cast."

"Maybe they don't know," said Franz, smiling. "Maybe it'll be you."

"See how he does that?" Linae giggled. "I love that." She rewarded Franz with another long, drawn out kiss on the lips before carrying on. "I got my fingers crossed on this one. I really think this could be my big break."

As we were enjoying our last drink of the evening, Delores wandered over from the dance floor. "Hey Bonnie, I'm going to take a walk down the beach with my new friends here." She lifted her chin to indicate the group behind her. "By the looks of things, you won't have any trouble finding a ride home." Bonnie smiled at Delores and the guy she'd been dancing with who was standing off to the side, and he waved and nodded in return. "Mike there's already volunteered to take good care of us," Delores said, throwing him a smile.

"Don't worry, I'll make sure she gets home okay." Mike gave a thumbs up.

"I figured," laughed Bonnie. "Have fun."

She slid off the bar stool and Delores stepped up with a shoulder hug. "You have a good time, too," said Delores, "I'll call you tomorrow."

"Talk to you then."

When our glasses were empty, Linae and Bonnie agreed that a stroll on the beach was the thing to do, and Franz and I were eager to oblige, knowing that we'd be getting a ride back to the camp and didn't have to worry about missing the bus. As we checked out the featured attractions at the pier's amusement park, Franz grabbed Linae's hand and pulled her toward the "Straw Pigeon" shoot. "Come on, baby. Keep your eyes on the prize now, 'cause I intend to win you something special."

The three of us watched as Franz downed the starting pigeons in two shots. Linae jumped up and down and held out her arms for a fuzzy, pink bear about the size of a large baby.

"Way to go, buddy." I slapped him on the back. "I know that ain't easy."

Linae gushed, holding her prize up like it was an Academy Award. "I always wanted a boyfriend to win me a carnival bear to pretty up my bed."

"Well, I always wanted a girl to win one for," said Franz. He wrapped his arms around Linae and lifted her off the ground, planting a noisy kiss on the side of her cheek.

Just after nine we piled into Linae's shiny blue convertible coupe, and she got behind the wheel, showing off with a quick drive down Ocean Avenue. The air was chilly off the water, but the breeze felt refreshing as Linae steered us across town toward Griffith Park. Winding her way past the stone entrance walls, she giggled as she reached in the darkness for Franz's hand. Arriving just outside the CCC, camp, she drifted to the side of the road, shifted the car into park and cut the engine. Franz swung open his door on the passenger side of the car and rushed around to do the same for Linae.

"A man who knows how to treat a girl like a lady is something special where I come from," she said. She made a formal showing of extending her arm and tipping her hand for Franz to take and help her step out. Franz tucked his head inside the car. "Be right back!" he winked and off they went.

Watching their quick departure, I barely had time to catch the back of Linae's sequined dress shimmering in the moonlight as they disappeared into the woods.

"Hmmmm," said Bonnie relaxing into me when I pulled her tighter. "I could never run off into the woods like that. Ever since I was a little girl, I've been afraid of the dark."

"Well, that's fine with me," I said, nuzzling her neck. "I like it here just like this."

With such an attractive woman in my arms, the desire to kiss Bonnie overwhelmed me and soon we were making out. When things became a little too hot, however, Bonnie pulled back with a nervous laugh. "They're gone a long time," she said. She sat upright straightening her dress and smoothing out her hair. "Franz sure is smitten."

"I don't know what's come over him," I said, catching my breath, surprised at the intensity of my desire that for several minutes didn't seem different from Franz's. "I've sure never seen him act this way before. It's like he's gone off the deep end or something."

When the lovebirds did finally emerge, Franz had one arm wound tightly around Linae's waist as they giggled and stumbled toward the car. He clicked open the door for Linae, and the moonlight revealed dark lipstick stained across his puffy lips and what looked like a hickey forming on his neck. It was only our close friendship that kept me from laughing out loud.

"Come on, Franz. Let's let these ladies go home. We got lights out in the camp any minute now. Time to call it a night." I climbed out of the back seat and helped settle Bonnie in the front passenger side. "Goodnight," I said, kissing her lightly on the cheek. "I'd like to see you again real soon if you're up for it. It's kind of hard during the week, but maybe this weekend if you're free?"

"Sure, I'd love to." said Bonnie.

"I need to get your number ..."

"I'm scribbling my number for Franz right now," said Linae, reaching inside the glove compartment for a small notepad and pencil. "Here, Bonnie, write yours down next to mine so these boys know how to get a hold of us."

When Bonnie had added her number, Linae tore the paper from the notepad and handed it to Franz. "Here ya go, sugar," she said. "Be sure and keep that in a safe place now."

"You don't have to worry about that," said Franz. "I'll call you tomorrow." He leaned in for one last smooch. We let the girls drive off, and then, following the car for a few steps, Franz cupped his hands around his mouth and shouted, "See you in my dreams, sweet thing."

On the path up to the camp barracks, Franz was euphoric. "It's not crazy," he insisted. "Anything that feels this good can only be one thing: crazy love."

"Take it easy, buddy," I said. "I know you're smitten, but ratchet it down a couple of clicks. You've only known her for a few hours."

"I know, Jake. I know it's fast, but I know this is it. I can feel it. I can just feel it, right here," he said, pounding his chest. "When a man feels this good ... when a woman makes a man feel this good, it can only be the real thing. Damn, Jake. My past might have been kinda' bleak, but my future's sure lookin' rosy."

"Okay, Franz. I'm happy for you. I really am. Come on though, let's hurry. I don't want to be late checking in. We don't need any problems back in the barracks."

The four of us kept up with one another in the coming months, Linae's car making all the difference in the world. We didn't have bus schedules to hassle with since she was more than eager to drive out to the camp every other night to hook up with "Franzie." Most times I went along and we'd pick up Bonnie at her apartment and head on over to Arnie's. On the weekends there were double dates for picnics in the park, roller coaster rides near the pier, walks along the shore line that Bonnie timed to make sure we didn't miss a sunset. It was obvious that Franz was head-over-heels for Linae, but I was falling in love too. Bonnie had captured my heart!

Once, at Franz's insistence, Linae drove us over to Venice and pointed out the boarding house where she worked, an over-sized white Victorian in need of a good paint job. She slowed so we could get a good look, and it looked respectable, but later I heard that it harbored more than a few cheap rooms that could be had for a night or two with maybe a girl to go with it. Afterward, we shopped for trinkets from the vendors that had set up shop along the Venice Beach boardwalk, and I spent ten cents on a shell necklace for Bonnie, who loved anything to do with the ocean. Later on, we watched and listened while Franz and

Linae had their fortunes read. At first I was reluctant to approach the gypsy woman who waved us toward her. The Malibu incident was still too fresh in my memory. As usual, Franz didn't hesitate though, and I relaxed when Bonnie let me hold her tight with my arms around her waist. I had fallen for her in a big way and was certain that she knew it. "You feel good," I whispered in her ear.

She lifted her chin. "You too," she smiled.

The old woman took her time peering into her well smudged crystal ball, and zeroing in first on Linae.

"Love is never easy," the gypsy started out in a hoarse whispering voice, holding Linae's palm up to the light. "The choice is up to you."

"Yeah, well, I've made my choice. Haven't I, honey? She squeezed Franz's hand before asking for more. "Tell me something I don't know," she giggled.

Linae's giggles disappeared though, when she inquired about her future as an actress and was told it was unclear as to whether or not she would ever become a big star.

"Are you sure?" she whined, clutching Franz's arm. "I have a huge audition coming up. I really have a good feeling about this one."

But the woman left Linae to pout on her own and turned her attention to Franz. Linae perked up only when halfway through the reading Franz was told he was destined to find "great love" to which he replied, "I've already found it!"

"Oh, Franzie," said Linea, "you're too much!"

"I don't want to know the future." I said quietly to Bonnie as we watched and waited: "I'm concerned enough about the present."

"If I knew she could look inside her crystal ball and tell me with absolute certainty what was in store for me, I guess I might be interested," Bonnie replied, "but I'm too much of a realist to believe in that stuff."

"Yeah, me too," I said. I hesitated before admitting, "I guess I kinda would like to know how my parents are doing though."

"Well, you don't need a fortune teller for that," Bonnie shrugged her shoulders. "Why don't you just write them a letter?"

Bonnie had become as much a friend to me as a love interest over the past few months and seemed content with our noncommittal connection. As an only child of divorced parents, she claimed she was in no hurry to marry, and I believed she simply enjoyed the ease of our relationship, free as it was from heavy conversations about the future.

"Already have." I replied. "I just haven't heard anything back."

"Do they know your address?"

"I put it on the envelope, as well as at the end of the letter just in case they ever wanted to answer."

The topic of the life I'd walked away from was painful for me and one it was difficult to get me to open up about. Bonnie never pushed me however, and accepted the fact that she knew little about my past, other than that I'd left home at thirteen and hadn't been back since. My story wasn't an uncommon one for the times, and she felt no desire to challenge my reticence.

CHAPTER SEVENTEEN

W E'D BEEN A YEAR IN the camp when word went out that the government was disbanding the Civilian Conservation Corps to concentrate on the war efforts. Pearl Harbor had been attacked and the country was reeling. Franz and I, along with a handful of others, were hired to stay on for several more months to tie up the work projects and leave the park in good shape. Though we appreciated the steady food and beds with real pillows, what we loved most were the great times we had in the company of Bonnie and Linae. The girls had added a layer of meaning to our lives neither one of us had ever experienced before, and we lived for the sight of Linae's big blue car shimmering up the drive. It was easy to get caught up in the war fever though, and the camp work itself had grown tiresome. As happy and content as we had become, we were going on twenty years old and longed for a life of more purpose and action. Toward the end of our stint, we decided to stop by a recruiting office and enlist in the army.

For me, serving my country was the next logical thing to do, a continuation of the structure and training we'd enjoyed at the camp, but for Franz military service was also a way to get Linae, who had hinted on numerous occasions that she found it hard to resist a man in uniform. Franz knew that after he served his time in the army he'd have saved some money, allowing him to start a life with her. There would be other benefits too, like schooling if we wanted it down the line, as well as medical care we'd receive for the rest of our lives.

Weeks before we signed up, I'd mentioned to Bonnie that I'd been thinking about it, and she had been supportive, if not enthusiastic. Linae, of course, was thrilled to hear she'd finally be dating a soldier, and couldn't wait to see Franz all decked out in his uniform. Nobody talked about the dangers as the focus was on the glory of defending our country. We were more than eager to fight the Nazi invasion blazing across Europe and like the other recruits of our day, were oblivious to the reality of life defined by war. The thought that I might not make it back never occurred to me at that time, and though I saw myself returning to Minnesota at some point, what I would "do" when the war was over was vague. And so, in the spring of 1944, when we were finally called up, we were only too happy to go.

As the day of our departure for basic training drew near, I rode the bus to Santa Monica one last time and walked the short block to Arnie's where Bonnie kept one of the booths warm waiting for me. The reality of saying goodbye was beginning to sink in and I was juggling mixed emotions. I tried not to think about the knot in my stomach as we shared an appetizer and ate French Dips one last time. We took our time strolling the shore line that I had come to love. Watching the full moon cast it's silver light way out over the water like a giant flood lamp, we pulled our shoes off and walked out toward the water, dropping to the sand above the edge of the break line, a safe distance from the incoming waves.

There was a prolonged silence between us. Bonnie was unusually quiet, as if she were a million miles away. "I feel like I'm only beginning to know who I am," I finally spoke up. "Franz seems so sure of himself right now and has such a clear vision of his future, but I don't know, Bonnie. I feel like I owe you more than that but …" I trailed off, my unfinished sentence a statement in itself.

"You don't have to explain anything to me." Bonnie responded in what had become her familiar, supportive way. "The only thing I know about myself is that I never want to leave California." She inched up and wrapped her arms around her bent knees. "I was born and raised on the scent of this ocean. I can't imagine not living near the water. The rest is as hazy as the fortune teller's vision of Linae's success as an actress." She smoothed the sand in a mound around her feet and picked out a few shells. "So many of my girlfriends are running off and getting married. Even Delores has given up her dream of becoming a stewardess to elope with Mike. She told me they're going to drive to Vegas to one of those little love chapels and even try and start a family before he ships out. I could hardly believe what she was telling me, but then I began to understand. I mean, he might not make it back."

"Is that what you want?" I asked. I turned to face her as I leaned back on my elbow. "You've always told me that you were in no hurry to settle down."

"Well, that's just it. I never thought so, but now I don't know." Her wistful reply to this delicate subject got my attention. "Lately I find myself thinking more about it. You know," she said, "with so much at stake and everybody going off to such far away places, it's kind of hard not to."

"Bonnie," I said, wanting to reach for her, but holding back. "I hope you know how much you mean to me, and I wish I could offer you more right now, give you something definite, but my future seems so uncertain I just don't think I can make any promises."

"Then you shouldn't, Jake."

I sat up and looked far out over the water as I struggled with the weight of the conversation. I felt so incredibly conflicted. My feelings for Bonnie were very real and it was hard not to ask her to put her life on hold for me. "I love you, Bonnie, and there's no one else I could imagine sharing a future with." I picked up a shard of sea glass and turned it over in my palm. It's sharp edges were long worn away by the sea. "But it isn't fair to ask you to wait for me. I have no idea what's going to happen. I don't even know what I'll do once this tour of duty ends."

"Jake, I'm aware of all that. I can't sit here and pretend I don't have feelings though. To be honest, there's a part of me that wishes you were giving me an engagement ring instead of telling me to go on with my life. I don't know …"

I glanced down and saw that she was silently crying. "Bonnie … don't," I said reaching for her, but she held up her hand and backed me off. "I'm afraid to make a promise I can't keep. It would just make things harder with so much of my life up in the air. It wouldn't be fair to either one of us." The truth was painful, but the timing wasn't right for us, and I was helpless to change it.

"I understand," she finally said, wiping her cheek with the back of her hand. "I guess I didn't expect to react this way. Of course you have to do what feels right. We'll let the future unfold, but I love you, Jake. You know that."

"Of course I know, and I'll always love you too. We're not going to lose each other. We'll be in touch the whole time I'm gone." I wanted to lighten the mood so I caught her and rolled over on her, leaning up on my extended arms, breathing in her now so familiar, sweet scent. "You're amazing. Do you always have to be so understanding? I want you to write to me. Will you do that? I promise you I'll answer as fast as I can. That, I can swear to."

"Of course I'll write, Jake. Just come back safe and sound and we can worry about the future then."

I stood up and reached for her hand. "Walk with me?" We sauntered back slowly toward where we'd left our shoes. "We head out in a week," I said as we brushed the sand from our feet. "How about a dinner with Franz and Linae one more time on Friday night?"

"Oh goodness, yes. Linae's already planning it. She's calling it the 'I'll never say goodbye' celebration."

Circling around to Bonnie's apartment, we kissed and whispered our farewells. It was sad and somewhat awkward, and I couldn't help but feel conflicted as I meandered down the street with my head down, my hands stuffed inside my pockets. My mind was dizzy as I reflected on our conversation, the faint scent of Bonnie's perfume clouding my head ... the touch of her hand on my face.

Bonnie had never opened up to me like this before, and I wasn't sure what to do about it. We had mostly shied away from serious topics like marriage and children ... pretty much anything to do with the future. The subject of the future of our relationship had never ever come up, but now I wondered if maybe all this time she'd been harboring feelings that she felt she couldn't express to me. Her sudden honesty had me all twisted up inside. What if I was making a mistake by not asking her to wait for me, or even to marry me as so many couples we knew were doing? Still, no matter how much I rationalized our situation, I couldn't bring myself to take a step forward. Though I was critical of Franz and Linae, I more than envied their wild and crazy ways.

Halfway to the bus stop a raucous laughter near the water's edge interrupted my reverie. It was so loud and disturbing that I turned my head. A group of sailors were partying around a bon fire, drunker than

I ever remember being. Then, as if I were watching a magic show, a familiar figure came into focus. Squinting hard, I forced myself to look twice to make sure it was her.

Linae, in all of her glory was nestled into the chest of a sailor who swung a whiskey bottle by his side and had his nose buried in her disheveled hair. I stepped onto the sand to get a better view, and when her eyes briefly shifted to mine, she reeled away, one hand feeling for the shoulder of her dress, the other tugging the sailor toward the water. I turned in disgust, fuming as I continued to the bus stop. Under the glare of the street lamp, I raged from every pore of my body. "Damn you, Linae," I swore out loud. "I can't believe what I just saw. How could you do such a thing? How the hell am I ever going to tell Franz?"

I snuck into bed while avoiding Franz who was at the tail end of a card game and hadn't so much as lifted his head when I walked in. After ruminating for what felt like hours, I decided to keep what I'd witnessed a secret, but holding it inside proved to be a lot more difficult than I expected. Hearing Franz sing Linae's praises every day was torture, and I debated whether or not to spill the whole story. I decided to wait until Friday when I assumed Linae would lay some flimsy excuse on Franz and cancel the big dinner. Instead though, she and Bonnie parked as usual in Linae's big blue car at the entrance to the camp and Linae eagerly returned Franz's display of affection, ignoring my hard stare. It was our final dinner, the last group squeeze into the booths at Arnie's before we shipped out, the final round of cold drinks. Together, we harbored an aggregate of mixed emotions.

After an order of drinks and a casual toast to each other, we chatted about how much we'd miss the good times we'd all had together. The place had become so familiar, almost "homey" to us. By the time the food arrived however, no one had brought up any of the heavier stuff. I sat back and reached an arm along the back of the booth behind Bonnie as I fumed all over again at Linae and struggled to participate in the conversation.

"Have you guys got everything ready to go?" Bonnie asked. "Delores told me Mike had a list a mile long of things he needed to pack. She's worried about him traipsing around Europe with such a heavy load once he adds a weapon."

"Oh, yeah." Franz replied. "I've packed my bag army style, so tight I'm afraid it's gonna bust a seam. Tell her not to fret. They're gonna' work him so hard in boot camp he'll be able to lift a tank off the ground." He paused a moment. "Honestly, I think boot camp scares me more than the war."

"Yeah." My laugh was forced. "I hear boot camp is where they break you if they can. It's no picnic, that's for sure."

"Every section of the military is pumped up about this, though," Franz added, giving Linae's shoulder a small squeeze. "Just like us, a lot of guys are trying to get in their last ounce of fun before they have to face the music."

"Hey, I saw some of that first hand just the other night," I said. "There were a bunch of crazy sailors and some women partying like animals on the beach."

I was boiling inside and zeroed in on Linae's eyes as I spoke. She ignored my reference though, and poured it on thick, ordering a double Scotch and doting on Franz as she always did with pecks on the cheek, hand squeezes under the table.

I seethed even more as I witnessed her using her acting skills to play out the scene as if she were making a movie. Finally, I confronted her more directly. "So, Linae, what have you been up to since we last saw you?"

"Work's got me tied up," she said, brazenly meeting my stare. "I didn't get the 'Lonely Tonight' part, but it looks like I'll be lonely every night anyway." Linae batted her lashes at Franz and flashed another masterful pout. "'Scuse me people. I've got to go to the ladies room." She nudged Franz, who scooted off the edge of the booth and stood up to let her out. "Don't miss me too much, sugar. I'll be right back."

"Guess I'll take a break, too" I said, sliding out of the booth and hurrying after her, hoping it wasn't too obvious.

As Linae set her hand on the door to the ladies' room, I caught her by the shoulder and spun her around.

"What the hell do you think you're doing?" I leaned in close to her face, squeezing her shoulders tight with both hands and nearly pinning her to the wall.

"Let go, Jake. You're hurting me," she said, turning her head from mine.

"No more than you're going to hurt Franz," I said with force. "I feel like I don't even know you, Linae. I never dreamed you'd turn out to be some kind of party girl who uses people with no thought for anyone but herself. Franz is about to go off to war and you're going break his heart now? What the hell, Linae!"

"I'm not gonna' break anybody's heart," she shot back. She squirmed to duck under my arm as I blocked her with my body. "Stop it, Jake."

I knew I was hurting her but I didn't care. "I feel like smashing you into this wall, but I won't 'cause I'm not that kind of a guy. But why, Linae? Why? Why Franz? Why him?"

"You don't know what you're talking about, Jake." she said.

"I know exactly what I'm talking about, actually, and so do you. It's gonna kill him, and you know it. Don't pretend you don't know how much he loves you."

"What you saw was harmless partying, Jake."

"Yeah, well it didn't look harmless to me. You break his heart now he'll be dead before he even hits the shores of France. You hear me? This would kill him faster than any bullet ever could, Linae." I was nose-to-nose with her, nearly touching.

"Don't be so dramatic, Jake. Go back to the table and stay out of it. Like I said, what you saw was nothing, and as long as you don't go telling Franz it was anything more than that he won't be hurt."

It was her cavalier attitude that disgusted me most, and for a moment I hated her.

"Like hell I'm over-reacting, Linae. I saw what I saw. Has all of this just been a big game to you? Do you even care for Franz at all?"

"Of course I care, Jake. Don't be ridiculous."

"He's in love with you, Linae, and he thinks you love him. Christ, he's building his whole life around you. He's expecting that you'll write him long love letters every day, and when he comes home that you'll marry him, move into one of those tract houses everyone's talking about and live happily ever after."

"My feelings for Franz are my business, Jake. And besides, I am going to stay in touch with him," she insisted.

"And break his heart later? Oh, that's great, that's really great."

"I keep telling you, Jake, you don't know what you're talking about. And besides, nobody knows the future. Anyway, you're one to talk - brushing off Bonnie the way you have."

"Now wait a minute, Linae!"

"No, you wait. Don't play holier than thou with me, Jake. What about you and Bonnie? Sounds to me like you're the one breaking hearts."

Her words caught me off guard and I had to work hard not to get thrown. "My relationship with Bonnie is none of your business, Linae. At least I'm honest which is more than you can say."

"Don't kid yourself, Jake. Honest hurts just as bad when you're breaking someone's heart."

"Don't try to change the subject, Linae. I'm not leading Bonnie on they way you're leading on Franz. It's dishonest."

"What it is, Jake, is also none of your business. I'm done with this conversation. Now get out of my way."

Suddenly, Franz poked his head into the narrow hallway and I quickly backed off. "Hey, where've you been? We thought you'd gotten lost getting back to the table," he laughed. Then, feeling the palpable tension in the air, he said, "What's going on?"

"Oh, it's fine baby," Linae answered. "Jake and I are just havin' a heart-to-heart about how worried I am for your safety, and how I want him to keep a watch out for you. Just doesn't seem fair all the good men going off to war. But come on, let's not talk about it anymore. I just wanna have a good time tonight. Go on back, and I'll be there in a sec."

Franz turned and left but Linae wasn't done yet.

"There ain't a girl I know, no matter what she claims, who in her heart doesn't want to get married to the love of her life. I don't know what you're thinking but trust me, Bonnie cares about you more than she's letting on. You'll always be wondering about the one that got away, Jake. Mark my words."

As I made our way back to the table, I decided that I would let my closest friend go off to war believing that the only woman he had ever loved would be waiting for him when he returned.

CHAPTER EIGHTEEN

WE BOARDED TRUCKS FOR THE long ride to the boot camp in the Mojave Desert the following week and there we learned, in no short order, what it means to be a soldier. A code of conduct was drummed into us by our officers and the consistent, underlying message was that if one soldier failed it was because the others had failed him.

The training was pure hell, but we were already in decent shape and found it easier than some of the other guys. Understanding that such rigorous training was preparing us for finally seeing some real action even made it exciting. When we received orders that we would be shipped overseas, however, the realization that I might never lay eyes on my parents or Bonnie again gnawed at me in the late hours when I should have been deep asleep. Instead, I tossed and turned, my head spinning with possible scenarios that would prevent me from ever returning home. As the time of my deployment drew near, I became increasingly disturbed about the fact that my parents had never responded to my initial letter, so I took out my pen and paper and wrote yet again, informing them that I would be shipping out soon. If my fate was that I die at war, I wanted them to know. In spite of worrying that I was dead to them both by now, I secretly held out hope for some kind of reconciliation. After so many years, I was more than ready to face my past.

"*You can write me at the APO address on the outside of this envelope,*" I wrote in distinct, blocky letters. "*I'm not sure when I'll get it, but I sure would appreciate hearing from you.*"

I checked the return address several times, secure in knowing that if my parents hadn't abandoned me in their hearts they'd be able to get in touch with me now. When two weeks had passed with no reply, however, any hope I had was replaced by a cold nagging sense of despair.

"I wrote to my parents weeks ago," I blurted out to Franz after dinner the evening of our last night at boot camp. We were in the final stages of packing up and going over our weapons. We'd been told we'd be shipping out sometime in the coming week and in spite of being occupied with these final preparations, I'd become even more obsessed with thoughts of home. "Yeah," I said. "I finally got up the nerve to write them again, but I've never heard back."

"Six years is a long time to be gone." Franz shrugged his shoulders.

"Long enough to be forgotten, it seems," I replied.

Franz paused for a second, letting his gun rest on the edge of his bed. "I find it's better when you don't expect anything. That way you can't be disappointed. Hell, I wrote my ma four times since we got here. Haven't heard a word. I'll keep writing, but it's something I just do now, like going off to war. I don't know what's coming, so I try not to think about it much."

"Is it really that easy for you, Franz? I mean damn, I miss my parents so much sometimes I can't sleep at night because I keep picturing my dad's face squinting in the sunlight and the funny way he used to chop wood. He'd lift the ax way back behind his head and I used to think he was going to fall backwards. And the way my mom used to sing church songs around the house. Her voice was so high and distinct. I didn't appreciate anything back then, but now I remember her voice sounded really good … pretty, even."

"I guess I just don't let myself think as hard as you do, Jake." Franz answered. "Sure I miss my family, but I guess I look at it in a different way." His tone was matter-of-fact. "I imagine I'll see them again someday, Lord willing, but what's meant to be will be. Nothin' I can do to change it."

"What do you say when the war is over we look up our families together, close a few gaps," I said.

"Sure," said Franz. "Wouldn't mind huggin' on my ma and some of my younger brothers and sisters. I barely knew them when I left. As for my pa, well, I've about let him go. For all I know he's either worn or worried himself to death by now."

We rubbed the polish deep into the creases of our boots, our conversation giving way to a silent understanding as we double checked our military packs. We'd been split into different platoons for what we'd come to know as "Operation Neptune," an assault phase meant to secure a foothold against the Germans in occupied France. By this point we'd heard plenty of horrific stories and the reality of war was beginning to sink in. Our youth could no longer protect us from illusions of invincibility. We knew full well that the danger we were about to embark upon was grave and the fear of death hibernated in the back of our minds. Still, we went forth with great hope for our futures which included being an integral part of winning the war.

✮ ✮ ✮

The call we'd been expecting for days now crackled over the ship's loudspeakers rousing me from a deep sleep. "Now hear this! Now hear this! All hands on deck!" The anticipation of what lay ahead fueled a rush of adrenaline that sent a chill down my spine. Moving as fast as I could, I pulled on my fatigues, tied up my boots and scrambled up the narrow stairs to join the gathering throng of men pushing forward into one of several Coast Guard landing vessels.

The small boats pitched and rolled in the choppy waters, eleven miles off the Normandy coast with no land in sight. We were all at the mercy of the heavy, salty waves that thrashed over the sides and soaked us soldiers already laden with guns and heavy equipment. After heaving my guts off the side of the boat, I rinsed my mouth with a swig of precious water from my pack. Embarrassed at my queasiness and stiff with cold, I returned to the business of helping bail out water with my helmet and barely noticed the sliver of the beachhead that had come into view and was dotted with plumes of smoke. There wasn't much any of us could do but pray as we moved closer to land engulfed in enemy fire. It looked as if we might make it, but suddenly our boat began lurching as it smashed against wooden stakes that the Germans had planted on the approach to shore. Before we had time to figure out what was going on, or even catch a breath, an explosion ripped a gaping hole on the leeward side of our boat as we were pummeled with machine gun fire. I watched in horror as splatters of blood hit my face and my bunkmate, a tough kid from a small town in Delaware, fell into the sea where several other bodies were already languishing in a swirl of red. Our vessel was sinking fast. Those of us who were left had no choice but to slide into the icy water and wade toward land in the chest high water, ducking and dodging to avoid the barrage of bullets whirring past our heads. Dazed and terrified and soaked to the bone, I lumbered forward under the weight of my load. By the time I hit the last several feet of water I was barely able to stagger the final soggy steps forward. Dropping to my knees and collapsing in the sand as the waves washed against me, I made one last futile attempt to get up, intent on reaching safer ground. Before I could pick up my head though, two soldiers yanked me back down and dragged me up the beach to where several men were huddled, sheltering under the chalk cliffs that ran along the coast. It wasn't until I was safe and dry that I realized they had saved my life.

It was days before those of us who had survived the assault had a chance to take full stock of the destruction and the dead. As we regrouped and reloaded while waiting for our orders, I sought out any information I could gather about the whereabouts of Franz. He had been expected to land along with the others on Omaha beach and it was no secret that his unit had taken the hardest hit. It was close to lights out after a rainy luckless day, when I came upon a gunner who claimed to have seen Franz's boat go down and directed me to the lieutenant of his platoon.

Most units were preparing to move further into the country side, but I was able to track down the lieutenant in question late in the day just as he was finishing up orders outside a truck loaded with soldiers waiting and ready to travel under the cover of night. When he stepped away, I approached him.

"Sir," I said, rendering a salute.

The officer returned the salute and reached inside his pocket for a cigarette. "What can I do for you soldier?"

"I'm looking for word on Private Franz Mueller," I said. "I believe he was a member of your platoon."

"Smoke?" he offered.

"Thank you, sir." I pulled one of the cigarettes from the outstretched pack even though I didn't smoke. For some reason, it felt like the right thing to do. Cupping his hand to protect the flame from the relentless wind, he offered me a light, in a demonstration of our connection. We each took a puff, the lieutenant inhaling deeply and taking his time to think.

"I'm sorry, son." The haze from the lieutenant's cigarette swirled around his head shadowing his dry, poker face. "Mueller was one of the best men I had. But there was a goddamn machine gun nest five hundred yards in. My guys got hammered. Your friend took hits in the legs, abdomen and chest … The medic said he was in bad shape when they carried him over there to the field hospital. Official word's not come down yet, but I'm guessing he didn't stand much of a chance with bullet wounds like that."

"Oh, God." I faltered through the shameless welling of tears that threatened to overcome me.

"Sorry, soldier. This is hard on everyone. If I were you, I'd check the field hospital." The lieutenant sucked in the last draw on his cigarette, then crushed it into the ground with the heel of his boot. "Your buddy might just have gotten lucky. If not, at least you'll know what happened to him, which is more than most."

As numbed as I was by the image of Franz lying half-dead in the field hospital, it was even more horrifying to imagine that I might be viewing him in a body bag. Saluting my exit, I thanked the lieutenant and raced to the far end of the camp where four large tents were framed together in an expanse of fallow meadow. The sky was black by the time I got to the field hospital, and the canvas flaps of the main tent's entrance were tied shut, a sign for visitors to keep out. Out of breath and undeterred, I began to unravel one of the knots on the door. A soldier on guard duty spoke to me from inside and stopped me in my tracks. "Hey! Hospital's shut down for the night."

"I apologize, sir. But I ran all the way over here looking for a friend of mine. Mueller, Franz Mueller. I just want to know if he's here. It'll only take a minute."

"Sorry, soldier. I can't let you in. The rules say to come back in the morning around nine. Doctor's rounds should be done by then."

Slowly, I turned around, retracing the steps back to my unit, terrified that Franz was alone fighting for his life or worse yet, had already passed on without a familiar face by his side. I wondered who would be notified in Franz's family if the worst had happened, and indeed if anyone cared. When I closed my eyes, Franz's face appeared, his wide-toothed grin ... his voice calling ... "Come on, Jake! Bodies on!" as we were about to make a jump. I was helpless to do anything to quiet my fears, and my dream offered little relief from the upheaval of the day.

CHAPTER NINETEEN

A S MUCH AS I SUFFERED with fears of Franz's fate, I woke up early the following morning with a strong sense that he was alive. Upbeat and pumped with fresh adrenaline, I breathed new air into my lungs as I sprinted to the front of the sprawling canvas hospital. My spirits were shattered, however, when I pushed aside the door flap. The first thing that hit me was the gagging odor of warm blood and open wounds. Holding my breath in the stifling room, I fought the impulse to cover my mouth and nose, taking a moment to compose myself. I took in the rows and rows of beds packed with injured men, many, who I knew would never see their families again. Overwhelmed, my heart sank even further when I noticed a soldier who looked to be about my age standing off alone in a corner, staring at the vacant tent wall. His left arm was bandaged and tied up in a sling, his right arm missing up to the elbow. As I glanced around for some direction, an enclosed circular area to my left caught my attention. The shoes of a team of doctors working behind it's thick rubber curtain were splattered with blood, serving as an exclamation mark to the sorrow that permeated the entire place. Scanning each bed in search of Franz's face, I was horrified by all of this human collateral, so many young men missing limbs, some scarred beyond recognition, others who had lost their minds. It was the unexpected stillness, though, that got to me the most - just the constant hum of fans pushing around the stale air. There were no cries of pain, no outbursts, no anguish. It was downright eerie and it tore at my heart as I scanned the room. When I was satisfied that none of the soldiers in the room was Franz, my eyes darted around for someone in charge.

"Excuse me," I said, approaching a nurse who had stopped rushing about to re-pin her cap on a mass of tangled, dark hair. "I'm looking for private Franz Mueller." I hesitated when I noticed the young soldier in the corner tilting his head to listen. I gave him a brief smile, but he only shuffled away, his face masked by the same dazed look. "They told me he might be here. I ..."

"Franz Mueller?" she repeated as she considered. "Over there, I believe," she said finally, repositioning a bobby pin to capture a fallen curl. She lowered her voice, pointing toward the entrance to an adjacent, smaller tent. "He's injured pretty badly. There should be a nurse back there to direct you, but I think Mueller's the third bed on the right."

Buoyed up by the fact that Franz was at least alive, I hurried to his bedside. A soldier lay either asleep or unconscious in that bed, his face swollen, his head bound up in a mountain of white gauze, a stringy I.V. dripping into his lifeless arm.

The heat of fear burned through my body as I stared down at the dying man. His face was disfigured, and I stared at him long and hard before I was certain that it wasn't Franz. Relieved, yet more anxious than ever to find him, I rushed to a nearby nurse. "I'm looking for a young soldier from North Platte, Nebraska," I blurted out. She turned her ruddy face toward me.

"What's your friend's name?"

"Franz Mueller," I pressed on. "The nurse over there, she said she thought he was in the third bed, but it's not him. His name's Mueller," I repeated, "Franz Mueller ... Is he here?"

The nurse picked up the patient chart that hung on the foot of the bed. "This is Mueller," she said calmly, letting her eyes meet mine. "Soldiers often don't look anything like themselves when they're this seriously injured, but even his dog tags are here." She held up the tags, laying them flat against the palm of her hand so I could read the imprint clearly.

"No, no," I insisted. "It might say that, but this is not Franz. That man is not my friend."

"Are you certain?" she asked. "Why don't you have another look." She gave the soldier in the bed a short nod and then repeated: "Believe me, a man's face can be unrecognizable when he's this banged up."

"Look," I said. My voice grew louder, breaking with despair. "We've known each other for years. He's like a brother to me. You've got to believe me. Please, I've looked hard and I'm positive it's not him."

"Well, if you're sure," she said. "There are cases of misidentification. I'll have to check into this, let my supervisor know, but for now, follow me." The nurse strode briskly out of the ward, motioning me to do the same. We wound our way back to the entrance of the makeshift hospital where she pointed to a truck idling off to the side. It's open canvas flap exposed what appeared to be at least three camouflaged body bags lying side-by-side.

"They're taking those over to the temporary grave site," the nurse said. "The transporter's name is Bill. Tell him Dorothy sent you over. He might be able to help."

"Thank you, so much." I walked over to the truck. "Are you Bill?" I called out to a soldier who appeared from around the driver's side.

"Sure am ..."

"The nurse back there, Dorothy, she said you might be able to help me. There's a soldier lying inside in a hospital bed who's not the friend I'm looking for, though the name on the chart and his dog tags say he is."

"Another messed up I.D., huh? Well, I got four bodies on the truck. They're all identified, but no harm checking. Who are you looking for?"

"Franz Mueller," I answered. I was desperate to find Franz, yet terrified to find him here.

The soldier jumped into the back of the truck and squatted down next to a body bag that had been placed beyond eyesight in the darker recess of the space. He slid the dense load halfway into the light, closer to the others, then double-checked the tag.

"Come on up, soldier," he said, motioning to me. "Friend 'a yours, huh?"

The body bags jostled with the movement as I hefted myself up next to him and felt the muscles in my back tense up. "Yeah," I said, "my best friend."

"Sorry for your loss. The temporary grave site's off limits, but we can open these up, maybe get lucky." He rotated the first bag and slid back the zipper of the enclosure, exposing the body inside.

I gazed at the young soldier's colorless face, eerily ghost-like in the shadowy light. Looking away, I exhaled deeply, releasing a wave of pent up emotion. "It's not him."

"Okay. We got a few more to go. Are you up for it?"

"Yeah, I guess so."

One by one, we checked the remaining body bags in the truck. "He's not here," I said, shaking my head in relief and frustration, the faces uncovered on the back of that truck already haunting me. "What could have happened to him?"

"Well, if he isn't on the truck or in the field hospital and they got his tags, then he's most likely already in the temporary grave. Missing in action, he'd still have his tags with him. I know it's not what 'you want to hear, soldier, but that's my best guess."

"Thanks. I'm gonna sweep the hospital tent one more time," I said, feeling more desperate than ever. "Maybe he's lying in one of those beds, and I just didn't recognize him."

"Sure wouldn't be the first time that's happened," said the soldier. "Or the last, I'm afraid." He shook his head as he turned to the task of sliding the bodies deeper into the truck, readying for transportation. "I'll make my run and be back here in an hour or so, then talk to the hospital staff. We'll have to put a call into our commanding officer and make a formal report whether you find him or not. Either way, we'll take it from here."

Back inside the field hospital, I took my time peering into the faces of every injured soldier there, bed by bed, row after row, praying, hoping, that one of them would be Franz.

"Where the hell is he?" I said to the same nurse who had taken me outside to Bill. By now carts of oatmeal and toast had been rolled in and breakfast was being delivered. Patients who could eat on their own were propped up with trays set on their laps, while nurses busied themselves cleaning and feeding others. I'd been methodical and quiet in my search so as not to disrupt their work, but I was unable to contain my frustration when the face in the last bed was not that of Franz. "Damn," I said. My voice was a little too loud and I felt several heads turn in my direction. "This is so messed up."

"Easy, soldier. Why don't you write his name down here and I'll keep an eye out. We've already alerted the higher-ups that there may be another misidentification."

Pulling myself together, I found my way back to the morgue truck and left my contact information with Bill. He was busy re-checking the list of bodies they'd delivered to the temporary grave site since the landing at Normandy over two weeks ago now. Working the confusion over in my mind, I queried him again. "I don't understand. How can my friend's tags be here, but he's not?"

"We sometimes get bodies with missing tags," he said, pouring over his records. "Often it's a case of the tags being blown off, or the ones that are pulled off a fallen soldier, having to leave the body under fire. Or dog tags get ripped off a soldier headed for surgery. Next guy comes in dead or injured with tags missing. Wrong tags get thrown on the wrong body. There's so many things could happen in this madness."

"Are you saying I may never find him?"

"Well, that happens, but like I said before, if somebody is MIA usually their tags are on them and they disappear together. But you say your friend's tags are here, so I'd say there's a good chance your friend came through this hospital. I got your information, so I'll be in touch if I get any news on my end."

"Thanks. I'd really appreciate that."

Strung out and discouraged, I walked slowly back to my tent barracks. My gut was telling me that Franz was still out there somewhere, alive, but I feared this could be just wishful thinking, and competing with this fragile optimism were images of him floating in the frigid waters off the coast of Normandy, his bloated body sunk deep in a watery grave, or that he was already lying in the temporary grave.

True, there was a body dying in a hospital bed with Franz's dog tags, but it wasn't Franz. If someone had pulled his tags off of him in the field, or found them, as Bill had said, they would have turned them in to those in charge and it would have been recorded. More than likely, Franz had been brought in injured or dead and, in the chaos, his tags had been stuck on the wrong body. Since he wasn't in the hospital, but his tags were, the most logical thing was that he was in the morgue, his body mislabeled. Still, I clung to the hope that Franz could still be alive, and as time wore on, I became even more tenacious about sticking to that belief.

We'd been ordered to hold tight on the coast for a few more days and many of the men sought out the support of one another. My grief, though, festered into a depressing jumble of recollections of years gone by with Franz, interspersed with haunting images of my mother weeping over my baby brother's dead body. The more I tried to control my thoughts and feelings, the more victimized I felt by them.

CHAPTER TWENTY

WHILE I WAITED FOR WORD about Franz, our commanders drew up plans for additional units, including mine, to move deeper into France, but the tenacity with which the German forces blocked the inland plains made progress slow. For almost a month I hung in there with the others, standing by for the word to advance, knowing I'd have to rely on my training to kick into auto pilot if I was ever going to lift my gun again. We were on constant alert, still shell-shocked from the rigors of D-Day and our frayed nerves left us feeling edgy and strung out. Then, on a day so hot and sticky that it spurred thoughts of the haying back home, a Mail Corps soldier tossed a dog-eared letter into the captured German bunker where I was hunkered down on watch with several of my comrades.

My heart raced at the sight of my name penned in my father's shaky scrawl. I tore through the envelope and as I read, his words stirred up feelings I had struggled to come to terms with for so many years. *"Son, hardly a day passes since you left that I haven't asked the good Lord to keep you in His graces."*

Tears blurred the page as I read each word, again and again.

"My prayers have been heard and your letter sure has eased my mind. Life here on the farm has changed a great deal. Your mother gave birth to twins a year after you left: a boy, Wills, and a girl, Claudia, who are mighty fine children. I'm sorry to tell you, though, that your mother, God rest her soul, died in the process of giving birth. Your mother loved you, Jake, in spite of her pain, and she wept many a night over the guilt she felt in driving you away. We're still here though, son, waiting for you to come home. I hope one day you will find your way back to us."

I sank back and let my tears flow freely in waves of grief, love, nostalgia and sadness. I cried for my mother, who died so young, and who had, I realized, lost all of her children in one way or another. I cried for my father who had only shown me love, and for the rough, lonely road he'd had to travel. I cried for Franz, with whom I'd shared so much, who might never kiss his mother's cheek or hug his brothers and sisters, never hear another swing band, never marry a red-headed girl. As my pain expanded, the images of the soldiers I'd seen in those body bags rushed in, and I cried too for all of the men whose lives were cut short and who would never see their loved ones again, or build families of their own. And finally, finally ... I wept for myself and for the little brother that had died so brutally so many years ago.

When I composed myself, I picked up the letter one more time. "*I hope one day ...*" I read the last line over and over until the possibility of returning home seeped down deep into my heart, and I knew at that moment that if I lived through the war, I would make it a priority to find my way home.

After the news of my family sank in, I wrote Bonnie telling her what I knew about Franz and what I hoped and feared as to his whereabouts, knowing she would pass it along to Linae. In truth, I could not have cared less if Linae never knew another thing about Franz, but I knew he would want her to know and I needed to honor that. As far as I was concerned though, Linae didn't deserve to know anything about him, in spite of the bundle of perfumed letters Franz had shown me one night in the barracks before we shipped out. Linae had written them all ahead of time so that Franz could carry them with him, and have something to read, "before I can write some more."

In the beginning, true to her word, Bonnie too had been diligent about getting letters off every other day, her loopy, distinct handwriting filling up pages of onion skin paper. Over time, the regularity stopped, however, and I sensed her drifting away. Her last few letters were filled mostly with the local gossip. Arnie's, she had reported, still packed them in every night, though the crowd had changed, and more locals mixed in with the low ranking Naval officers and assorted sailors from the base in San Diego. Bonnie saw Linae around town from time to time, she wrote, always the center of attention, always on the arm of a different sailor.

"Linae's having about as good a time as a single girl can have," Bonnie had written. *"She landed a part as an extra in a movie starring Rita Hayworth - something about a woman named Gilda. She seems not to have a care in the world, other than the whereabouts of the next party, though she tells me she writes to Franz every day."*

Of course, hearing that Linae partied with other men while writing to Franz every day infuriated me to no end, but I was glad that I'd never let on to him what I witnessed that night on the beach. I was certain now that I'd been right about her all along, and I wondered once again how Franz could have fallen so hard for such a woman, even as I knew that he didn't stand a chance against her gaudy glamour, the sexy provocation tantalizing him to the point of breaking and taking advantage of his vulnerability. The guy was putty in her hands. Why Linae had taken up with him in the first place, however, was a mystery I could never understand, no matter how much I tried. It was obvious she liked it when men adored her, and Franz more than fit the bill in that regard, but she was so controlling I don't know how he stood it. As if he were some overgrown kid, she was always fussing over him straightening up his shirt and dabbing his chin with a napkin, or making sure he wore his hat in the sun. In my view, it was all pretty insulting, though Franz never seemed to mind. "I suppose," I thought, "if Franz is dead, he died believing that Linae truly loved him and that's all that mattered." Later, when Bonnie gave Linae the news about Franz, she reported that Linae had burst into tears and had to be escorted out of Arnie's. *"I stayed up all night with her, Jake,"* Bonnie had written. *"She was so broken up. I don't know. She's taking it really hard. She doesn't even want to go to Arnie's anymore. I think she may have loved him after all."*

✫ ✫ ✫

I wrote my father every chance I got, adding a note or two for Wills and Claudia, and later for old Aunt Liddy who, I learned, had moved up from Kansas to help raise the twins. Each correspondence fed my homesickness. As time wore on I became more and more preoccupied with questions about my family: What were the twins like? How did my aging aunt manage with small children now that she was more than seventy years old? Mostly, though, I thought about my father and prayed that he was still strong and in good health. When flashes of the accident wrestled their way in, I fought to replace them with fantasies of walking through a planted field at sunset, or pitching fresh cut hay into a wagon, maybe brushing down a wet horse, and most wonderful of all, feeling my father's embrace once again.

The luxury of such self-indulgent thoughts however, were quickly replaced by the realities of war. At last my platoon received orders to advance. We moved ahead, navigating the narrow back roads of the French countryside past fields and farms, through crumbling villages blasted wide by bombs, their once picturesque stone buildings now defaced by bullets, some crumbled to the ground. We pushed on past orchards and bald hills littered with abandoned tanks and trucks, the bloated corpses of decaying farm animals lying alongside those of dead Americans and Germans, all rotting in the mid-day sun. Every lifeless body we passed tormented me with fears of what could have become of Franz. There had been no word at all about him, and it became more and more difficult to believe that he was still alive. I turned my head away from the detritus of war as I reflected on all of the trials we had survived together over the years - how we had begun bonding on that first train ride to the west coast, then zig-zagging the country in search of work. We were constantly starving and dependent on the kindness of strangers. I thought about how our lives had improved working in the CCC camp, and then our overwhelming belief that our futures were brightening when we joined the army. We had signed our names one after the other, on the very same day. "What was it all for?" I thought. "What could ever have happened to him?"

For months I trudged through Europe with my comrades, forcing the Germans to retreat and taking back town after town. The long marches wore down even the sturdiest of men until we began to call ourselves "the weary warriors." In spite of our fatigue though, our spirits were fueled by reports of further Ally victories and for the first time we began to talk about an end to the war. Then, on June 27th, 1944 we joined a long line of American trucks that rolled through the rubble in the aftermath of the fighting that had liberated the small French town of Cherbourg. War-weary villagers peered out from behind curtained windows, then threw open their doors at the sight of the American flags waving from the stream of tanks and trucks. Shouts of congratulations and gratitude filled the air. "Merci! Bien Fait! C'est magnifique! Extraordinaire! Merci beaucoup!" They pushed bottles of wine, bread, baskets of apples and cheese at us, so grateful to be alive and free of the Nazi foothold that had held them for so long. Every man in my platoon joined the celebration. Our voices rivaled the crowd's as we joined in, pumping our fists toward heaven and crying out, "Viva la France! Viva la France!" None of us could have known it then, but that the sweet taste of victory was about to get even better.

Two months later, we found ourselves in Paris where the city had already been liberated after four years of German occupation, and the beautiful wide boulevards and parks once again teemed with life. I fell in love with the charm of the city that romanced me at every turn, and when I prayed in the great cathedral of Notre Dame I felt the magnificence of the architecture and reflected on the millions who had worshiped there before me. I visited as often as I could, kneeling to light votive candles, one for Edwin and one for my mother who, both of whom died so young and so tragically. A third candle I lit for Franz. Struggling to pray the troubles from my heart, I desperately tried to soak up the healing powers of such a holy place. Many afternoons I sat alone in one of the outdoor cafes, captivated by the rhythm of the French language, so melodic and distinct from anything I had ever heard. It was in these moments, surrounded by the beauty and history of the city, that occasionally a feeling of peace would wash over me, but it was fleeting, and the guilt of enjoying life without Franz quickly replaced it.

The war was not over quite yet, however. Orders to head out came down two weeks later, and we began an arduous trek north. By the beginning of December, my platoon was at the center of a long convoy of trucks and tanks making our way into Belgium, and I was pleased when we halted and set up camp below a line of forested hills near the picturesque village of Wiltz. It was peaceful there, with all the charm of a Christmas card, but the tranquility only allowed me more time to miss my family and worry about what had become of my friend. One day I hiked into town and checked in at the field hospital which had been set up in an old church that had been chipped away by mortar shells but was serviceable just the same. That afternoon, and whenever I could steal away some time in the days following, I visited the injured soldiers, sharing conversation or reading a book out loud, often playing a hand of cards or helping one of them write a letter home. Somehow the company of these men made me feel closer to Franz.

I hadn't heard from Bonnie in weeks, and in my loneliness I penned a hasty note to her and then to my father, notifying him of my new location. I was hoping we'd stay in Wiltz long enough for me to receive some return letters. As we waited for new orders we enjoyed a bit of the holiday spirit here among the evergreen trees on the peaceful side of the hill. Some of the guys built a snowman with a wreath of pine around his head and a dead branch stuck in his hand in a nod to the war. Someone even strung a small nearby spruce tree with popcorn and candy wrappers. As I watched the local children sledding, it brought back snowy days at the farm when Henry and I would belly land old tires down the icy hills behind his house. It was easy to relish the beauty of the season here in the quietude with plenty of food and warm fires, but like so many things in life and war, all of it was uprooted in a single day.

About a week before Christmas, we woke up to news that the Germans had pushed through the line, breaking the Allied hold. A thick fog blanketed the ground, adding a ghost-like eeriness to the bitter day and the old familiar spark of fear spread through the ranks like fire. We scrambled to assemble our gear for combat as units from other divisions rushed in to lend support, rolling through the small cobble-stoned town to the edges of our billeted camp. Standing in formation to begin the journey inland, we could make out the dark figures of the

German soldiers in the distant hills etching the virgin snow with their descent, like long lines of insects. It was a frightening sight to behold, and I knew then that we were in for a tough fight.

For days we faced off with the Germans gun-to-gun. We were desperate for support to break through the treacherous weather, but Mother Nature was stubborn and showed us no mercy. Disoriented and running out of steam, the rank and file kept falling back, not knowing if we would be able to survive another onslaught. When news filtered down that our comrades in other platoons were being captured and marched off to prison camps, a new level of fear took hold. That night for the first time in a long time, I got down on my knees and prayed, asking God's mercy to keep us safe.

Weeks passed with little relief from the fighting but then one day we woke to find the sky beyond the forest had brightened and the fog had cleared. That afternoon a roar of muddy trucks and jeeps pushed through with enough men and supplies to reinforce our position. The siege that had nearly sent us all to our graves was over.

The following morning after a scramble of eggs and sausage, we received the news that the allies were winning. Once again we were headed to victory. With our spirits buoyed, we rested up knowing that in two days we'd be trekking deep into the German countryside. There was a renewed sense of urgency to our course now, a feeling that perhaps all of the suffering had not been in vain. But like so many times before, it wasn't long until our relief turned to horror as we came face-to-face with some of the unimaginable nightmares that had preceded us.

☆ ☆ ☆

"Let's get a move on!" my commanding officer shouted as we loaded up the trucks along a roadblock set up to intersect German cargo trains. We'd been breaking down the camp for more than an hour in the quiet beauty of a chilly, but otherwise idyllic April morning. A soft mist fell around us, turning the surrounding evergreens a vivid green, and the air was heady with the scent of pine as our boots crunched down on the wet balsam needles. We had been told earlier that a detachment of troops from the 9th Armored Infantry Battalion was on their way to liberate a large concentration camp called "Buchenwald" that the Nazi's had established near the town of Weimar. We'd worked late the previous night under the brightness of a full moon, carrying out orders to set up a blockade across the rail tracks that would halt any trains headed in that direction. With our job completed, we were anxious to get going and make it to Buchenwald itself where, if the rumors were true about the horrors of the camps, they would need all the assistance we could give. Several trucks were already idling, ready to move on when the familiar sound of a locomotive chugged somewhere off in the distance. My gut tightened up just as it had every time Franz and I had hopped a train.

"Heads up! I want every man in action."

We scrambled, reaching for our guns and hauling ourselves up to attention. None of us had ever overtaken a train before, and we were on edge, not knowing what to expect.

Within minutes, a glaring headlight came into view beaming through the fog. As the engine ground to a halt, a group of us wasted no time climbing on board. Descending upon the engineer, his brakeman, and several German guards, we seized the guard's weapons and ordered all of them to disembark. "Bewegt euch! Move it!" we shouted pointing our rifles. The prisoners stepped to the ground with their hands on their helmets and one of our men, who spoke fluent German, stepped forward with the first lieutenant and questioned the engineer. The rest of us fanned out along the sides of the boxcars and stood by on full alert.

"Wohin gehst du? Where are you going?"

"Weimar."

"Weimar?" Our lieutenant turned and strode a short ways down the line, planting his boots in front of the first of the boxcar doors. "And what are you delivering to Weimar?" He pulled a pistol from his belt and blew the lock off as another young soldier rushed in and slid open the heavy door.

"Oh, God!" We drew back in horror as a throng of emaciated people squinted into the light, their hollowed eyes sunk deep inside their sockets, their boney arms and legs barely able to support their bodies. It looked as if an entire cemetery of ghosts had risen up, with hundreds of the living dead all packed into a single cattle car. The stench was nauseating.

"Wo komst du denn her?"

"We're coming from Auschwitz," one of the inmates replied hoarsely. Up until now we'd only heard stories of the concentrations camps, but it was almost impossible to imagine that such atrocities could be true and nothing had ever been confirmed. There was no denying the rumors now, though. Car after car was busted open exposing its human cargo and the magnitude of their living hell was overwhelming. The majority here were men, and most were too weak to move, but a few of the stronger ones inched forward, their smiles exposing rotting or missing teeth. Driven by compassion, we shared whatever we had on hand: K-rations, blankets, a knife, a canteen of water. One officer was so moved that he took off his over-coat and wrapped it around the shoulders of a shivering elderly man. The truth was, the man probably wasn't much older than the soldier giving up his coat, but he was so emaciated and broken down that he appeared decades beyond his years. More than anything, we assured each of them that help was on the way and that they were now free. "You don't have to be afraid anymore. The nightmare is over."

News of our discovery was radioed to the command post and within an hour a scout vehicle jumped the tracks with a message that the liberation at Buchenwald had begun and that American troops were expected to reach the camp sometime that afternoon. "I got a convoy of trucks behind me rolling in to assist you," the driver said, casting his eyes on the multitude of human misery before him. "Looks like they can't get here fast enough." We were assured that a small field hospital and a kitchen unit with plenty of food would be set up on the spot and that the sick and dying would be treated there. In spite of this good news, however, the situation was so dire that I couldn't help but wonder how many of these people would survive even if we could provide unlimited aid.

"We'll keep our boots planted until first truck arrives, but then be ready to move out," our sergeant filled us in. "There is no time to waste."

Less than an hour later we were on the road.

As horrifying as the scene was that we'd just left, we were not prepared for the carnage that greeted us when we entered Buchenwald late that afternoon. Everywhere bodies were piled up near buildings and in corners, as well as on the beds of open trucks intended for transportation to mass graves. The camp had technically already been liberated, but the scene was beyond anything that we had ever witnessed before and it was almost impossible to fathom. Over twenty thousand prisoners languished throughout the compound stuffed into segregated barracks lined with wooden bunks, four tiers high, crowded with starving men in various stages of dying. Most were too weak to move on their own, others appeared to be not much more than skeletons covered with skin. My eyes wandered like the lens of a camera snapping up images of the gruesome truth of the unforgivable cruelty and incomprehensible suffering that had gone on here for so long. They were images that would haunt my dreams for decades and live inside me forever.

☆ ☆ ☆

On May 8, 1945, the Nazi's surrendered, and the war officially ended. I listened to the broadcasts on the BBC with my fellow soldiers as London and New York exploded in celebration. Relief and peace, defined the mood as people everywhere drank and lifted their voices, dancing and shaking their heads in astonishment at the realization that the hell on earth was finally over.

I, too, was grateful to have made it through alive, and was ecstatic that the long bloody battles had ended. Within hours I penned a hasty letter to my father telling him that I would be pounding up the old porch just as soon as I was able to arrange my discharge. For the first time since I'd closed the door behind me, I didn't hold back, though my heart ached with apprehension. After all these years, I was prepared to take my first real step on the long road home, and in spite of all our plans, Franz would not be by my side.

As I was biding my time with the others, waiting for the call on the plane that would transport us back to the states, the mail orderly tossed me a telegram from Bonnie.

"Franz has been found alive. Recuperating. V.A. hospital Los Angeles. Letter to follow."

"Oh, my God! Oh, my God!" I yelled, waving the telegram in the air like a victory flag. Breathless with joy, I read the words over and over inviting the news to dispel every last modicum of disbelief before I finally folded up the telegram and tucked it fervently into my chest pocket. Throughout the day I pulled it out so many times to re-read it that by evening the creases were already showing signs of wear.

A week later, when Bonnie's letter finally arrived, I tore it open, devouring it with as much relish as I would a home-cooked meal.

"Apparently, when Franz was found on the beach they'd given him up for dead, but a medic in the field managed to get a faint heart beat on him. The day after the invasion, they shifted him to a transport plane when a vacant spot turned up at the last minute. He was flown to a hospital in London where he lingered for over a month and the prognosis was not good. Somehow he hung on and regained consciousness and was later able to identify himself.

Apparently, the tags got switched right there in the field hospital. Franz was ID'd as the other guy. During the battle, that other soldier suffered a severe head injury and died three weeks later wearing Franz's dog tags. There had been a huge mix-up.

After the mistake was sorted out and Franz was strong enough, they transferred him to the V.A. hospital in Los Angeles and he called Linae right away. She rushed over and began dropping by every day. Franz has since been released from the army, but they've still got him recuperating in the rehab unit of the hospital. Linae told me that they wrote you once, but perhaps you never received the letter because they never heard back from you. Truth is, I just found out about this myself. Franz was in such bad shape that I believe they might have been overwhelmed by not knowing how things were going to turn out. He's made a lot of progress though, and Linae has been a big part of his recovery.

He's doing well but I think you should be prepared, Jake. He has lost one of his legs."

CHAPTER TWENTY-ONE

WITH THE WAR BEHIND ME, I spent my time waiting for my discharge papers to come through. Though I fantasized, to the point of obsession, about what it would be like to feel my foot step up on the creaky boards of the old front porch back home, the news about Franz changed everything, and there was no doubt in my mind that I had to stop in L.A. first. But there was something else too. Even though things between Bonnie and me had cooled, my heart ached to see her, and I allowed myself to imagine what it would be like to hold her in my arms after so much time.

I woke up in the middle of the night and wrote her a long letter professing my feelings and sharing my plans to come to Los Angeles. When I strolled over to the post office on base to mail it the following morning I was excited to find a letter from Bonnie waiting for me there. My pulse quickened. I was sure she too had come to realize the depth of her feelings for me in anticipation of my return and the synchronicity of it all made my heart sing. It was all going to come together. I stepped outside and found a private shady spot on the grass, tore open the envelope and read it eagerly. Bonnie's sure, sweet voice came through loud and clear as I read the words, and when they sank in, I fell back, too stunned to even speak.

"*It's taken me awhile to write this letter, Jake,*" *she wrote,* "*but I need to let you know that I've met a wonderful man. Last night, Ted surprised me with a proposal and a ring, and I accepted. Sometimes love has a way of finding us when we least expect it. Funny how things happen, but it looks like I will be making my life in California after all. I want to thank you for the wonderful times we had together. I'm looking forward to getting together when you get home and introducing you to Ted. I think you'll really hit it off. You have a lot in common. Safe travels. See you soon."*

I don't know why I was so shocked that Bonnie had moved on with her life. "Of course she moved on," I admonished myself. After all, hadn't I told her not to wait for me? The truth was that I had subconsciously taken it for granted that she would wait, and that when I was ready she would still be there.

Pulling my letter to Bonnie from my pocket, I tore it in half and dropped it inside the trash outside the post office door. I brooded endlessly, kicking myself for being so cavalier about my relationship with her. The irony was that this is what I had feared most for Franz, and now it was happening me. I was miserable and desperate to hang on to her. After all of my imaginings about our life together, I could not picture her with another man, and as I went about my chores I beat myself up, haunted by the warning that Linae had dropped months ago in the weeks before I shipped out: "Love don't come around that often, Jake. I know how Bonnie feels about you, and I'm pretty sure you love her too. Like I said before, you'll always be wondering about the one that got away."

In the middle of another sleepless night days later, I scribbled an anxious reply, *"Bonnie, I don't know what I was thinking when I told you not to wait, but please don't do this. I love you and can't imagine my life without you. I realize now that I was a fool to leave you so alone and now, more than anything, I want to get back together and work things out. Please think about it. I'm asking you with my whole heart to give me another chance."*

No sooner had I written *"give me another chance"* than I crumpled the paper in my fist and threw it against the wall. It was over between us, and I deserved it. I'd lost her, and it was too late to change it. For days I sulked and berated myself. I couldn't let go of my fantasy of how perfect life would have been with Bonnie. It took me weeks and many sleepless nights, but one day I woke up determined to move on, and I forced myself to dash off a short reply. *"I won't pretend that I'm not upset. I was looking forward to the possibility of rekindling what we once had and creating a future together, but what matters most is your happiness, and I wish you all the best. I'll never forget the great times we had together, and I will always remember you for the lovely, kind, supportive woman that you are."* For one whole day I agonized over how to sign it, but finally scribbled *"Love, Jake"*, sealed the envelope and tossed it in the mailbox before I could change my mind.

Two weeks later on August 3, 1945, I boarded an army transport plane for the long bumpy flight to California. Within forty-eight hours I was watching the world go by through the window of a bus in Santa Monica. I was excited and nervous but also sad about the fact that Franz was not on the seat beside me. He was even more on my mind though when I disembarked two blocks from Arnie's, then took a slow stroll on the beach to collect my thoughts. It was a perfect summer day, warm and clear with a small breeze blowing in off the ocean. My spirit was uplifted by the natural beauty surrounding me, in such sharp contrast to the life I'd been living since leaving home. The sun was always shining here, so endless and bold, glistening off the blue crests of waves that curled up onto the sand. When I arrived at the Santa Monica Pier, I rested on one of the benches along the wide boardwalk and let my mind drift as I watched two sailboats racing in the off-shore wind. When one of the boats tacked inland, I glanced around. Not far down on the beach, two young boys, only a little younger than Franz and I were when we'd hit the rails, were digging trenches deep into the sand. They roared with laughter when a wave predictably crashed in, filling it with water and washing it away. The sight of the boys tugged me to my feet. I headed back to the road and signaled a cab.

Unsure of what I would find when I arrived at the Veterans Hospital, a cold sweat rose up on the back of my neck as we pulled into the circular drive-way of a large rehab unit. I stepped out of the car and passed some bills to the driver without waiting for my change. "Sir!" he yelled through the rolled down window, but I waved him off and kept moving. Pausing outside an awning-covered door at the entrance to the mission-style building, I leaned against the wall and closed my eyes, struggling to grasp the magnitude of what it must have been like for Franz to lose a leg. I knew that many soldiers had lost limbs in the war, but this was Franz, my best friend, and it was a tough reality to swallow. Of course, I was just happy that he was alive, but my God, how our lives had changed.

⁕ ⁕ ⁕

I found Franz sitting up in a wheel chair parked in front of a window, the pant leg of his right leg folded under, conspicuously missing through the rails of the chair. When I knocked weakly at the door, Franz wheeled around and his face broke into a broad grin. "Jake!" he yelled, and my reserve dropped as I rushed across the room to embrace him, hardly able to speak for the lump that was lodged in my throat.

"Damn, Franz. You sure are a miracle," I said. "I've never been so happy to see someone in my life!" I hoped that I was hiding how shocked I was by the gray pallor of his face and his gaunt look, but when our eyes met I could see that he was still the same old Franz. The hug we exchanged expressed a depth of feeling that our words could not. "Jesus, Franz," I said, "I've been sick about you for months. To tell you the truth, it was getting harder and harder to trust that you were even still alive."

Franz laughed. "Yeah, well from the sound of things you had good reason to suspect that. The last thing I remember is wading toward shore and a burning sensation in my chest. After that everything went black."

"I looked for you everywhere that first week after we hit Normandy," I said. I kept shaking my head, locked on Franz's eyes, hardly believing that we were together here in this room. "It scared the hell out of me when I discovered a dying man wearing your tags. And the worst part was that no one knew what had happened, other than that there was a damn good chance you'd been killed."

"I'm sorry, Jake. That must have been a real nightmare."

"It was. But forget me. I'm just so happy to see you sitting here in the flesh. Bonnie filled me in with what she knew, but what the heck really happened? I need details, man."

"Well, like I said, I have no memory of the ordeal until the part where I heard some nurses in the hospital calling me by the wrong name. At first I couldn't even muster enough energy to speak up."

"You mean you couldn't say anything, but you could hear what was going on?"

"Yeah, I couldn't get my eyelids to open, let alone spit out a word. I was in some kind of deep fog that felt like it was so heavy on my body I couldn't function. I could hear these English accents clipping away in the background though. They'd be fussing about before they'd get around to me and then it'd be, 'Ralph this and Ralph that' until I couldn't stand it anymore. It irked me to the point that I forced myself to summon the strength to battle through the imprisonment of the stupor. 'Name's Franz Mueller,' I blurted out one day. I hadn't spoken for so long that it came out barely louder than a whisper, but an orderly heard me loud and clear. I'm telling you, Jake, the look on his face was enough to make what I'd been through almost worth it!"

"That's the craziest damn thing," I said. "You think you ever would have opened your eyes if they hadn't been calling you Ralph?"

"Dunno," Franz answered, shifting his weight in the wheel chair. "Turns out my dog tags had been mixed-up with a soldier named Ralph. You can imagine how both of our families have suffered terribly as they tried to sort it out."

I listened in silence.

"But, you and me, Jake." Franz's voice trailed off as if he'd decided to say something else. "We're still here. Sometimes I can't even believe it."

"Maybe what my dad used to say is true after all," I said. "Ain't nothin' can keep a good man down!"

"Yeah, well, I guess we're living proof," Franz laughed.

Our throats were plenty dry by the time we had reminisced about our years on the road and shared detailed stories of the war. It took awhile, but eventually, I got up the courage to steer the talking toward a more intimate subject.

"Have Bonnie and Linae been by?"

"Yeah, they've both been here."

There was a short hesitation, and then Franz went on. "Bonnie told me about your mother, Jake. Sure was sorry to hear about that, but I'll be damned. You got a brother and a sister?"

"I know, right? It's been a lot to take in. I can hardly believe it myself."

"I think I know more about your family now than I did when we were riding the rails together. You figurin' to go home like we planned now that the war's over?"

"Yeah. I had to see you first, but other than you and …" I held back Bonnie's name and went on. "It's really about all I've been able to think about these past few weeks. I'm heading there in a few days, as soon as I'm done here."

"Makes a lot of sense, Jake. I'm glad to hear it and you know what else I'm figurin' right now?"

"What?"

"What I'm figurin', buddy, is that I sure could use a cold one."

"Couldn't agree more," I laughed. "There were times when just the thought of returning to Arnie's kept me alive, I think!"

"Feel like pushing an old gimp?" he laughed. "I can manage myself, actually." Franz grabbed his crutches and threw them across his lap: "But hospital regulations, you know."

"Be my pleasure," I smiled. No way was this injury going to keep Franz's spirit down. He was still the same old Franz.

I stepped out to the nurse's station and dialed a cab, then wheeled Franz to the elevator. When the cabdriver sounded his horn, we made our way outside. Sitting in the car with Franz and riding through the streets of Los Angeles, I felt like we'd been down this road before, the countless times we heard Linae honking to hurry us off the beach or outside the CCC camp when she'd come to pick us up. I could still see her twisting the rear view mirror to touch up her lipstick. And how many drives had we made in that big blue car with the top down, the wind slapping against our faces, our hats in our hands. I started picturing Bonnie in my head though, and those thoughts sobered me.

"I guess Bonnie told you she's engaged," I said. I found myself bracing now that I had broached the subject.

"Yeah. Sorry, buddy." Franz shifted his weight. "She did tell me." He cleared his throat before he went on. "I knew she was seeing someone, but I didn't realize how serious it was until she told me he had proposed."

I turned my face to the window. "It messed me up at first," I said. "I was such a fool. How could I leave a beautiful girl like Bonnie behind and expect her to be here when I got back?"

"You never seemed interested in anything serious," said Franz. "Maybe it wasn't meant to be, buddy, but I am sorry. I really am."

"Yeah, I know. Thanks." I sunk further into the seat. "It was my fault though. I learned another huge lesson the hard way. You just can't take people for granted."

"Don't be so hard on yourself, Jake. We were young. The war changes things ... changes people, clarifies a lot of things. You just weren't ready. No shame in that."

"Maybe," I said, "but it doesn't feel good whatever the reason. For years I've been tormented by wishing I could go back and change the choices I made as a kid. Now, I wish I could do that with Bonnie."

"Yeah, I guess we all have our regrets, but seems the only thing to do is look ahead, not back. I know that's what I'm doing."

When the cab pulled up to the curb, by the time I'd handed the driver a few bills, Franz had already maneuvered himself out of the car. I was prepared to take it slow as we made our way to the entrance of our old watering hole, but Franz surprised me by the ease at which he navigated with crutches on his one leg. He seemed to accept all that he'd been through, and I found myself wondering if I'd ever be able to do the same. We slid into one of the worn leather booths, and two cold Ritter Brau's were set before us. Damn, it felt good to be back.

"It looks like you're getting along just fine, Franz." I tilted my head and let the cold beer work it's magic. "Pretty soon I'll have to hustle to keep up with you!"

"Yeah," Franz smiled. "At first I was feeling pretty sorry for myself, but once I got into physical therapy things began to change. I saw guys worse off than me, and I snapped out of it pretty fast."

"Well, nothing makes me happier than to see you doing so well."

"Thanks, Jake. I'm good with my life right now. What about you? When are you planning to head home?"

"Like I said, I'll be leaving in a few days, but I was hoping we could spend some time together before I took off."

"Yeah, I'd like that," Franz answered. "We've got a lot to catch up on."

"What about Linae? You seen much of her lately?"

"She's been by."

"Has she cracked the movie business yet?"

"She doesn't talk much about the movies anymore. I think she may have moved on."

"She still drivin' that blue Olds?"

"Oh, yeah, still drivin' …"

I brought Linae's name up at several intervals over the course of our time at Arnie's, but the conversation never went anywhere. Franz was always vague and eager to change the subject. After awhile, I dropped it, figuring that Franz had found out about her running around and just didn't want to talk about it.

✬ ✬ ✬

It was mid-morning the following day when I grabbed a coffee-to-go down the block from my small motel and set out for the hospital again. Franz and I had plans to sit in the courtyard around the V.A. and visit before heading to Arnie's for lunch and then maybe head to the beach after that. I found him in his room in good spirits, dressed and ready to roll, and for a moment I almost forgot that he'd ever been injured. I backed a wooden chair up against a wall opposite his bed. "So what are you thinking of doing when you're all healed up? You haven't said a word about your own plans."

"Well, I've been fitted for a leg prosthesis and …" but before he could finish his answer, the door flew open and Franz's face lit up. "Funny you should ask, Jake." He smiled wide at Linae who was framed in the doorway with an oversized pocketbook clutched in her hands.

"Hello, boys," she said in her best movie star voice. She sauntered into the room and plunked her bag down at the foot of Franz's bed.

Given what I had assumed had transpired between the two of them, I was shocked to see her. Her makeup and hair were, as usual, a little too done-up, but she was clad in an uncharacteristically conservative suit, though the peachy, low-cut camisole visible underneath the jacket barely contained her breasts. "Some things," I thought, "never change."

"Hey there, Jake," she glanced my way. "It's been awhile, but I suspected you'd show up here one of these days now that the war's over. Glad to see you come back lookin' so good."

Truth is, I shouldn't have been so dumbfounded at the sight of Linae waltzing in like she was Bette Davis in a feature film. I knew she'd been around and such, but the whole dramatic entrance thing caught me off-guard and mingled with the old negative thoughts I'd harbored toward her throughout the war. I wasn't quite sure how to respond, but I managed to be civil: "Hey, Linae. What's up?" I said, trying for Franz's sake to hide the disgust I was feeling.

Ignoring my question, she unpinned her hat and glided across the room to plant a big kiss on Franz. "Hey, baby," she said, rubbing a smudge of lipstick from his lower lip. "How's my favorite guy?"

Franz returned her affection with a prolonged kiss, then turned his attention back to me. He sat up tall in his chair and assumed a somewhat auspicious posture. "We got some news for you, Jake. Me and Linae are getting married and then moving back to Oklahoma in a few weeks, just as soon as I get my new leg. Linae's mama passed away over the winter and there's a big old house sitting there empty, just waiting for us."

"But ... when did this happen?" I stumbled over my words, unable to hide the bewildered look on my face. "You didn't say anything. I didn't even know if you were still seeing each other."

"Didn't mean to mislead you, Jake. We just wanted to tell you together," said Franz. "I always knew she was here for me, even when we couldn't write. Seein' this woman's face in my dreams is what kept me alive. We've both been through hell and back in our own way, but there was never a doubt in my mind that we'd live with each other forever."

"What he's sayin' is true," Linae chimed in with her eyes fixed on Franz, flashing him a smile. "I love him, Jake. I always have. Just didn't know my own feelings before. It took a relationship with a loser to make me realize what I'd walked away from. I know I did wrong, but he's forgiven me and we're gonna be married. I mean to keep nursing him back to health for as long as it takes and then we'll settle down and grow old together. I was raised in that old three story house and we can't wait to call it our own."

"Yeah, Jake, we got a shot at making us a B & B," Franz chimed in, as excited as I'd seen him since that first night he'd set eyes on Linae "Linae's got experience running a place, and I'm pretty good with numbers. Heck, we're even thinking of opening a little bar on the main floor where she can get her singing career going."

Linae slipped an arm around Franz's shoulders and hugged him close. "Never did get my big break into show business, but it don't matter now. I know I've found something better."

"I'd like you to be my best man, Jake," said Franz assuming a more serious tone. "I know you'll be heading out to check in on your family, but it'd mean a lot if you stood up for me before you take off. We're planning on going to City Hall next week as soon as we can get our license. Linae's already asked Bonnie to be her Maid of Honor, and Bonnie's agreed. Said she'd be happy if you joined us as a tribute to our friendship. Whadda ya say, man? There's no one else I'd rather have."

I sat in my chair with a million thoughts competing for attention as I listened to the two of them lay out their plans for a life of perfect bliss. It all sounded good now, but I was leery about how Franz would get along with such a major disability. I also wondered about Linae's commitment long term, whether or not she'd be able to stay faithful. Jumbled into all this also, was my nervousness about seeing Bonnie again, and about how I'd feel when we all got together.

Linae broke up my reverie. "I know what you're thinking, Jake," she said. "You're wondering how me and your old buddy here are gonna make it, aren't ya? Well, I can tell you, Jake, I'm not marrying a leg. I'm marrying a man. He's gonna be fine. We're both gonna be fine."

And with that comment every ounce of skepticism that I had harbored these past few years melted away. I looked at Franz and Linae as they stood before me with their crazy dreams, full of so much hope, and when our eyes met I knew things couldn't be any other way. "I'd love to stand up for you, Franz. There's nothing I'd like more than to see my best friend marry a beautiful red-headed girl. Congratulations to both of you. This is the happiest news I've heard since Franz came back from the dead. Come on, it's not too early for lunch and a toast. Drinks on me at Arnie's."

☆ ☆ ☆

The following Saturday I hustled myself down to City Hall where Franz and Linae had gathered to make their new life official. As nervous as I'd been for the past week about seeing Bonnie, my fears were allayed as soon as she walked into the room. She looked more sophisticated than I had remembered her. She'd grown up a lot while I'd been away and wore a hat that softly framed her face and a dress that dress showed off her slim waist. Her perfume was different than what she used to wear, something exotic that I couldn't place, but I liked it. Just looking at the light in her eyes, I was certain that there would always be a part of me that loved her. I wrapped my arms around her with a generous hug and a peck on the cheek, but there was no time for small talk. "Hi, Bonnie," I said. "You're as lovely as ever. It's so good to see you."

"It's wonderful to see you too, Jake. I was so relieved when I heard you were back safe and sound. You look great."

Another couple stood behind us waiting to get married once Franz and Linae had tied the knot. Franz, all decked out in a shark skin suit with a silk hanky stuffed inside the pocket, couldn't stop grinning. "Let me fix this, baby," Linae said, fiddling with a white carnation she'd stuck on Franz's lapel.

Linae looked beautiful in a creamy silk taffeta dress that was about as tight as a dress could get, and along with that, true to form, she wore a short cropped jacket that in no way hid her cleavage. In heels, she towered several inches over Franz, and her flaming hair was swept up in a French roll with a lavish white camellia that seemed determined to shed every one of its petals down her back. "Most beautiful woman in the world," Franz said, glancing my way as she fussed over him.

Having received my discharge papers just days before, I had spent thirty bucks on a dark summer weight suit with a wide lapel and a blue checkered necktie. The salesman in the clothing store had made a big deal over the suit. He pointed out its modern style and great fit. I felt like a real adult the second I slipped into the jacket.

Once we were all in place, the portly judge cleared his throat and opened his book, peering at us through wire spectacles that looked too small for his face. "Shall we begin?"

Before he could say another word though, Linae piped up, using a tone that only she would dare to take with a Justice of the Peace. "Now, Judge," she said, "as much as I am willing to pledge my life to this man, I am questioning my ability to obey as it says in these vows, and I know the men don't have to obey. I am wondering if we might just strike it from my section, the woman's that is. I can love him until death, Judge, but I'm not so sure I can obey. You know, 'until death' could be a very long time and obeying ain't, I mean isn't, my strong suit."

"Listen to me, young lady," said the judge who'd seen more than his share of quirky people. "You are entering into the most important union between a man and a woman, so if you're having second thoughts ..."

"Oh no, sir," she interrupted. "I was just wondering about that itty-bitty part ... the 'obey' thing ..."

"Well, we're partaking in a civil marriage ceremony here today, and the word 'obey' is not part of the vows so you don't have to worry. Now, is there anything else you object to because I don't want any interruptions once we begin."

"Oh no, Judge. I'm good now. I'm good."

"Shall we begin then?"

When the I do's were repeated, the judge invited Franz and Linae to join hands. "Repeat after me ... "

By the time Franz had uttered "and hereto I pledge you my faithfulness," Linae was in tears, and the Judge paused to let Bonnie step up and hand her a handkerchief.

"Can we proceed, young lady?" he said. The judge softened his demeanor only a little and adjusted his glasses.

Linae sniffled, blew her nose and dried her eyes while Franz slid one of his crutches over to me and threw his arm around her. "I am sorry, Judge," she said. "It's just that no one's ever wanted to marry me before … nobody's ever loved me enough."

After taking a couple of moments to compose herself, Linae was finally able to repeat her vows. "By the authority vested in me by the state of California, I now pronounce you man and wife," the Judge concluded, motioning to the door attendant for the next couple in line. "Congratulations. May you live a long and happy life."

Franz gathered his new wife close with his free arm and delivered a long deep kiss. "Thank you, Judge," said Franz before he turned toward Bonnie and me and announced: "I gotta be the luckiest man alive!"

Stepping out of City Hall into the bright California sunlight, the four of us piled into Linae's Oldsmobile, with a line of beach buoys hanging off the bumper and "Just Married" that someone - I guessed Linae herself - had painted across the trunk. After we all had a chance to properly celebrate at Arnies, the newlyweds planned to head to the Beverly Hills Hotel, where Linae had splurged and booked them the bridal suit for the night. The plan was that when Franz was fully functioning with his new leg they'd make the long drive out to Oklahoma and sight-see on the way. "I hear there's a couple 'a good clubs in Palm Springs," said Linae, always looking for a good time. "I'm planning on breaking out my trousseau there, as we are most definitely staying over a couple of nights to party it up."

The top was down. It felt warm, but the breeze picked up once we hit Santa Monica, and we parked as close as we could get to Arnie's, snapping pictures on the boardwalk, then engaging a passerby to take a group shot. Back at Arnie's, we toasted each other with champagne and a wedding cake that Arnie had gussied up special for the occasion, even placing a plastic bride and groom on the top.

"Ya never know," said Linae, gulping her champagne. "We might even have a couple 'a kids. Franzie wants kids and I think I'm maybe warming to the idea."

"Whatever makes you happy, sweetheart," Franz grinned. "You're all I need, and whatever comes along after that will only add to the treasure I've already got."

I smiled, sinking back in the booth and turning my attention to Bonnie for the first time. "I never did get a chance to congratulate you, Bonnie. I really am happy for you. Franz has told me that he's a great guy." As I spoke the words I realized that I truly was happy for her. There were still so many unanswered questions in my life, and as much as I cared for her, it wasn't the right time to be making plans with anyone.

In the end we all hugged and brushed away a few tears as we lingered on in our farewells. I wanted to take my time saying goodbye to Bonnie, so I asked her if it was okay to get dropped off with her at her apartment and maybe have a walk around the block. "I don't mind at all," she said. "In fact, I'd really like that."

Linae pulled the car up to the front of Bonnie's apartment and we called out 'congratulations' and waved and watched them until they were out of sight. "I understand that you couldn't wait for me, Bonnie," I said, "but I wish it could have been different between us. I'm sorry I couldn't make a commitment to you. I really am."

"I know, Jake, but the timing just wasn't right," she said, pausing a little ways down the street and meeting me with her eyes. "We had some great times though, didn't we?"

"Best times of my life."

"You'll always have a special place in my heart, Jake," she said. "I'm happy to have found someone who loves me and shares my dreams, but I'll always remember you. I hope you find someone special, too."

She stepped up and planted a warm kiss on my cheek. We strolled the rest of the way in silence. As I watched her make her way up the stone path to her front door, I knew once again that I'd been a fool to let her slip away. "Goodbye, Jake," she said. "Take care. Keep in touch."

"Will do," I said. "And hey, Bonnie ... I ... congratulations."

CHAPTER TWENTY-TWO

THERE WAS BY NOW AN ache in my heart, a constant raw desire to get back to the farm and as I dug through my duffle bag for a decent shirt, I came across the old dishtowel my mother had embroidered with Edwin's name. My homesickness soared as I smoothed out the tattered cloth as if it were a fine piece of linen. I wanted to feel my father wrapping his arms around me. I wanted to see the old farmhouse, the trees and pastures, touch the animals, smell the fresh cut hay, taste the raw milk. More than anything, I wanted to be back in the only home I'd ever known. Three days later, with the "**EDWIN**" dishtowel tucked deep inside my jacket pocket, I sat on a polished bench in the L.A. Union Station waiting for the streamliner headed east. All around me was the commotion of uniformed service men on their way home, along with the other hundreds of people on the move. I was struck by the irony of how many years Franz and I had ridden the rails and had never even glimpsed the inside of a train terminal. As I waited, I tried thumbing through an L.A. Times, but my mind was so unsettled I couldn't concentrate. Folding the paper in half, I set it on the seat beside me. Eventually, I got up and ducked inside a gift shop where I picked out a pocket knife for my father and a hair comb for Aunt Liddy. At another shop nearby, I plunked money down on the counter for two children's lunch boxes: a "Lone Ranger" for Wills and a "Nancy Drew" for Claudia.

I was so lost in my fantasies and fears about what would greet me when I got home, that the roar of the train as it pulled into the station caught me by surprise. The modern, clean look of the engine and cars was so unlike those that Franz and I used to ride that for a moment I felt unworthy of even boarding it. Once in my seat though, there were even more wonderments to take in, and I wished Franz had been with me to share the experience. I laughed to find that my seat reclined, but even more mind boggling, I discovered that there was a club car for drinking and a dining car for eating. The whole ride was a far cry opposed to our days of hiding in dirty, empty boxcars, or worse yet, stuck on a ladder between cars the way Franz and I had done the night we nearly lost our lives.

As I settled into the luxury of the train, I found I could relax most in the club car sipping a cold beer and watching the world go by. When I spotted an expansive field in the middle of nowhere, I thought of my mother and how she was always there for me when I got out of school, waiting with open arms in the Stiver's pasture between our land and the schoolhouse. The images were so vivid that I turned my whole body toward the window and allowed myself the luxury of a good cry, knowing I would never have the chance to make things right with her. As the train sped eastward, I prayed I would someday be able to make peace with all that had happened in my life, and that I'd feel a part of what was left of my family once again.

After two days, we pulled into the Minneapolis stationed and I grabbed my bags and stepped into one of the cabs that sat idling at the curb outside. The air was cool and the city trees looked full and green. I thought the bushy trees signaled a first-rate growing season and I couldn't wait to check out the summer crops. The ride out to the farm confirmed my hunch, and, with every passing field my anticipation grew. As the old homestead came into view, I could see that time had done its work here, too. The barbed-wire fence that still ran along the driveway was rusted deep, and the barn door - no surprise - needed a coat of paint, as did the house itself. The taxi's tires grated against the loose gravel as it pulled up to a stop at the house I had called home so long ago. Before I had even paid the driver, the screen door swung open and my father, slightly bent over but still vigorous, stepped out onto the porch. I fumbled the driver my money and leap-frogged up the creaking steps.

"Dad," I cried, wrapping my arms around my father. The familiarity of him rushed back: the ever-present scent of the farm on his clothes, the strength of his embrace, and most of all his love that had comforted me in my darkest times. We clung to each other in the joy of the moment, as well as in the sadness of all that had been lost.

"It's good to see you, son," he whispered in my ear. He held me at arm's length, taking in all of the changes I'd undergone since I'd left home so many years ago. "It sure is good to have you home."

Aunt Liddy, even heavier now, and favoring a bad hip, limped out onto the porch and draped her arms around us both. "And look whose finally come back 'round," she said, her laughter mingling with our tears of happiness. "Jake, it's about time you came home."

"It's so good to be here," I said and I meant it even more than I imagined I would.

When my eyes had adjusted to the reflective overhang of the porch, I caught sight of Wills and Claudia who looked lost as they stood against the wall near the front door, somewhat bashful but excited to meet this mysterious older brother they'd heard so much about.

"Look who's here, kids," said my father, beckoning them to join us. "Jake, this is your sister, Claudia, and your brother, Wills. They've sure have been waiting a long time to meet you."

"Hi," I said, feeling awkward. I stepped forward and extended my hand to Claudia and then to Wills, but their touch melted my reserve, and I pulled them into my arms. Wills reminded me of myself as a skinny, light-eyed eight-year-old, and Claudia, I thought, had our mother's eyes and her soft brown hair that was always escaping around her face. "Hey, look here. I brought you both something." I dug into my duffle bag and watched their eyes light up when I handed them their lunch boxes.

"And this is for you, Dad," I said, pulling out the pocket knife in a black felt case.

"Thanks, Jake," my father said, letting the shiny blade glide from it's sheath. "You know how much I love a good knife and this one looks mighty fine."

"I still got the jackknife you gave me, Dad. I can't tell you how much comfort it's given me over the years."

Aunt Liddy wasted no time twisting the tortoise-shell comb into the side of her hair bun. "Fanciest comb I ever saw," she said, as tickled with her gift as the children. "But enough standing around on the porch. Come in, come in where I got food cookin' up. It's much too hot to be lingering around out here," she scolded us in the familiar tone that used to grate on me as a boy, but now brought a smile to my face.

As we settled in the living room, I was flooded with emotions that at moments threatened to overwhelm me. Steeling myself, I shifted my attention to the twins who hadn't left my side and who begged for stories of where I'd been and what I'd seen. I obliged them until Aunt Liddy announced that supper was nearly ready. "Leave Jake alone now children. Let him wash up before we eat."

Refreshed, I sat down at the old family table, overcome with joy by the kind of home-made feast I'd dreamed about for all these years: fried chicken, peeled potatoes, corn scaled fresh from the cob and hot bread that I smothered with light brown gravy.

After dinner, before the dishes had even been cleared, Wills and Claudia began to compete for my attention. Wills pulled out several pieces from a collection of wooden animals he kept on a shelf in my old room that had now become his. "I whittled them with only a little help from dad," he whispered in my ear. Not to be outdone, Claudia sidled up next to me claiming to have created special drawings of me. "Before I knew what you looked like in person," she said offering me a sample of her work.

When Aunt Liddy had sliced us each a piece of her famous apple cake, the five of us lingered around the table, sharing even more stories late into the night until my father shooed the yawning twins off to bed. We pushed back our chairs and walked our coffee cups to the sink.

My dad gave me one of his knowing looks. "You remember your friend, Henry?" he said.

"Sure do."

"Surprised us all by marrying a girl he'd met when he entered one of his herding dogs in the competition at the state fair."

"This year's fair?"

"No, it was a year ago. Seems she helped him with the registration form and before we all knew it, they were farming just south of town with a baby on the way. Bought the old Dixon farm I heard."

"Baby?"

"Yes, they have a little girl. I saw Jess in church a couple of weeks ago and she said everybody's doing fine. Named her Rosalee, if I recall right."

"So Jess Stivers is still around?" I said.

"She was gone for the longest time, but it seems she's moving back from the city. Said Minneapolis was too big for her taste."

The mention of Jess's name got my attention. "Oh, really?" I said. "What was she doing in Minneapolis?"

"She'd gone out there to get herself a teaching certificate and now she's going to be taking over one of the classrooms at the new school they built two blocks past the church. When I told her you were on your way home she said to tell you hello and to come by. I guess it will be nice to have some of your old friends around."

The news about Jess being back in town set off a flood of emotions, and I knew I'd be stopping by her classroom sooner rather than later. I'd always had a soft spot for her in my heart and there was no denying the fact that I was more than a little excited to see her.

"Yeah, dad," I said. "Maybe you'll let me borrow your car and I'll drop in on her in a day or two?"

"Whenever you want, son. Keys are on the hook by the door."

I turned to Aunt Liddy and encircled her with a strong hug. "How do I ever thank you for how welcome you've made me feel here tonight?"

"You're being home is all the thanks I need, Jake. We've been thinking about this day for a long time. Lived for it, really."

"It's a great day," said my dad, and I embraced him too.

"It certainly is," I agreed. "One that I fantasized about for quite some time now, too."

I laid myself out on the same davenport I used to curl up on as a kid, grateful for the welcome I'd felt since I'd stepped through the door. My shattered self was healing with every hug, every conversation and I felt uplifted in every muscle of my body. It was that good to be home. In the foggy hours of the night however, scenes of the horrific accident that had forced me to leave flashed through my head. The old pain crept back, and I was overcome by feelings for my mother and Edwin. There was an uncertainty about my future here, and I began to question whether or not I belonged here for the long haul. Could I really stay and make my life on this farm after all that had changed and all I'd been through? I drifted in and out of a fitful sleep, disturbed by dreams that fueled my insecurity and would haunt me for days.

At dawn, I found my father in the kitchen leaning over the counter. "Mornin', Jake. You up with the birds or the rooster?" he said, the same as if I'd been a boy of six. He grinned, motioning to the coffeepot bubbling on the stove as he sliced up some of Aunt Liddy's leftover apple cake onto a plate. "I got up extra early just so I could be here to see your face when you walked in! It's such a blessing to have you home, son. Back where you belong."

I smiled and poured myself a steaming cup and pulled a kitchen chair up to the table. My father filled me in on another change in the house. "I can't always count on Liddy to make the breakfast anymore," he confided. He rested his elbow on the worn hickory tabletop, his thick fingers soothing his brow. "You'll have to make do with my dishing up the leftovers."

"I thought she seemed a little more frail. What's going on?"

"Well, her mind's gotten even more feeble and her hip's always throbbing. Keeps her away from many of the household chores, though she outdid herself last night."

"Yeah, I did notice her limping. How long has that been going on?"

"It's been on and off for years, but lately it seems much worse. Claudia does her best to help, but I'd like my baby to stay focused on her schoolwork, maybe get a job off the farm someday."

"I understand, dad." I nodded in agreement. As he spoke, I began to realize the magnitude of the burden my father had been carrying alone all these years, and I wondered again what role I would play in this family now. It was one thing to be welcomed back, but another to truly be a part of things again.

When we finished our coffee, my father left to wake up Wills and was soon leading him into the kitchen, setting the end piece of apple cake before him with a glass of cold milk. After he had crammed the last few crumbs into his mouth and washed it all down with a final swig, they headed out to the barn to harness Justice and Noah to a buckboard that had been bought for the kids. I followed, unsure if I was meant to be included, but we weren't even half-way through the farmyard when Wills turned and ran back to grab my hand. "Come on, Jake. Hurry up!" I allowed him to pull me forward and then broke away.

"Last one to the wagon is a rotten egg!" I yelled, then slowed a bit to allow him to pass. When the horses were ready, I swung myself up into the driver's seat they'd left free for me. I hesitated with memories of the last time I'd held these reins.

"It's been a long time, Jake. You reckon you still got the feel for it?" My father smiled in my direction and I smiled back. "Pull 'em up, but not too tight. Just enough to let them know you're in control."

"I remember, Dad."

Reveling in the old familiar feel of the reins in my hands, I inhaled the moist country air deep into my lungs. We drove out to the field edge and pulled up near the grove. By now the sky was lighter with bands of ivory and pink swirling beyond the distant low-mounding hills as we pulled the wagon to a stop, and I jumped down off the seat stroking the horse's heads. I remembered how angry I'd been at them after the accident, desperate as I was to share the blame. With time and maturity though, that had all dropped away, and I could finally see things as they were: two spooked animals and a young boy caught up in a tragic accident. I walked a dozen or so paces toward the field edge before stopping to gaze, trance-like, over the land. My heart filled up as memories of the day Edwin died rose up inside of me. As I choked back the tears, the raising and lowering of my shoulders betraying the emotions that overwhelmed me even as I struggled to forgive myself.

"What's wrong with Jake?" Wills turned to our father anxiously. "Is he crying?"

"He's alright," my father answered. "We'll just let him be. Sometimes a good cry is what a man needs."

Composing myself, I came around and hoisted up into the driver's seat. Forcing a smile to hide the longing that ached anew inside of me,

I put my arm around my little brother. The three of us watched the sun inch into the sky, the pastel hues morphing now into an orangey glow.

"You come back to stay, son?" My father kept his head to the sunrise and allowed the question to hover in the newness of the day.

"I'd like to, Dad," I said, "but I'm not sure what staying even means just now."

"Well, we got haymaking just round the corner. Sure could use the help."

"I know, but ..." I hesitated, unsure how to communicate the deeper meaning of my reply.

"Go on, son."

"I don't know, dad. I guess I'm not sure where I fit in anymore. I mean, I'm real glad to be here, and you've all gone out of your way to make me feel welcome, but I feel so bad about everything that happened." I stopped, unsure of how to speak about my guilt and the fear of rejection that I'd harbored for so many years. Wills had been intently listening to our conversation and jumped in.

"What happened, Jake? What's Jake talking about, Dad?"

"Nothing that needs going over now, Wills. Don't you worry." Then turning his full attention back to me he answered: "I'm not worried about the past. And you shouldn't be either. Life goes on, son. Accidents happen and mistakes are forgiven. You're my son, Jake, and there's nothing I'd love more than having you settle here as long as you like."

I took hold of the reins, then gazed out again across the expanse of rich farmland that lay before me, allowing the magnitude of my father's statement to sink in. It was a healthy farm but too much for my aging father to manage alone, that much was clear. After several long moments, I turned to face him.

"I guess I'll stay for the haying and see how things go," I said.

My father broke into a wide grin.

"Yeah!" shouted Wills. "You're staying! Wait 'til Claudia hears!" Wills's childish excitement lifted the weight of the moment, and I reached over and hoisted the boy between my legs.

"Come here, little brother," I laughed. "You ever driven these horses before?"

"No," said Wills, shaking his head, and looking to our father, the familiar pleading in his eyes.

"Guess so," said my father. "No one better to teach you than Jake."

My heart warmed with the compliment, the depths of which my little brother would never know.

"Papa says, 'yes,'" Wills said grinning with childish excitement as he fixed his eyes on me. "What do I do?"

"Just sit right here, real tall, and grab hold of these reins with me," I said, taking his small hands in mine. "We're gonna drive the wagon together. Steady in the hand now. You've got to show you're in control." As we cracked the reins, I added: "Promise me you'll never take the horses out on your own though, Wills. You hear me?"

Author's Note

THE WAY BACK 'ROUND IS a work of fiction. The story, characters, events and their timing come from my imagination. The setting is the depression era which began with the Stock Market crash in 1929, ending with the U.S. entering WWII in 1941 and continuing on through the end of the war in 1945.

This was a unique time in history. Millions of people had no jobs and even farmers, were wiped out by storms and drought unlike anything anyone had ever experienced before. The middle of the country was particularly hard hit, and "The Dust Bowl" sent people west to places like California where they thought they could find work and a way to survive. For many though, it was not the utopia they had dreamed of, but rather a tough place to eke out a living. It was not uncommon for teenagers and kids from hard hit homes to ride the rails and crisscross the country in search of work. This was the world in which the main characters of this story, Jake and Franz, found themselves.

I've taken broad strokes to some of these historical events and fiddled with some details. I would like to give a special thanks to my cousin, Will Wolf, for allowing me to embellish on a scene from his own book: *When Kids Ran Free*, a story he wrote about his boyhood in western North Dakota. When Jake and Henry go ice fishing and freeze their pants legs into stove pipes - this is a direct experience Will had as a kid himself. Thank you, Will, for preserving all of those memories!

Discussion Guide For The Way Back 'Round

1. What is the meaning behind the quotes the author has chosen for the three "Parts" of the novel and how do they apply to those particular sections? What is the trouble suggested in Part I and how do the characters reactions cause consequences for each other? Can you see any incidents in your own life where someone's reaction to a circumstance changed the outcome? What about Part II - what are the key "moments" that take Jake and Franz's friendship to a new level? Why, in the end, is it important for a person to have something they feel they can fall back on? What other things in life could a person fall back on, if not their family, and did Jake have any of these?

2. Discuss the relationship between Jake's parents, Albert and Sarah. Did they have a good marriage? Do you think Albert could have done any more to help his troubled wife? What about his son? What was good and what could have been better? How did their reaction to Edwin's death affect Jake? Do you see anything similar in the world around you?

3. Is Sarah a good mother? Is she a good wife? What are her issues? Does the birth of Edwin solve or not solve any of her problems? How does Jake fit into this and does he help or make things worse? How does she change through the course of the story?

4. Do you know anyone who has lost a child or suffered a family tragedy of this magnitude? Are there any similarities between their dealing with their own situation and the way the characters react in *The Way Back 'Round*? Is there any way to predict how someone will react to a tragedy? How would you help someone who has lost a child or been through something horrific?

5. Talk a bit about parenting. How does Sarah's strictness and control over Jake affect him? We know it stifle's him, but is there also anything positive about it? Does Sarah realize what she's doing to Jake? How does the relationship between Jake and his mother change? Do they love each other? Do you think that Albert should have stepped in and stood up to his wife more often on Jake's behalf? What makes a good parent?

6. What causes Jake to run away? He claims it is the guilt he feels over Edwin's death, but is there more? How does Jake see himself at this point? What do you think would have happened to Jake if he had stayed on the farm with his parents? Do you believe that he could be forgiven? How does the author handle forgiveness in the novel? Does Jake's mother ever forgive him? What does it mean to forgive someone?

7. Discuss the pros and cons of life on the road for Jake and Franz. What do they learn?

In one of the jungle camps "Mo" gives them the speech about what it means to be a man?

"You're a man when you got yo'self some responsibilities and you can handle 'em. Like when you got a woman and a couple 'a babies depending on you. Ain't nothing better, as long as you can handle it. But if something should happen, you lose your work and you can't even buy food 'cause the money's dried up and there ain't no jobs, then your manhood goes down the swamp. You feel like nothing. Oh, you still got the wife and the babies ain't going anywhere, but you ain't no man in the 'spectable sense, anymore. The world done strip you of that." Mo goes on to say that Deadfoot is still a man "'cause he sends money home whenever he can."

What is Mo telling the boys about manhood? Does Mo's idea of what it is to be a man still hold in today's times? Many families suffered during the depression. What are some of the similarities in this modern day era of struggle and economic uncertainty?

8. Life on the road is tough, but the boys are also met with kindness too. Discuss the people they meet along the way – the Mexican family, Angel and Manuela, the Texas farmer, Joe Barton and his wife, Evelyn, then Mo and the other hobos. How is this contrasted with the evil they encounter - the Bulls, the way the migrants are treated and finally, in the end, the ultimate evil of the concentration camps? How do you think these events influenced the boys? What do they take away from these encounters?

9. How does the friendship between Jake and Franz develop? What are the key moments in the novel that move their relationship forward and does the author succeed? How do Jake and Franz help each other make it through the tough times? How important is friendship in your life?

10. Franz, the boy who'd never been in love, dreams about someday marrying a red-headed girl. How important are goals and dreams in a person's life? What are Jake's dreams? Do the boys realize any of their dreams and if so, which ones? What steps do they take toward their dreams?

11. The author contrasts the structure of the Conservation Corps Camp with leisure time when the boys hit LA and hang out at "Arnie's bar in Santa Monica. How do the boys react to this? How important is the balance between structure and leisure time in a young person's life? Which is more important and how do you strike the balance?

12. How do you feel about the character Linae? Linae is cheap, flashy looking and likes to party. Does it make you think about how you judge other people? Does she redeem herself in the end? Compare and contrast her to the quiet, safe Bonnie. Who has more heart? Does the author make a fair judgment in the way she develops these women?

13. Let's go back to friendship. Do you think that Jake should have been honest with Franz when he saw Linae partying with the sailors on the beach that night? Jake held back out of concern for his buddy shipping out into a danger zone. Was this the right thing to do or do you think he should have told Franz the truth as the events unfolded?

14. When Jake receives a letter from Bonnie telling him that she has become engaged to another man, Jake is devastated. Discuss his reaction. They obviously have a connection, but it doesn't go forward. Why? Who do you think is responsible? Could they ever end up together?

15. Do you believe that Linae is sincere when she says to Jake: "I'm not marrying a leg, Jake. I'm marrying a man." What does she mean? Why does the relationship between Franz and Linae work?

16. Jake still has the dishtowel his mother embroidered with his brother's name "**EDWIN**" inside his duffle bag when he returns home as a grown man. Why did he keep it with him all those years? What is the significance of mementos or family heirlooms? How did the meaning of this modest towel sustain him through so many hardships and for so long?

17. When Jake arrives back on the farm, old Aunt Liddy, in spite of her dementia and aching hip, has cooked up one of his favorite childhood feasts - fried chicken, potatoes, gravy, her apple cake. Jake is comforted and lulled by the familiar food that only his family can create. Discuss why food is so comforting and why specific family traditional food is a gold coin in the memory bank of children. What foods are remembered in your family? Do you have one to pass on?

18. In the end, Jake is reunited with his father who lays the burdens of his life at his son's fee. There is a half brother and sister that have been born since he went away, his father is aging, and the farm is too much for him to handle. Was Jake's decision to stay the right one and where do you see Jake's life going from here? What will it take for his dreams to be fulfilled?

I would love to hear from you so please feel free to drop me an email at brendasorrels@aol.com

Please visit on Facebook: www.facebook.com/brendasorrels and Pinterest http://www.pinterest.com/brendasorrels/boards/
You may also contact me through my website at: www.brendasorrels.com which is also the home of my blog and news of upcoming projects!

Copies and E-readers versions of this book may be ordered through Amazon.com, Barnes& Noble.com or Lulu.com

YOUNG PRAIRIE WIFE

Coming soon from Brenda Sorrels

YOUNG NATHANIEL BARTELL, HAVING LEARNED the truth of his identity returns to Gustafson Corridor to begin his life with Emma, a beautiful young girl he met at a dance. Their love is tested, when early on, they are met with their own sudden tragedy. Emma is unable to cope, and her vulnerability leads her into a precarious situation where a bad choice is made that nearly destroys their marriage. The consequences compound an already stressful situation and it's unclear if things can ever be resolved.

Young Prairie Wife picks up at the closing of *The Bachelor Farmers,* but completely stands on it's own. It is a story of what happens when a family begins to live the truth. It is also the story of a young couple who learns the hard way some of life's greatest lessons. This is a novel about a new beginning, about love and loss, marriage and parenthood. *Young Prairie Wife* reminds us that when there is real love and forgiveness, the possibilities are endless.

About The Author

THIS IS THE SECOND NOVEL of Brenda Sorrels, author of *The Bachelor Farmers,* a love story set in northern Minnesota in the winter of 1919. She grew up in Fargo, N.D. and headed east to Manhattanville College in Purchase, N.Y. She now lives in Dallas with her husband and small dog, Charlotte - spends summers in writing in Connecticut.

Visit her website at: www.brendasorrels.com